"Kathleen Fuller's *The Teacher's Bride* is a heartwarming story of unexpected romance woven with fun and engaging characters who come to life on every page. Once you open the book, you won't put it down until you've reached the end."

—AMY CLIPSTON, BESTSELLING AUTHOR OF *A SEAT BY THE HEARTH*

"Kathy Fuller's characters leap off the page with subtle power as she uses both wit and wisdom to entertain! Refreshingly honest and charming, Kathy's writing reflects a master's touch when it comes to intricate plotting and a satisfying and inspirational ending full of good cheer!"

—KELLY LONG, NATIONAL BESTSELLING AUTHOR, ON *THE TEACHER'S BRIDE*

"Kathleen Fuller is a master storyteller and fans will absolutely fall in love with Ruby and Christian in *The Teacher's Bride.*"

—RUTH REID, BESTSELLING AUTHOR OF *A MIRACLE OF HOPE*

"*The Teacher's Bride* features characters who know what it's like to be different, to not fit in. What they don't know is that's what makes them so loveable. Kathleen Fuller has written a sweet, oftentimes humorous, romance that reminds readers that the perfect match might be right in front of their noses. She handles the difficult topic of depression with a deft touch. Readers of Amish fiction won't want to miss this delightful story."

—KELLY IRVIN, BESTSELLING AUTHOR OF THE EVERY AMISH SEASON SERIES

"Kathleen Fuller is a talented and a gifted author, and she doesn't disappoint in *The Teacher's Bride.* The story will captivate you from the first page to the last with Ruby, Christian, and engaging characters. You'll laugh, gasp, and wonder what will happen next. You won't want to miss reading this heartwarming Amish story of mishaps, faith, love, forgiveness, and friendship."

—MOLLY JEBBER, SPEAKER AND AWARD-WINNING
AUTHOR OF *GRACE'S FORGIVENESS* AND THE AMISH
KEEPSAKE POCKET QUILT SERIES

"Enthusiasts of Fuller's sweet Amish romances will savor this new anthology."

—*LIBRARY JOURNAL* ON *AN AMISH FAMILY*

"These four sweet stories are full of hope and promise along with misunderstandings and reconciliation. True love does prevail, but not without prayer, introspection, and humility. A must-read for fans of Amish romance."

—*RT BOOK REVIEWS*, 4 STARS, ON *AN AMISH FAMILY*

"The incredibly engaging Amish Letters series continues with a third story of perseverance and devotion, making it difficult to put down . . . Fuller skillfully knits together the lives within a changing, faithful community that has suffered its share of challenges."

—*RT BOOK REVIEWS*, 4 ½ STARS, ON *WORDS FROM THE HEART*

"Fuller's inspirational tale portrays complex characters facing real-world problems and finding love where they least expected or wanted it to be."

—*BOOKLIST*, STARRED REVIEW, ON *A RELUCTANT BRIDE*

"Fuller has an amazing capacity for creating damaged characters and giving insights into their brokenness. One of the better voices in the Amish fiction genre."

—*CBA RETAILERS + RESOURCES* ON *A RELUCTANT BRIDE*

"This promising series debut from Fuller is edgier than most Amish novels, dealing with difficult and dark issues and featuring well-drawn characters who are tougher than the usual gentle souls found in this genre. Recommended for Amish fiction fans who might like a different flavor."

—*LIBRARY JOURNAL* ON *A RELUCTANT BRIDE*

"Sadie and Aden's love is both sweet and hard-won, and Aden's patience is touching as he wrestles not only with Sadie's dilemma, but his own abusive past. Birch Creek is weighed down by the Troyer family's dark secrets, and readers will be interested to see how secondary characters' lives unfold as the series continues."

—*RT BOOK REVIEWS*, 4 STARS, ON *A RELUCTANT BRIDE*

"Kathleen Fuller's *A Reluctant Bride* tells the story of two Amish families whose lives have collided through tragedy. Sadie Schrock's stoic resolve will touch and inspire Fuller's fans, as will the story's concluding triumph of redemption."

—SUZANNE WOODS FISHER, BESTSELLING AUTHOR OF *ANNA'S CROSSING*

"Kathleen Fuller's *A Reluctant Bride* is a beautiful story of faith, hope, and second chances. Her characters and descriptions are captivating, bringing the story to life with the turn of every page."

—AMY CLIPSTON, BESTSELLING AUTHOR OF
A SIMPLE PRAYER AND THE KAUFFMAN AMISH BAKERY SERIES

"The latest offering in the Middlefield Family series is a sweet love story, with perfectly crafted characters. Fuller's Amish novels are written with the utmost respect for their way of living. Readers are given a glimpse of what it is like to live the simple life."

—*RT BOOK REVIEWS*, 4 STARS, ON *LETTERS TO KATIE*

"Fuller's second Amish series entry is a sweet romance with a strong sense of place that will attract readers of Wanda Brunstetter and Cindy Woodsmall."

—*LIBRARY JOURNAL* ON *FAITHFUL TO LAURA*

"Well-drawn characters and a homespun feel will make this Amish romance a sure bet for fans of Beverly Lewis and Jerry S. Eicher."

—*LIBRARY JOURNAL* ON *TREASURING EMMA*

"Treasuring Emma is a heartwarming story filled with real-life situations and well-developed characters. I rooted for Emma and Adam until the very last page. Fans of Amish fiction and those seeking an endearing romance will enjoy this love story. Highly recommended."

—Beth Wiseman, bestselling author of *Her Brother's Keeper* and the Daughters of the Promise series

"Treasuring Emma is a charming, emotionally layered story of the value of friendship in love and discovering the truth of the heart. A true treasure of a read!"

—Kelly Long, author of the Patch of Heaven series

The
TEACHER'S
Bride

OTHER BOOKS BY KATHLEEN FULLER

THE AMISH LETTERS NOVELS
Written in Love

The Promise of a Letter

Words from the Heart

THE AMISH OF BIRCH CREEK NOVELS
A Reluctant Bride

An Unbroken Heart

A Love Made New

THE MIDDLEFIELD AMISH NOVELS
A Faith of Her Own

THE MIDDLEFIELD FAMILY NOVELS
Treasuring Emma

Faithful to Laura

Letters to Katie

THE HEARTS OF MIDDLEFIELD NOVELS
A Man of His Word

An Honest Love

A Hand to Hold

NOVELLAS INCLUDED IN
An Amish Christmas—A Miracle for Miriam

An Amish Gathering—A Place of His Own

An Amish Love—What the Heart Sees

An Amish Wedding—A Perfect Match

An Amish Garden—Flowers for Rachael

An Amish Second Christmas—A Gift for Anne Marie

An Amish Cradle—A Heart Full of Love

An Amish Market—A Bid for Love

An Amish Harvest—A Quiet Love

An Amish Home—Building Faith

An Amish Summer—Lakeside Love

An Amish Family—Building Trust

An Amish Family—Surprised by Love

An Amish Homecoming—What Love Built

An Amish Heirloom—The Treasured Book

The TEACHER'S Bride

AMISH BRIDES *of* BIRCH CREEK

KATHLEEN FULLER

ZONDERVAN

The Teacher's Bride

Copyright © 2018 by Kathleen Fuller

This title is also available as a Zondervan e-book.

Requests for information should be addressed to:
Zondervan, *3900 Sparks Dr. SE, Grand Rapids, Michigan 49546*

Library of Congress Cataloging-in-Publication
Names: Fuller, Kathleen, author.
Title: The teacher's bride / Kathleen Fuller.
Description: Grand Rapids, Michigan : Zondervan, [2018] | Series: Amish
brides of Birch Creek ; 1
Identifiers: LCCN 2018029044| ISBN 9780310355076 (trade paper) | ISBN
9780310355090 (epub)
Subjects: | GSAFD: Love stories.
Classification: LCC PS3606.U553 T43 2018 | DDC 813/.6--dc23 LC record
available at https://lccn.loc.gov/2018029044

All Scripture quotations, unless otherwise indicated, are taken from The
Holy Bible, *New International Version®*, NIV®. Copyright © 1973, 1978, 1984,
2011 by Biblica, Inc™ Used by permission. All rights reserved worldwide.
www.zondervan.com

Any internet addresses (websites, blogs, etc.) and telephone numbers in this
book are offered as a resource. They are not intended in any way to be or
imply an endorsement by Zondervan, nor does Zondervan vouch for the
content of these sites and numbers for the life of this book.

All rights reserved. No part of this publication may be reproduced, stored in
a retrieval system, or transmitted in any form or by any means—electronic,
mechanical, photocopy, recording, or any other—except for brief quotations
in printed reviews, without the prior permission of the publisher.

Publisher's Note: This novel is a work of fiction. Names, characters, places,
and incidents are either products of the author's imagination or used
fictitiously. All characters are fictional, and any similarity to people living
or dead is purely coincidental.

Printed in the United States of America

18 19 20 21 22 / LSC / 5 4 3 2 1

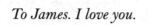

To James. I love you.

GLOSSARY

ab im kopp: crazy, crazy in the head

aenti: aunt

appeditlich: delicious

boppli/bopplin: baby/babies

bruder: brother

bu/buwe: boy/boys

daed: father

danki: thank you

Dietsch: Amish language

dochder: daughter

familye: family

frau: woman, Mrs.

geh: go

grossvatter: grandfather

gut: good

gute morgen: good morning

gute nacht: good night

haus: house

Herr: Mr.

kaffee: coffee

kapp: white hat worn by Amish women

kinn/kinner: child/children
lieb: love
maedel: girl/young woman
mamm: mom
mann: Amish man
mei: my
morgen: morning
mudder: mother
nee: no
nix: nothing
onkel: uncle
schee: pretty/handsome
schoolhaus: schoolhouse
schwester/schwesters: sister/sisters
sehr: very
seltsam: weird
sohn/sohns: son/sons
vatter: father
ya: yes
yer/yers: your/yours
yerself: yourself

CHAPTER 1

I can't believe she came here without letting us know ahead of time."

Ruby Glick paced outside on the front porch. She doubted her older brother, Timothy, and his wife, Patience, realized she could hear their conversation through the screened windows—a conversation about her. Maybe he shouldn't have told her, in a kind but firm way, to wait outside while he and Patience talked.

"Timothy," Patience said, her voice gentle and one hundred percent a reflection of her name. "You're not making much sense. I don't understand why you don't want *yer schwester* to stay with us."

"Favorite *schwester*," Ruby whispered. And only *schwester*, but that was a technicality.

Timothy paused long enough for Ruby to hear a woodpecker drilling in the distance. "Patience, I love Ruby, but she's a walking disaster. Which means a whole lot of problems for us."

Uh-oh. Ruby recognized the firmness in his voice. This was

Timothy when he was standing his ground. She chewed on the inside of her lip and brushed away a stray fallen leaf with the toe of her black sneaker. This wasn't a good sign. Not at all. Not to mention her feelings were a little hurt. Yes, she'd been called a walking disaster before. And yes, it wasn't far from the truth. But that didn't mean she liked hearing it spoken behind her back.

"I can't believe you mean that, Timothy," Patience said, sounding surprised.

Ruby backed away from the window. Maybe she should have written to Timothy before she arrived unannounced on his doorstep ten minutes ago. That would have been the polite thing to do. But since she'd made her decision to come to Birch Creek only yesterday, there wouldn't have been enough time for him to receive a letter from Lancaster. That, and of course the fact that she couldn't wait to get here.

She tugged on her index finger. If Timothy didn't let her stay here for a while, it would ruin her plan. And her plan was perfect, if she said so herself. Unfortunately, she hadn't been in Birch Creek very long before her brother hurled a monkey wrench into it.

She sighed. She didn't want to trouble anyone, except trouble was her middle name according to her parents, Timothy, and more than a few people back home. But not anymore. She straightened her shoulders as she heard Timothy's dairy cows lowing in the pasture behind the house. She was different now. As of twelve hours ago, she had turned over a new leaf. Somehow, she would convince her brother that was the truth.

The front door opened, and she swirled around, hopeful. Timothy scowled at her, shoved his hat onto his head, and took off for the barn. Ruby's shoulders slumped.

Patience walked out behind him and put her hand on Ruby's arm. "This isn't like Timothy."

Ruby glanced at her. "When it comes to me, it is."

Patience gave her an encouraging smile. "I'll *geh* talk to him some more. While I do that, you can put *yer* things in the spare bedroom."

"Are you sure?" Ruby said, brightening. There was hope after all.

"Positive." The expression in Patience's gentle brown eyes grew resolute. "You're our *familye*, and you're staying here in our home. That's final."

Impressed, Ruby grinned. She hadn't thought Patience would be the kind of wife to go against her husband's wishes. Ruby didn't exactly endorse that behavior, but since Timothy was being unreasonable, she was glad Patience saw it her way. She threw her arms around her sister-in-law. "*Danki*, Patience. I promise I won't cause any trouble."

Patience smiled. "Of course you won't." She glanced at the barn and then at Ruby. "Will you keep an eye on the *kinner* while I *geh* talk to him? They're down for their naps, but Tobias might wake up in a few minutes."

"Of course." She opened the screen door, careful to make sure it didn't slam behind her, and went inside. She loved her nephews and hadn't seen them for a few months, not since Timothy and his family last visited Lancaster. One of the perks of coming here was that she could spend time with the little boys.

Ruby took her suitcase upstairs. Timothy's house wasn't that big, and she had been here a few times before, although the last time had been three years ago. She started to set the suitcase on the spare room bed but then paused. Should she unpack now?

Despite Patience's assurances, she wasn't sure if Timothy would relent. *Lord, change his mind, please.*

She set the suitcase on the floor, making sure she was quiet. She slipped off her shoes and went into the hallway. She'd passed Tobias and Luke's room a few moments earlier. Maybe she should peek in on them. When it came to children, she was confident, and at twenty she'd had plenty of babysitting experience.

When she looked inside their room, she smiled. Oh, her nephews were so sweet. Luke, of course, was still in a crib, and Tobias lay on a small bed. A wooden baby gate stretched across the threshold, much like the one she and Timothy had when they were young. Of course, Timothy never tried to escape his crib or his bedroom like Ruby had. She was the reason for the baby gate. As their mother had said time and time again, Ruby had been the *difficult* child.

She bit her lip and stepped back from the bedroom, not wanting to wake her sleeping nephews. Her heart pinched, but she ignored the familiar feeling, as she had so many times over the years. It wasn't as if her parents were wrong. Problems did seem to follow her no matter what she did and despite her best intentions. But she was an adult now, and something had to change. Or rather, *someone.* She had to learn how to be better. To be more acceptable. To be like Timothy and everyone else she knew. And the way to start that transformation was to get married.

At least that was what Ruby had decided. There was a bit of a glitch, though. Although she was ready to find a husband, the single men in her community weren't exactly lining up to propose. That also hurt her feelings a bit, but she had somewhat of a reputation back home. Not a salacious one, though. Just the thought of having *that* type of reputation made her face heat. But she'd been in enough scrapes and caused enough complications that the men stayed far away.

The lack of matrimonial contenders sparked the idea of coming to Birch Creek. It was a thriving community. It was also full of young men who knew her only as Timothy's little sister. She fully intended to use their lack of awareness to her advantage.

She slid down the wall next to the children's bedroom until she was seated on the floor. Then she pulled her knees to her chest, resting her chin on them. She'd had plenty of time to think on the bus ride here from Lancaster. Plenty of time to puzzle out how she was going to land a husband. Also plenty of time to suspect that this might not be the best way to go about it. But she had never been one to sit back and wait for something to happen. Perhaps that tendency also needed further consideration, but right now she was too excited about her plan. After all, it was the first time she had a plan about anything. If she followed it, she was certain she would have a potential husband candidate by Christmas. Or at least a date. *Maybe I should concentrate on that first.*

Ruby smiled. Yes, she would prove to herself and everyone else that she had finally matured into a responsible, sensible adult. They would no longer see her as a walking disaster, leaving chaos in her wake. It was time to introduce the new Ruby Glick to the world.

Timothy grabbed a pitchfork and threw some straw into an empty stall. The horses were out in the pasture, which was a good thing, because they would have experienced a surprise straw shower. Never mind that he'd just put down fresh bedding that morning and he was creating a new mess to clean up.

Patience walked in, but he ignored her. Finally, she said, "Timothy, you can't turn Ruby away."

He jammed the pitchfork back into the straw. Patience might be right, but he didn't want to acknowledge that fact. He didn't have a good reason to turn away his sister, and deep down he didn't want to. But he had enough to worry about right now. He'd just purchased a dozen more dairy cows, which brought his herd up to thirty. He had two small children and a spouse who was keeping plenty busy as a midwife because Birch Creek was experiencing a baby boom. He was on the school board, and a month ago the community decided to draw lots for a district minister. He'd been chosen, and now he had those duties to add to his plate.

These were all good things. He was blessed, and he knew it. He and Patience were in a far better situation than when he first moved here after their wedding. At the time he'd been unsure about leaving Lancaster behind to live in a community with an unwelcoming bishop. But Patience wanted to stay in Birch Creek, and the land here was cheaper than in Lancaster, which allowed him to own his own farm instead of working for his father back home. Emmanuel Troyer, the former bishop, had left, and since Freemont Yoder had become the new bishop, Birch Creek and its various businesses had thrived.

But he was overwhelmed at times, feeling pulled in different directions. Which was why Ruby showing up without warning had knocked him off-kilter. He didn't need his troublemaker of a sister upending everything.

"Stop ignoring me," Patience snapped.

That got his attention. He tossed the straw and leaned the

pitchfork against the stall. "I'm sorry, *lieb*." He walked to her and brushed off a strand of straw that had landed on her *kapp*. "I'm confused, that's all."

"About Ruby?"

"*Ya*." He loved his little sister, but sometimes he didn't understand her. He'd tried to over the years, chalking up her troublemaking nature to immaturity. But that explanation went only so far. For some reason she courted disaster, even when she was trying to be helpful. He wondered what his parents thought about her coming here. *Maybe it was their idea.*

"She's a sweet *maedel*, Timothy. She's also *yer schwester*. We don't turn our backs on *familye*."

He looked at his wife. He'd met Patience almost seven years ago when she was visiting Lancaster, and he'd fallen in love the moment he saw her. Now he was more in love with her than ever, and her kindness was one of many reasons. "You're right," he said, touching one of the ribbons of her *kapp*. "She can stay. But only for a few days."

"She asked to stay indefinitely, remember?"

"Don't you wonder why?"

"*Ya*, but it's none of our business, even if she is staying with us. We need to respect her privacy."

He wasn't going to win this. "Fine. She can stay as long as she wants. But I'm stating for the record that I warned you about her."

Patience scoffed. "You make her sound like a complete—"

"Disaster?"

"How can you talk about her that way?"

Timothy blew out a breath. "Patience, when she and I were *kinner*, she burned down the barn."

Nodding, Patience said, "I remember you telling me that.

You also said it was an accident. She knocked over a lit lantern. That can happen to anyone."

"*Ya*, but what I didn't tell you was that it was our second barn burning."

Patience's mouth dropped open. "You mean she burned down the first one too?"

He nodded. "I know she doesn't mean to, but she gets distracted." Timothy remembered how distraught Ruby had been over both events. She was ten years old the first time, fourteen the second. None of the animals had been hurt, and the second barn was a little salvageable after the fire. "Stuff like that happens around her all the time. Trouble, bad luck—whatever you want to call it, it follows her like a starving stray dog." Right now, he wasn't prepared for whatever havoc his little sister might cause next. Not that he ever could be.

After a long pause Patience said, "She's not a *kinn* or teenager anymore."

Timothy crossed his arms. "I realize she's an adult now. I'm just not sure I can trust her."

Patience touched his beard, her beautiful brown eyes taking on that soft look he couldn't resist. "What about grace, Timothy? Doesn't *yer schwester* deserve some?"

It wasn't her expression that worked on him this time. It was her words. Ruby could be frustrating, and she'd made plenty of mistakes in her life. *Haven't we all?* It wasn't as if he was perfect, even though his mother often said he was close to it. "You never fussed, and you never broke the rules," she would say, usually when Ruby was within earshot. He frowned. That had to be a pretty big burden for her to bear. "*Ya*," he said, his distrust for his sister changing to compassion. "She does."

"That's the Timothy I know." She put her arms around his waist. "And love."

He gave her a half-grin. "There will have to be ground rules, even though she's twenty."

"I think that's fair."

"And she'll have to find a job. She stays out of most trouble when she's busy."

"She could help you around here." When he stiffened, Patience laughed. "I'm kidding. I'm sure she can find work somewhere else." She kissed him on the cheek and stepped out of his embrace. "The *kinner* should be up by now. I asked Ruby to watch them for me."

"Thank God we don't have many breakables," Timothy muttered.

"I heard that." Patience walked out of the barn.

Timothy smiled and shook his head. He couldn't resist that little dig. He swept up the mess he'd made, checked on the cows and horses in the pasture, and then went back to the house.

When he walked into the living room, he saw Ruby sitting in the middle of the floor, playing with Tobias and Luke. Luke was in her lap chewing on a teething ring and Tobias was stacking wooden blocks into a short, crooked pile. When they toppled over Ruby clapped. "Yay, Tobias! You did it."

"It fell," he said, sticking out his bottom lip.

"*Ya*, but now you can build *yer* tower all over again. Wouldn't that be fun?"

Tobias grinned and started stacking the blocks as if he hadn't been pouting a few seconds before.

Patience appeared at Timothy's side. "She's really *gut* with the *kinner*," she whispered.

"*Ya.* She is."

Ruby looked up and smiled, and Timothy wondered if she'd heard them. He hoped she had. She deserved the compliment.

Patience went to Ruby and picked up Luke, whose chubby hands were already stretched up and reaching for his mother. She cradled him against her hip and then reached out her hand to Tobias. "Let's *geh* get a snack." Tobias nodded and clambered to his feet, knocking over his blocks. The tower and Ruby forgotten in anticipation of a snack, he followed Patience and Luke into the kitchen.

Ruby started putting the blocks in the small wooden crate where Patience kept them. "The *buwe* have grown since I last saw them," she said, placing the last block in the bin and pushing it toward the coffee table. The crate knocked into a table leg, and a glass of iced tea on top toppled over. "Oh *nee,*" she said, rushing to upright it. She used the hem of her dress to wipe up the spill. "I'm sorry, Timothy."

He smiled a little as she frantically mopped up her mess, not surprised that she'd spilled something. She'd been here for over an hour, after all. "It's all right, Ruby."

She got up and stood in front of him, and he was surprised the tea wasn't dripping from the hem of her dress. "I'll be more careful."

To her credit, when things did go wrong, she always tried to make them right. He realized he'd been too hard on her when she first arrived, and he needed to make amends for that. "We're happy to have you stay with us as long as you want," he said.

Her eyes brightened. "Are you sure? You didn't say that a little while ago."

"Because you surprised me," he said, feeling a little bad that he might have hurt her feelings. "You know I don't like surprises."

She nodded and looked up at him. "I should have told you I was coming ahead of time."

He went to her and patted her shoulder awkwardly. While he was affectionate with his wife and children, he was usually reserved with the rest of his family. Their parents hadn't been very demonstrative, and they were a quiet pair. Ruby and her bright, boisterous personality had always been a challenge for them to understand and accept. "I'm glad you're here."

Her grin grew wide. "I'm glad to be here. And you'll see, Timothy. I've changed. I'm a better person now." She tilted up her chin. "I can't wait to prove it to you."

"Just promise me one thing," he said, his tone turning serious.

"Anything."

"*Nee* lanterns in the barn." He didn't want to bring that up, but he had to start the ground rules now.

Regret flashed in her eyes, but then it was replaced by determination. "I promise. *Yer* barn is safe while I'm here."

Dear Lord . . . I hope so.

"The dog ate *mei* homework."

Christian Ropp looked at the seven-year-old boy in front of him. He knew Malachi Chupp was lying. He also knew his parents, Jalon and Phoebe, would be horrified if they knew their son was telling a blatant fib to his teacher. Like the rest of the parents he'd met during the past month since he started teaching at the Birch Creek school, they were interested in their child's total education, both academic and character. And right now Malachi's character was in question.

"I see." Christian folded his hands on his desk. "Which dog ate it?"

Malachi paled. "What?"

"Which one of your dogs ate your homework?"

"Uh . . ."

"You don't have any dogs, do you, Malachi?"

The boy's face turned red as he looked at the tips of his shoes. "*Nee.* I only have Blue. He's a cat."

Christian glanced at the rest of the classroom. He was pleased to see the older students, who sat in the back, were still focused on their schoolwork. But the younger ones had started fidgeting in their seats, some of them leaning forward and listening, as if they couldn't wait to see what kind of punishment Malachi would receive. But Christian didn't dole out punishment. He administered correction.

He glanced at his lesson plans. Reading Group B was scheduled to go to the front table in less than a minute, which meant Malachi would have to wait for his correction. However, Christian presumed the period Malachi spent worrying about consequences was sufficient motivation to put an end to the lying. "See me after school, Malachi."

Malachi barely lifted his head. His blue eyes were filled with remorse, another indication that this was unusual behavior for him. He nodded, shoulders slumped as he trudged back to his seat.

Christian pushed back from his desk and stood. "Reading Group B, please come to the table."

Three six-year-old children climbed out of their chairs and went to the reading table, their reading books in hand. He didn't group according to ability but to age, which was easier with the population of the school. He preferred to organize his students by skill level, but he was still learning what they could and couldn't do. For now, grouping by age was the correct choice.

The rest of the afternoon went smoothly, with only one disruption from one of the Bontrager boys. They made up a third of the school's population. For the most part they were well behaved, but they were also boys, and they couldn't seem to keep completely free from making a commotion. This time it was Nelson, who threw a paper wad at his brother Jesse right before dismissal.

After he dismissed the rest of the students for the day, Christian motioned for Malachi and Nelson to come to his desk. Both boys dragged their feet as they made their way to the front of the room.

"Nelson," Christian said, handing him a dry erase marker, "please write *I will not throw paper at my brother* twenty times on the white board."

Nelson grimaced and nodded, taking the marker from Christian's hand.

Christian then turned his attention to Malachi. "Let's go outside."

Malachi's eyes widened, and he followed Christian out of the schoolhouse. They walked down the three steps and to a large oak tree several yards from the building. The weather was warm, but hints of fall came from the few yellow, red, and orange leaves scattered around the base of the tree. A buggy drove by at the same time a car zipped down the opposite side of the road.

Knowing they were sufficiently out of Nelson's earshot, Christian turned to Malachi. "Why did you lie to me about your homework?"

Malachi kicked at one of the leaves. "Because I didn't do it."

Christian frowned and looked down at the little boy. "You should always tell the truth, Malachi—"

"But I didn't want to get into trouble."

"—even if it means you'll get into trouble. Because you lied, you have committed two infractions—first not doing your homework and then the lie."

"What's an infraction?"

"A violation of the rules. You broke the rules," he added, making sure Malachi understood exactly what he had done. While he didn't want to water down his vocabulary, since he fully thought exposing his students to uncommon words was a vital part of his communication with them, he didn't want to be too esoteric.

"I know." Malachi looked down at the ground again. "I'm sorry."

"You are a bright student. I don't understand why you didn't do the work. You would have gotten everything correct."

"I don't like homework," Malachi muttered, kicking at another leaf. "It's boring."

Christian balked. Although he knew he shouldn't take a seven-year-old's critique to heart, he couldn't completely ignore it. He spent hours preparing lessons to make sure the activities were educationally stimulating. During his school years and beyond, he couldn't wait to learn. Even now he enjoyed nothing more than reading a good book and expanding his intellectual horizons. "Boring," he mumbled. "You think my homework assignments are boring."

Malachi looked straight at him. "You said to tell the truth."

Hoisted on his own petard. He should have expected that from Malachi. He wasn't giving him empty encouragement when he said the boy was smart. He was highly intelligent. "That I did," Christian admitted, setting aside his own ego—which he should have done in the first place—and focusing on the problem at hand. "Now, to address your consequences."

"What are those?"

"When you do something against the rules, you have consequences. That's part of discipline."

"I don't want discipline," he said, a flicker of fear in his eyes. "I want to *geh* home."

Now the boy was being overly honest. Perhaps a lesson for the whole class on when it was appropriate to speak and when one should be kept silent was in order. "After Nelson is finished, you will clean the classroom."

"The whole thing?"

"Yes. The whole thing."

Malachi glanced away, but relief was evident on his face. "Okay," he muttered.

Once that was settled, they went back to the schoolhouse. As soon as they stepped foot inside, Nelson ran toward them. Behind him was a slanted, and rather messy, list of sentences. The last line was nearly illegible, but Christian decided not to comment on it.

"Ready to *geh*, Malachi?" Malachi usually walked home with the Bontragers since the families were related by marriage and lived close to each other.

"I have to clean up the classroom." Malachi stuck out his lower lip.

"I can help you do that," Nelson said.

Christian shook his head. "Malachi must do this himself. You may wait outside on the playground for him."

Nelson gave Malachi a look, and Malachi nodded. After Nelson left, Christian graded papers while Malachi took out the trash, wiped all the white boards, straightened the desks, and swept the floor. The entire process took twenty minutes. "That's enough, Malachi," Christian said, taking the broom from him. "You may go home now."

Christian had just finished speaking when Malachi dashed out the door. The open window near his desk faced the playground, and Christian could hear him and Nelson talking loudly outside. "That took a long time," Nelson said.

"*Ya.* It wasn't any fun, neither. I'm never going to lie to the teacher again."

Christian managed a small smile. He glanced over the room, noticing right away what Malachi had missed during his cleaning. Imperfection was to be expected. He was a slight boy, a little shorter than average height, and he couldn't be expected to dust the top of the tall bookshelf or to reach the corner of the white board to erase the day and date. He also hadn't cleaned up the line of dust left behind by the dustpan. But overall, his effort was acceptable.

Christian finished sweeping the floor and cleaning the board, and then he straightened a row of the desks that were still out of alignment. He hung the broom and dustpan on the pegs near the front of the schoolroom and returned to his desk to finish grading papers. This part of teaching could get a bit tedious some days. But for each paper, he made sure to look at each answer, make a few notations for correction, and write an encouraging word or two before recording the grade in his grade book. An hour had passed by the time he finished grading. Then he moved on to his lesson plans, which he scheduled out at least three weeks in advance.

It was nearly dark by the time Christian locked up the schoolhouse. He carried his lunch cooler home, along with his lesson plan book. He still had a few things to add to the plans, but he could do that after supper.

When he reached the small house he shared with his younger sister, Selah, he went inside, headed for the kitchen, and placed his lesson plan book on the table. Selah was standing at the kitchen counter, slicing carrots. "Where did those come from?" he asked, setting his cooler near the sink. Since they'd just moved here during the summer, they didn't have a garden. "Did you go to the store?"

"*Nee.* Mary Yoder dropped them off." Mary was the bishop's wife. Selah continued to slice, her gaze focused on the cutting board.

"What are you making for supper?"

"Vegetable stew."

He looked at the pieces she'd sliced off and frowned. "I advise you to cut them smaller."

"They don't have to be perfect." Selah shoved the knife blade through another carrot.

"Small pieces will heat up faster than large ones, thus speeding up the cooking process."

She blew out a frustrated breath. "You know everything, don't you, *Chris?*"

He flinched at the shortened version of his name. But it was his own fault. After the school board hired him, he'd shaken each of the board members' hands. "Welcome to Birch Creek, Chris," Freemont had said. "Is it okay with you if we call you Chris?"

"Of course," he'd answered, wishing to keep in the members' good stead, especially the bishop. "Chris is fine." The name had stuck, and he regretted not correcting Freemont at the time, especially when Selah taunted him with it. It was too late to change it now.

She suddenly set down the knife a little harder than necessary. "Maybe you should do it, then."

He wondered for a moment if she was angry with him, only to dismiss the thought. He'd done nothing to inspire anger. He'd only made a logical food preparation suggestion. Perhaps she did need a little instruction in that department, however. "If you insist," he said, picking up the knife.

Selah muttered, but Christian didn't understand her. Now he suspected she was annoyed with him—which wouldn't be the first time, nor the last. Such was their sibling relationship, although at times he wished there wasn't so much strife between them as of late. With a shrug he began cutting the carrots into medallions of equal size.

"I suppose it's pointless to ask if you washed *yer* hands." Selah pulled a soup pot from one of the cabinets and dropped it on top of the stove.

He flinched at the banging sound. "I washed them before I left school." He always made sure to wash his hands several times a day. Good hygiene prevented illness from spreading among the student population, and it was important that he set the example for his pupils.

As he worked on the carrots, he heard Selah moving around behind him—the sound of water running as she filled the soup pot, the scrape of the peeler as she peeled the potatoes, and then the whoosh of the gas element as she turned on the stove. He had three carrots left when she came up behind him.

She glanced at the cutting board. "You're not finished yet?" She let out a sigh and walked away. "The rest of the ingredients are already in the pot."

He quickened the pace, but not at the expense of making the carrots uneven. When he'd finished he set down the knife and turned to her. "They're now ready for your stew."

She took the cutting board and knife and dumped the carrots into the pot, barely looking at his careful handiwork.

He bristled. She could have at least said thank you. "Do you need assistance with anything else?"

Her light-brown eyebrows knitted. "I'm capable of making stew, Christian. Despite what you might think."

"I never said you weren't."

She looked at him, let out another sigh that sounded rather long-suffering, and then shook her head and stirred the stew.

She seemed overly annoyed with him, far beyond any reasonable response to his taking over the cutting of carrots. No need for her to have such a strong reaction to that. Deciding that vacating the kitchen was the best course of action, he said, "If you don't need anything else, I'll be outside taking care of Einstein."

"You do that."

He left the house, the last rays of daylight illuminating the path to the barn, and took in a breath of the fresh, early-fall air. Other than his sister's attitude, and the issue of people calling him by a name he didn't particularly like, he was content in Birch Creek. Here, he was able to pursue his goal of becoming a teacher, one that had initially surprised both his parents. His mother was now supportive. His father . . . well, better to not dwell on how he felt. Neither of them had been too happy when Selah had insisted on moving with him.

Her decision had puzzled Christian, and he had more than a moment of hesitation before he agreed. Why was she so eager to leave family and friends behind? He had a compelling reason—his job. She had . . . He didn't know what she had here. They'd never been close. Despite that, he had to admit it was nice not to live alone. And sometimes Selah was fine. Pleasant, even. But her unpredictability was beginning to bother him.

He set his problem with Selah aside—whatever the problem was—and gave Einstein his oats. As his horse ate, he swept the barn of every strand of stray hay. The barn was nearly as tidy as his classroom, and he worked to keep it that way. He made sure Einstein had fresh water, and then he went back inside the house.

As he entered the kitchen, the savory scent of the stew simmering on the stove filled the air. He glanced at the clock. It was nearly seven, and they rarely ate earlier than that during the workweek. That was late for some families, but not for him and Selah since he often stayed at school so long. Strangely enough, that was one thing his sister never complained about.

Assuming Selah was upstairs in her room—his room was on the first floor next to the downstairs bathroom—he checked the stew and tested one of the carrots for doneness. Determining that it wasn't quite soft enough, he rinsed the fork, placed it in the sink, and then picked up his lesson plan book and went into the living room. He sat down on the chair nearest to the wood-stove, which hadn't been lit since late spring. It wouldn't be long before it would be running most of the time.

He opened the book and pulled a folded sheet of paper from the front pocket. He unfolded it and skimmed it.

GOALS:

1. ~~Secure a teaching job.~~
2. ~~Purchase/build a house.~~
3. Get to know people in the community.

Once he had the teaching job, accomplishing his second goal had been fairly easy. Two widowed sisters, Tabitha and Melva, had put their house up for sale the week before he and Selah arrived in Birch Creek. The small home had been affordable, and he quickly purchased it, glad the house was already up to the *Ordnung's* standards and he didn't have to worry about removing the electricity and putting in natural gas.

Number three, however, was proving to be a bigger challenge than anticipated. The residents of Birch Creek were friendly enough, but he hadn't connected with them. That wasn't anything new. He owned several books on how to make friends and communicate with people for a reason. Yet he hadn't been able to put that knowledge into practice, at least not the way Selah could. She had quickly made friends with Martha Detweiler, the only single woman her age in the community, and she was genial with everyone else. In contrast, Christian had yet to have more than a five-minute conversation with anyone.

He had long ago come to terms with the reality that he didn't need friends. He was satisfied with his career and his books. And the Lord, of course. His faith was highly important to him. He wasn't a complete outcast, but he enjoyed his own company. His social standing had never been a problem before.

That had to change, though. Because if he didn't become more integrated into the community, he wouldn't accomplish the last goal on his list:

4. Get married.

Christian stared at the words. He hadn't told anyone else that he wanted to find a bride. Although he was only twenty-one, still on the young side, getting married was the next logical step in life. A job, a house, marriage. Then after getting married he'd have children. That, apart from a few outliers, was the way of life among the Amish. When he joined the church, he had chosen to embrace every part of that life—marriage and family included.

However, he'd encountered another problem he hadn't anticipated: Birch Creek had very few single women. Other than Selah, he knew of only two: Martha Detweiler, whose family had moved here two months before he arrived, and Cevilla Schlabach. Cevilla was out of the question, since she was in her eighties, although she looked and behaved more than a decade younger. Martha, however, was a possibility. She was twenty and quite pretty, although looks weren't that important to him. He just didn't know much about her, so he'd have to make an effort to learn more soon.

Christian folded the paper and put it back in his planner, and then he picked up *The Diligent Classroom* to read while he waited for the stew to finish cooking. He relaxed as he focused on the chapter on classroom management, which was much easier to think about than determining a way to get to know Martha.

Other than a few hiccups like today, his students were well behaved overall and interested in learning. But he couldn't let down his guard or he would have chaos. And if there was one thing Christian Ropp would not allow, in his classroom or in his life, it was chaos.

CHAPTER 2

On Sunday morning, Ruby left for church with Thomas, Patience, and her nephews in their buggy. Luke cuddled in Patience's lap in the front seat while Ruby sat in the back next to Tobias.

"Jesus loves the little children," Ruby sang softly as she put her arm around Tobias, who leaned against her. "All the children of the world . . ." She sang songs to her nephew until they arrived at Naomi and Bartholomew Beiler's home.

Timothy parked the buggy, helped Patience and Luke out, and then took Tobias from Ruby. "We'll see you at the service." He walked away, holding Tobias's small hand and keeping his steps short so his son could keep up.

Ruby smiled. She wasn't surprised that Timothy was a good father. She climbed out of the buggy and stood by Patience, noticing all the buggies parked around them. "This crowd is a bit different since I was here before Luke was born," she said to Patience.

"It definitely is." Patience carried Luke on her hip, but he was squirming to get down. His parents had told her he'd started crawling a few weeks ago, and last night Ruby saw him trying to pull himself up, with a little help from the coffee table. He didn't quite make it, landing on his bottom just as he reached his tiptoes. "We've had several families move here and quite a few weddings since then. It's been wonderful to see how our little community has grown and blossomed. The Lord surely has blessed us."

Ruby nodded. She'd known from Patience's letters to her mother that Birch Creek had grown, but she hadn't realized how much.

"I want to say hi to Sadie for a minute before the service," Patience said. "I'll see you inside." She walked over to a small group of women who were carrying babies with one arm and holding on to toddlers with their other hands.

Ruby slowly followed behind her, taking in the crowd of people gathered near the barn and in the Beilers' front yard. Although so many of them were strangers to her, Ruby did recognize several people from her visit three years ago. She saw Seth and Ira Yoder, the bishop's sons, standing near the Beilers' white house. They were talking with some other young men. Her gaze fell on Seth, the older of the brothers. If she remembered right, he was close to her age and Ira was only two years younger. Wow, they had grown a lot since the last time she'd seen them. Seth was tall and wiry, while Ira was a few inches shorter and stockier. Both were nice looking. She made a mental note to find out if they were available.

A dash of unease came over her. This didn't seem the right way to go about getting married. Being this calculating—which she never was—seemed wrong. But as her parents had put it to her more than once, it was time for her to engage her brain more than her heart. There was more than one way to find a spouse, other than waiting around for love to happen. Her parents had been set up with each other by a mutual friend, and Timothy and Patience had exchanged letters for a year before they were engaged. She was simply being intentional about it, carefully weighing her options. That had to be why she was unsettled. She'd never been intentional about anything, especially nothing this important.

As she was bolstering her confidence in her decision to hunt down a husband, she kept her gaze on Seth. He really was handsome, his sand-colored hair visible under a black hat, his white shirt and black vest fitting him well. Although she could see only his profile, she thought he had a nice smile too. Was that a dimple in his cheek? She took a step forward to get a better look, only to bump into something solid. Or rather someone. "I'm so sorry," she said, turning to see whom she'd knocked into.

"Apology accepted."

Ruby found herself looking into the startling blue eyes of a man who had the blankest expression she'd ever seen. Thick black eyebrows were set in a straight line over those eyes. He had high cheekbones, a long nose, and unsmiling lips that were set in the same type of line as his eyebrows. She also noticed he didn't have a beard. *Obviously single.* "I didn't mean to run into you. I wasn't paying attention."

"You clearly weren't."

She couldn't tell if he was upset at their minor collision, but she wasn't going to let a little run-in keep her from being friendly. "Hi. I'm Ruby Glick. I'm visiting *mei bruder*, Timothy, for . . . for a while." No need to tell anybody she was planning to make Birch Creek her permanent home if her quest was successful.

"Nice to meet you." His tone remained flat, and his expression stayed the same. Blank. Unapproachable.

Awkward. "Well," she said, moving away from him, "I should get to the barn since the service will be starting soon. Nice to meet you too. Good-bye."

He didn't respond as he turned and walked away.

What a strange man. She could cross him off the list of potential husbands. She wasn't interested in someone who couldn't be bothered to say good-bye.

Ruby went inside the barn and sat down next to Patience, putting Seth and that other strange man out of her mind. It was time to prepare her heart for the service. For the next hour she focused on singing, prayer, and worship, completely involved in the service . . . until Freemont started giving the sermon.

Not that the bishop wasn't a good preacher. He had a quiet way of speaking, the importance of his message more in his words than in his tone. Still, it didn't take long for her to be distracted. No matter who was speaking, she always struggled to concentrate during sermons. She sat on her fingers as she glanced around the barn, making sure to look with only her eyes as she kept her head as motionless as possible. She didn't want to draw attention to herself.

The Beilers didn't have a huge barn, like the Stoltzfus's massive one back home in Lancaster. The space did accommodate the community comfortably, though. She saw Timothy sitting next to two men, one with dark-red hair and freckles, the other with black hair and a gorgeous profile. She had no idea who they were, but they both had beards, so she moved on with her perusal. She saw the man she'd run into sitting on the bench behind them. He was staring straight ahead, his posture perfectly straight, his palms on his knees, and he appeared to be listening intently. Upon further inspection she had to admit he was a decent-looking guy. He was no Seth Yoder, but he was okay.

She felt a pinch of guilt and inwardly chastised herself for being shallow. Looks weren't everything. In fact, they meant very little to her, other than to catch her initial attention. And it wasn't like she was the prettiest girl around, not by far. Besides, she'd decided early on that the most important qualities in a potential spouse were his strength of faith and kindness. Of course, he had to be good with children, and a sense of humor was important, considering her ability to get into a pickle or twenty. But it would be nice if she was at least attracted to her future husband.

"What's wrong?" Patience whispered.

Uh-oh. She'd been caught. Ruby turned to her sister-in-law, hoping her face wasn't as red as it felt hot. *"Nix."*

"You're frowning and staring at Chris Ropp."

Her cheeks heated up more, and she faced the front, forcing herself to pay attention to Freemont's sermon. Chris. Funny, he didn't look like a Chris. She imagined him with a more formal name. Like Edward or William, although William wasn't much of an Amish name. If she was going to scout out husband prospects, she needed to be subtle about it, even though subtlety wasn't exactly in her wheelhouse. Wait, she was supposed to be concentrating on the sermon. She cleared her thoughts. With great effort she managed to keep herself from looking at Chris, Seth, or any other man for the rest of the service.

When the service ended, everyone went outside. It was a beautiful fall day with few clouds in the sky. Some leaves fluttered to the ground here and there, but most of them were still clinging to their branches. Patience had lingered behind in the barn, talking to another friend. Ruby figured she'd eventually learn everyone's names.

She didn't see Patience, but she did spy two women who looked to be in her age group. They were standing by the front porch of the house, near the steps. She went to them, thinking it was a good time to introduce herself. When she reached them, she smiled. "Hi. I'm Ruby Glick. I'm visiting *mei bruder*, Timothy."

The shorter of the two gave her a sweet smile. "I'm Martha Detweiler. We just moved here a few months ago." She turned to her willowy friend. "This is Selah. She's new here too."

Selah nodded, but she didn't say anything. In fact, she looked past Ruby's shoulder as if her attention had been suddenly drawn elsewhere.

"Welcome to Birch Creek," Martha said. "How long will you be visiting here?"

Ruby glanced at Selah, who was still looking past her. Or was it through her? Either way, Ruby thought she was being a little rude. "I'm not sure," she said, turning to Martha, who, unlike Selah, was paying attention to their conversation.

"Will you be here next week?"

Ruby nodded. "I plan to be."

"*Gut.* You'll be here for the singing."

A grin broke out on Ruby's face. There was no better place to meet an eligible bachelor than at a singing. She'd made the right decision to come to Birch Creek after all. "That sounds nice." She tried not to sound too excited. The last thing she wanted was for Martha or anyone else to find out what she was up to. "I'm looking forward to meeting everyone."

"I should warn you, though," Martha said, "the group is a bit unbalanced."

"What do you mean?"

"She means we're the only single women here." Selah tilted her head and looked at her. "Now there's you, obviously."

Ruby was too intrigued to be bothered by Selah's curt response, not to mention her assumption that she wasn't taken. "The men outnumber the women?"

Martha nodded. "By a lot. Let's see, there's Seth and Ira Yoder, the bishop's *sohns.* Then the Bontrager boys—Devon, Zeb and Zeke, who are twins, and Owen, but he's only seventeen."

If Ruby had been alone, she would have done a cartwheel. She'd hit the bachelor jackpot—if she was interested in jackpots, of course. Which she wasn't. No gambling allowed.

"You forgot *mei bruder*, Christian," Selah said. "I mean *Chris.*" She gestured to a buggy across the yard. "He's standing by himself, as usual."

Ruby turned and saw the man she had bumped into earlier. He was alone, his arms at his sides, looking as blank as ever. Christian. That name suited him better.

"He'll be at the singing," Selah said.

Martha looked surprised. "He will? He's never come to any gatherings before."

Selah shrugged. "I guess he's decided to show his friendly side. I'm sure it's in there somewhere."

The women chuckled as Ruby glanced at Chris again. He looked a little forlorn standing off by himself. Then again, he was somewhat odd. Maybe he liked being alone.

She turned to Selah and Martha, and she couldn't help but size them up. Martha smiled, and Ruby fought a tiny bit of jealousy. She was very pretty with a perfect figure, and the green of her dress complemented her fair skin and blond hair. Selah was lovely, too, but in a different way. Her eyes were the same blue as Chris's, although her hair was a lighter brown than his. They both had those straight eyebrows, but while Chris's seemed not to express any emotion, Selah's resembled a scowl.

Despite that, Ruby had no doubt the young men in the community were interested in her, and in Martha too. But she didn't see that as a problem. With the ratio of men to women, the odds were in her favor. She would focus on that instead of what she lacked in beauty and grace. Still, it would be good to know a little bit about her competition. "Are either of you seeing anyone?" she blurted.

Selah looked surprised at the question. "That's rather personal."

"I'm sorry." She needed to remember to think before she spoke. That was part of the new Ruby too. "You're right. I shouldn't have asked that."

"It's okay," Martha said. "I have a feeling we'll be *gut* friends soon anyway." She smiled. "To answer *yer* question, *nee*, I'm not seeing anyone."

"I should check on Chris." Selah abruptly shot past Ruby and headed toward her brother.

Ruby cringed. She hadn't meant to put off Selah. "She's annoyed with me."

Martha shook her head. "I don't think so. But she is private. Both of the Ropps are." She leaned forward. "They're also a little strange," she said in a low voice. "Not in a bad way. Just . . . different."

"Oh." She understood different. She'd been different her whole life. When she was little she was too noisy and busy. When she was a teenager she was too clumsy and inattentive. As a young adult she was too friendly and too excitable. She was always too much.

But she could change. She could be a proper woman, a proper wife, and a proper mother. And she would prove it not only to Timothy, but to everyone. Most of all, she would prove it to herself.

Christian stood by the buggy, surveying the different small groups that always broke off and met together after the service. He found it fascinating that no matter how large a group was, it always self-divided mostly according to age and gender. Some of that was the Amish way, but he'd noticed this tendency even in English groups.

His gaze landed on his sister and Martha. The two of them had become friends, which Christian might be able to use to his advantage. He'd never want to do anything to cause a problem for Selah, but he might be able to convince her to mention him to Martha as a possible marriage prospect.

Then he saw that woman—Ruby, he thought she'd said—flounce over to them. She was a bundle of energy, and he had observed how she'd tried to sit still during the church service. Rather immature, in his estimation. Since she was just visiting the community, he dismissed her as a possible spouse, although she was decent looking. Her hair was a typical light brown, and he had noted her vivid blue-gray eyes.

Which left him with Martha. A nice young woman, but as of right now he didn't have any feelings for her. Not that it mattered, since feelings were immaterial. Marriage needed to be based on mutual respect, not love. If the emotion came later, that would be acceptable, but it wasn't a prerequisite to securing a date or pursuing a relationship.

Selah came toward him, a frown on her face. "It wouldn't hurt for you to mix and mingle with people, Christian."

He'd intended to, but then he got caught up in his marriage thoughts. "I will," he said, although everyone was dispersing now. No group lunch had been planned for this afternoon, and families were returning to their own homes. "After the next service."

"Sure you will." She rolled her eyes and faced Martha and Ruby. "I heard you met our visitor."

"Our?"

"Ours as in the community, Christian. You know, the one you're a part of?"

"You seem quite testy this morning, Selah. I would think a sermon as fine as the one Freemont gave would have encouraged you."

She lolled her head at him, gave him an annoyed look, and then looked back at Ruby and Martha.

"I met Ruby. She seems like a nice woman," he said.

"Oh? She's a little nosy, though."

For some reason that didn't surprise him. "How is Martha today?" He had little interest in Ruby, and he needed to turn his attention to his possible future bride.

"Why don't you *geh* ask her *yerself?*"

His palms suddenly and annoyingly grew damp. Nerves. He had them every time he thought about approaching Martha, which was part of the reason he'd hung back after the service. He'd had several opportunities to speak with her, but he couldn't bring himself to do it. "She's leaving," he said, relieved that she was walking toward her family and thus giving him a reprieve. "I'll have to speak with her another time."

"*Right.*"

Her response jabbed at him, as if she were treating him like her personal pincushion. "Sarcasm doesn't suit you."

"And I never thought you'd be such a chicken."

"I'm not a chicken. And if you're trying to bait me into an argument, you won't succeed."

"I'm well aware of that, Iceman."

He detested that nickname, which had been given to him when he was in elementary school. Selah was the only one who continued to call him that, and even though he told her in no uncertain terms that he disliked it, she didn't hesitate to use it when she was frustrated with him. She'd used it a lot lately.

"I'm ready to *geh.*" Selah got inside their buggy.

Christian started to turn, catching a last glimpse of Ruby. She picked up a dandelion and blew. White fuzz floated in the air. Such a childish gesture from a grown woman. He unhitched their horse and joined his sister in the buggy.

The ride home from the Beilers' wasn't too long, but that didn't keep the silence between him and Selah from feeling strained. He should ask what was bothering her. Then again, she might just snap at him. Considering he was her older brother, that would be disrespectful. It would be easier if he minded his own business. But when he glanced at her and saw the shadowy frown on her face, he couldn't stay quiet. "Is something wrong, Selah?"

"*Nee.*"

But the heavy sigh she heaved told him differently. "Clearly you're dodging the question."

"Clearly it's none of *yer* business."

And that was why he didn't get involved. He gripped the reins, telling himself she was in one of her moods and he shouldn't take it personally. But a part of him did, and like always, he shut down that part of himself.

They didn't speak for the rest of the ride home. Christian wasn't too worried. As a young woman Selah was prone to up-and-down moods, per the psychology books he'd read last year. Hormonal changes were a part of that too. He would leave her to her pouting and scowling, and perhaps she would be friendlier later today.

Besides, he had other things to focus on. He wouldn't work today, but that didn't keep him from thinking about his students—especially Malachi. Perhaps the boy had a point about the work being boring, considering his intelligence. This week he would develop some assessments for his students to see if they were being educationally stimulated. He'd been bored in school, but never bored with learning. Still, procedures had to be followed in the classroom, and not completing homework had to be addressed.

Then there was Martha. He had to approach her sometime. Obviously, Selah wouldn't assist him. Surely there was a way to get over these paralyzing nerves. He needed to conquer them, and soon. He had no reason to delay marriage—and he didn't intend to.

"What are *yer* plans for this week, Ruby?" Patience set a plate of sausage links on the table.

"Helping you," Ruby said as she poured milk for her nephews. She spilled a little bit on the table and wiped it up with the bottom of her apron. She secured the tops of their sippy cups and put the milk back in the gas-powered fridge.

"I do have some sewing to catch up on." Patience sat down just as Timothy walked into the kitchen. He'd been outside doing the morning chores.

"I can watch the *kinner* for you while you sew." Ruby put her hands in her lap and waited for her brother to wash his hands. The toe of her shoe tapped on the floor. When she heard it, she froze. *Sit still, remember?*

Timothy sat down, and after a silent prayer of thanks, the family started eating breakfast. "The cows were eager to get out in the pasture this morning," Timothy said as he buttered a slice of toasted bread.

"Do you need any help with them?" Ruby asked.

Timothy paused, the bread halfway to his mouth. "Uh, *nee.* I've got everything under control."

"I'm sure you have some chores I can do after I help Patience."

He shook his head and crammed the toast into his mouth.

Patience put a few pieces of oat cereal on Luke's high chair tray. "Timothy, you could use a little help. I'm sure Ruby can help you with the hay bales."

Ruby and Timothy looked at each other. "You didn't tell her

about the time I sent all the bales tumbling out of the loft?" Ruby asked.

He shook his head. "I forgot about that one."

"How could you forget?"

"Because so many other accidents stick out in *mei* mind. Like when you decided to give the cat a bath."

"Oh." She grew serious. "That didn't turn out the way I expected."

"Tobias, drink *yer* milk," Patience said. She turned to Ruby. "What happened?"

"What didn't happen?" Timothy picked up his fork and pointed at her with it. "She decided the cat needed to smell better."

"I was only six," Ruby said.

"So she took the cat—who was about the size of a fox, mind you—and stuck him in the kitchen sink."

Ruby looked down at her plate. "He didn't like that too much."

Luke started to bang on the table, so Patience gave him a few more Cheerios. Tobias was busy spreading his scrambled eggs on his plate.

"He didn't like it at all." Timothy started to laugh. "He was sopping wet and leapt out of the sink onto the counter. *Mamm* had just finished washing the breakfast dishes, and they were drying on a towel. They scattered onto the floor, and Ruby tried to catch him by grabbing his tail. He let out a screech that would curl *yer* hair, and then he streaked through the living room, where *Daed* was cleaning his boots in front of the fireplace."

"With black shoe polish," Ruby said, her voice barely above a whisper.

"Oh *nee*." Patience lips twitched.

"This wet, scared cat leaps into *Daed*'s lap and spills the black shoe polish all over the stone hearth."

Ruby shrank back in her chair. "Remember, I was six," she squeaked.

"He ran through the shoe polish, and then he dashed all over the furniture like his tail was on fire." Timothy guffawed. "*Daed, Mamm*, and I were all chasing him."

Patience laughed. "What were you doing while all this was happening, Ruby?"

"Crying in the corner."

Timothy stopped laughing. "That's right. You were. It wasn't that bad, Ruby."

"I broke *Mamm*'s favorite dish."

"The cat broke *Mamm*'s dish," he said gently.

"But it was *mei* fault." Even now the guilt over the destroyed dish hit her as if it had happened an hour ago. *Mamm* had made *Daed* a special breakfast for his birthday, and she had served the blueberry pancakes on that dish. Since it was a family heirloom, she used it only on special occasions.

"You *were* only six." Timothy patted her hand. "I'm sorry. I shouldn't have brought up that story."

"*Nee, nee.* It's funny looking back on it now." Except that it wasn't. Not to her.

"What happened to the cat?" Patience asked.

"He pulled the curtains off the window before Timothy caught him."

"Then I did have to give him a bath because he was covered in shoe polish."

Ruby nodded. "And I helped *Mamm* clean the furniture." She sighed. "Fortunately, the polish didn't stain too badly."

"Well, you're not six anymore, and Timothy never polishes his boots." Patience smiled. "No worries about that happening here."

"Besides," Timothy added, "we don't have a cat."

"Kitty?" Tobias said, looking up from his eggs. "Can we have a kitty?"

The three adults chuckled, and Ruby felt a little better. Timothy could tell many stories about her, and the cat story wasn't even the worst one. *Use* yer *brain, Ruby.* How many times had she heard that? Well, now she was going to. There would be no more disasters, or broken heirlooms, or complete bedlam surrounding her. But she was glad her brother didn't have a cat.

Later, when Timothy went out to speak to a potential milk buyer and Patience brought out her sewing, Ruby took her nephews outside. She took the cover off the sandbox and played with them for the rest of the morning, forgetting about the past and even forgetting about her quest to get married. She held on to Luke to make sure he didn't put sand in his mouth while she helped Tobias scoop sand into a small plastic bucket with a tiny, bright-red shovel.

While Tobias played, she glanced around her brother's dairy farm. He had done well for himself, and she was happy for him. One day she hoped to have the same kind of life—peaceful and happy. That was possible, wasn't it?

CHAPTER 3

*T*he week passed quickly for Ruby. She helped Patience with the chores and spent time with her nephews. She twice offered to help Timothy milk the cows, but he refused. She thought he looked more tired than he should at the supper table after spending the day working on the farm. But she couldn't force her brother to let her help, and while she was a little frustrated about that, she also understood. She didn't exactly have the best history when it came to helping out in barns.

On Saturday she accompanied Patience on her midwife visits. First, they stopped to see Sadie Troyer, who was expecting her first child. Ruby observed Patience as she asked a series of questions about how Sadie was feeling, if she felt the baby kick, and if she was eating well. Sadie was five months along, Ruby found out, and a little nervous about the pregnancy.

"I just don't want anything to happen," Sadie said, touching her slightly rounded abdomen. "Aden tells me not to worry, and

I know I shouldn't." She lowered her voice. "But sometimes I can't help it."

Patience took her hand. Ruby knew the women were good friends. "It's normal to feel like this with the first *boppli*," Patience said. "Sometimes the second, and the third . . ." She smiled. "But Aden's right. You don't need to worry. It's not *gut* for you or the *boppli*. When you feel anxious, the best thing you can do is pray. If you can take a walk and pray—or do something else physical while you're praying—that's even better. And, of course, you can always come and talk to me. You're in *gut* hands, Sadie."

Sadie nodded, her expression more relaxed. "I know. *Danki*, Patience. I'm glad you're with me through all this."

After they left Sadie's, they went to Irene Troyer's. Irene was married to Aden's brother, Sol. They spent a shorter amount of time there since this was Irene's second child. She was six months along, and her one-year-old son, Solomon Jr, was sleeping in a playpen in the living room.

"Could I speak to you privately?" Irene asked, glancing at Ruby.

Patience nodded. "Of course." The women stood from the couch.

"Do you mind watching Solomon for a few minutes, Ruby?" Irene asked. "He probably won't wake up. He didn't sleep well last night, and he was tired this morning."

Ruby nodded, and the women left. She scooted to the edge of her chair. The playpen was in plain sight, and she could see the rise and fall of Solomon's soft breathing through the white mesh of the pen. A shock of red hair stood straight up on top of his small head, and he was a bit chunky. He was also adorable.

She couldn't help but smile. Children were such a blessing.

She couldn't wait to become a mother someday. Hopefully sooner than later.

A few minutes later, Irene and Patience entered the living room. Just as Irene predicted, Solomon had kept sleeping. But he must have sensed his mother was back, because he let out a small cry. His eyes opened, and he fussed a little more.

Irene bent over and picked up her son. He laid his head on her shoulder and she patted his back.

"I'll be back to check on you next month," Patience said. "But if you have any questions or problems, you let me know right away."

"I will. *Danki*, Patience."

As Ruby and Patience climbed into the buggy, Ruby thought about how impressed she was. Patience was kind and professional with both Sadie and Irene. Ruby didn't know much about what a midwife did, other than help with the birth of babies, but she could see there was more to it than that. Patience was an encourager, a confidante, and someone her patients depended on. She was a wonderful midwife who knew what she was doing.

They headed in the opposite direction of Irene's to pick up Tobias and Luke, who'd been spending the day with Patience's parents. Timothy had gone to a livestock auction with Jalon Chupp and Adam Chupp, cousins who owned a large farm, a little more than two miles from the Glicks'. Ruby was beginning to learn who was who in the community.

She glanced at the landscape as Patience drove. Unlike where she lived in Lancaster, which was busy not only with Amish but plenty of English—both residents and tourists—she hadn't seen too many cars on the roads out here. Birch Creek inhabitants didn't experience the bustle of traffic, the smell of exhaust, or the blare of a car horn from an impatient driver. In this area were acres of country land, some with houses, gardens, and farms. Others were large, unspoiled fields. Ruby's last visit here had been a short one, but now she had time to take in the beauty of Birch Creek.

"I hope you weren't too bored today," Patience said, interrupting Ruby's thoughts.

"*Nee*, not at all. *Yer* job seems fulfilling."

"It is. I plan to be a midwife as long as God allows."

Ruby nodded. It must be nice to be that fulfilled, that secure in knowing that what you're doing is part of God's plan. She had always felt so adrift, working a few different jobs but nothing ever really sticking. She'd been a clerk in a store for a little while, but the job was uninteresting, and her boss wasn't too happy when she knocked over product displays two days in a row. She wasn't too upset when she left that position and started cleaning English houses. She cringed as she thought of that job. She'd been fired from it when she was dusting and accidentally broke a client's expensive crystal vase that had been a twenty-fifth wedding anniversary present. That had taught her not to work around breakables.

Then she worked on a dairy farm for a little while, which was why she felt confident offering her services to Timothy. But shortly after, the owner retired and sold off his stock. Jobs were a little hard for her to find after that, so she took in sewing and babysat when she could. She didn't mind sewing too much, and of course she enjoyed babysitting. But neither job brought in much money or the type of fulfillment Patience had in her work.

"Have you ever thought about being a midwife?" Patience asked.

Surprised at the idea, she shook her head. *"Nee.* I wouldn't be *gut* at it."

"How do you know?"

"I'd be worried that something would *geh* wrong. It's too important a job for me to do."

Patience smiled. "That's why you train for it. If you want to learn, I can teach you."

Ruby looked at her. "Are you saying you need an assistant?"

Patience shrugged as she pulled the buggy into her parents' driveway. "I've been thinking about it. A lot of *bopplin* have been born in Birch Creek lately. Fortunately, the births were spread out over time, but if the community keeps growing at this pace, I won't be able to keep up." She pulled the buggy to a stop and turned to Ruby. "You're still not sure when you're going home, *ya?"*

Ruby nodded.

"Don't you miss Lancaster? *Yer* friends, *yer familye* . . . maybe even someone special is waiting for you?"

She couldn't think of a single person who would miss her. All her childhood friends were married and starting their own families. Over the past two years they had all become more distant. They seemed to want to talk about only one topic— their husbands and children. The ones who didn't have any children yet wanted to talk about their future children. She had nothing to add to those conversations, so she stopped engaging in them.

Then there were her parents. They were probably glad to be rid of her for a while. She knew they loved her, but they were often frustrated with her, and she felt guilty about that. And she was keenly aware of having zero marriage prospects back home.

What was the point in going back there? She threaded her fingers together in her lap. "I need a change of scenery," she said.

"Or a new start?"

Her gaze shot up at her sister-in-law. Did Patience suspect something? She wouldn't be surprised. She'd caught Ruby staring at Chris Ropp in church Sunday—not that she was interested in him. Patience was smart, but could she draw the correct conclusion from that? Ruby decided she couldn't, but she vowed to be more careful with her words and actions.

Patience didn't seem bothered that Ruby hadn't answered her question. "Why don't you pray about it?" she said.

"Staying in Birch Creek?"

"About being *mei* assistant." She tilted her head, her expression pensive. Then she smiled. "I would love for you to help me."

Ruby could hardly believe Patience was serious. "You're not afraid I'll ruin something?"

She chuckled. "Of course not. You worry too much about making mistakes, Ruby. That might be part of the reason you make so many." Before Ruby could respond, Patience got out of the buggy and looped the reins around the hitching post.

Well, no one had put it to her that way before. Was that why she was so clumsy and awkward? Because she was tense all the time? She realized some truth was in those words, but she didn't believe that was the only reason. As much as she could remember, she hadn't been tense as a child, yet she'd caused plenty of problems then. The bathed cat and the burned barns were prime examples. With her track record, it was hard not to be stressed—which meant she had to think carefully about Patience's offer.

Patience's parents, Josiah and Mary Anne, were a kind

couple. They were also weary looking after spending the morning and part of the afternoon with a baby and a toddler. Ruby eagerly gathered Luke in her arms and snuggled him against her while Patience picked up Tobias and spoke with her mother. Her father plopped down in a chair.

"This is why you have *kinner* when you're young," he said. "Those *buwe* are full of energy."

"They take after their father," Patience said.

"More like their *mamm*," Mary Anne corrected. "You were a handful when you were young."

"Really?" Ruby was surprised to hear this.

"Absolutely. When she was little we had to lock the doors so she wouldn't escape."

"She liked to explore." Her *daed* scratched his gray beard. "Usually in the middle of the night."

Patience laughed. "I grew out of that phase, though."

"You did. But until then you kept us both busy."

Luke tugged on the ribbon of Ruby's *kapp*. So she hadn't been the only rambunctious child in the world, although her parents seemed to believe she had. Then again, Timothy had always been the perfect child. Always followed the rules, never got in trouble, made straight *A*s in school, kept the same job from age fourteen to when he moved away. Until he married Patience. When he left for Birch Creek, her parents, especially her mother, were heartbroken. Since they didn't like to travel, they had visited Timothy and Patience only two times in the past five years. But her mother wrote to him often, and, dutiful son that he was, he wrote back. He and Patience had also visited Lancaster several times, making sure the grandparents got to see their grandsons. Which was the *perfect* thing to do.

Ruby had yet to hear from her parents, and she'd been in Birch Creek a week. She frowned as she gently took the string of her *kapp* out of Luke's hand. How hard was it to send them a letter? Or even a postcard? Then again, she hadn't written or called them either, so she had no right to complain.

When they arrived back at Timothy and Patience's house, Patience settled Luke down for an afternoon nap in his crib. Ruby figured the baby should nap well since he'd been fighting sleep on the buggy ride home. While Patience was upstairs with Luke, Ruby helped Tobias select a children's book off the bottom shelf of the short bookcase against the wall in the living room. He wanted to hear nursery rhymes, so Ruby pulled out a book whose cover had a picture of a goose wearing a frilly bonnet. She handed the book to Tobias, and he drifted to the couch and climbed up on it. Ruby sat down next to him and started to read.

Hickory, dickory, dock.
The mouse ran up the clock.
The clock struck one,
The mouse ran down,
Hickory, dickory, dock.

"*Mamm*," Tobias said, pointing to the book. "Goose. Goose."

Patience, who had entered the room while Ruby read, nodded. "That's *yer* favorite, isn't it?"

Tobias took the book from Ruby's hands and held it out to Patience. "Read. Read."

"Ruby's reading to you, Tobias."

With a shake of his head, he said, "I want you."

"It's okay," Ruby said, getting up from the couch. "He hasn't seen you all day."

"All right." Patience sat down and took the book from Tobias. As she started reading about going around a mulberry bush, Ruby slipped into kitchen.

She thought about her parents again. She really should call them. Maybe they did miss her. She had to admit she was missing them, along with the pot roast and potatoes *Mamm* always made on Saturday nights. About now the rich scent of the roast would be wafting around the house, and her mother would be putting finishing touches on a peach pie or banana pudding, two of her father's favorite desserts. Thinking about that made her hungry and also a little homesick. She hadn't expected to be.

Ruby went through the mudroom, out the back door, and around the house. The phone shanty was at the end of the driveway. She shut its door behind her, but then cracked it open. It had been a warm day, and the shanty was stuffy.

She dialed her home phone number. After five rings, she almost hung up, thinking her mother was probably too busy making supper to answer the phone. She was putting the receiver back in the cradle when she heard her mother say, "Hello?"

Ruby brought the phone to her ear and smiled. "Hello, *Mamm.*" It was so nice to hear her voice.

"It's about time you called, Ruby. How is Timothy doing?"

"He's fine." She leaned against the wall of the shanty, anticipating her mother's next questions. "The *buwe* are doing well and so is Patience. Timothy has a terrific *familye.*"

"Is he getting enough rest? I worry about him working too hard. He always gives one hundred percent in everything he does."

She'd heard that a time or two before. She also decided not to tell her mother that Timothy might be overworked. "He's getting plenty of sleep, *Mamm*."

"What about eating? When he came to visit last year, he looked a little thin."

Ruby sighed. Apparently *Mamm* would never stop fretting over Timothy, even though he was a grown man. "He's fine, *Mudder*. Patience takes *gut* care of him."

"*Humph*. I'm not so sure about that."

"How are you and *Daed* doing?" Ruby asked, deciding to change the subject.

"We're fine." Ruby listened as her mother detailed what she and her father had been doing for the past week, which mostly consisted of *Daed* working at his job as a bricklayer and *Mamm* visiting various friends in the community, followed up with delicious suppers and tranquil evenings. "It's been quiet and peaceful," she said. "Just the way we like it."

Ruby swallowed. "I'm glad."

"I need to finish up supper now. Tell Timothy how much we miss him. And make sure you stay out of trouble. Don't be a bother to *yer bruder*."

"I won't—" But *Mamm* had already hung up.

Ruby set the receiver in its cradle and stepped out of the shanty, her throat tight. *She didn't ask how I was doing. Didn't say she missed me.* Maybe that was because she didn't. *Peaceful and quiet. The way we like it.* Clearly, they were happier when she wasn't around.

Fine. They could feel that way for now. And for now, she didn't even need them. She had her own goal to reach, one she hadn't thought much about this past week. She was changing that right now. She was going to get married, and when she did she would move to Birch Creek permanently. Then her parents would miss her. Respect her. Want her around.

She wiped her burning eyes and headed down the road. She would need to put her plan in motion, and fast. Except she realized her plan wasn't much of a plan beyond "find a husband." Then she remembered the singing Martha mentioned. That was happening tomorrow evening. *Wonderful.* At the singing she would take a first step to becoming someone's bride. As far as she knew, she'd have her pick of candidates. Seth Yoder immediately came to mind, but she mentally set him to the side. She needed to keep her options open. *Although he is very schee . . .*

Ruby wasn't sure how long she'd been walking down the road when a massive tree caught her attention. She stopped, amazed by its size and splendor. The tree was situated in a large pasture, which surprisingly, since it was perfect for grazing cows, had tall grass and no fencing.

She turned her attention back to the tree. An oak that huge must have been growing in this field for years, and the trunk was thicker than any she'd ever seen. Curious, she walked toward it, feeling a slight change of temperature as she walked under the cooling shade of its immense canopy. She touched the bark of the tree as she began to circle it. She imagined the stories a tree like this could tell.

Suddenly she stubbed her toe on something. Assuming it was one of the tree roots that had made its way above ground, she looked down, determined to watch her step. Wait, it wasn't a tree root. She'd hit her toe against a book. Someone must have left it here. The area did seem like a quiet place to read. Maybe a name was written inside the cover. If so, she would try to return the book to its owner.

But when she bent to pick it up, she was startled by a loud snore. She lifted her gaze to see Chris Ropp leaning against the tree's trunk, fast asleep.

What was he doing out here? Quietly, she crouched, picked up the book, and rested her elbows on her knees as she looked at the title. *A Man's Guide to Understanding Women.* She let out a chuckle and then slapped her hand over her mouth.

Chris opened one eye and then the other. They both grew wide and he sat up straight. He blinked once before snatching the book from her hands. "What do you think you're doing?"

She hurried to stand, lost her balance, and landed on her behind.

He was on his feet by now. His blue-eyed gaze bore into her. "Were you spying on me?"

"*Nee.*" She clambered to her feet and brushed the grass off the back of her dress. "I don't spy on people." She couldn't help but glance at the book in his hand.

He put both hands behind him. "If you're not sneaking around, then why are you here?"

That was a nosy question. "I could ask you the same thing." Unless he owned this pasture, which meant he owned this tree. Which meant he had every right to be here and she . . . didn't.

He lifted his chin. "I'm always here on Saturday afternoons, weather permitting. I enjoy the peaceful setting. It allows me to read, to contemplate, and to pray."

"And to understand women, apparently," she mumbled.

Chris's cheeks turned slightly red. "My reading material is none of your business."

"Do you really think you'll figure out women by reading a book?"

He averted his gaze while somehow still managing to come across as haughty. "I have learned a great many things from books." He turned to her. "You should try reading one."

Did he think she was dumb? Of all the nerve. "I read plenty of books," she said, crossing her arms over her chest.

"Oh? What genres do you enjoy?"

"I like, um . . ." Oh dear. When was the last time she'd read a book? Not lately, she had to admit. But she would admit that to herself, not to him. "I like fiction," she said. There. That should satisfy him.

"Any particular kind?"

She grimaced. "There's more than one kind?"

He shook his head. "Never mind." He picked up his hat from the ground and started to move past her.

"You think I'm stupid, don't you?"

He waved his hand at her in a dismissive gesture. "I don't know you well enough to make that assessment."

"But you just insulted me." She dropped her arms and put her hands to her sides. "More than once . . . I think."

He paused and then he turned and faced her. "I apologize, then. But I'm not the only one at fault here."

"What do you mean?"

"I find it incredibly rude that you would not only sneak up on me while I was napping, but then be meddlesome enough to peruse my reading material."

Her mouth dropped open. She had never heard anyone speak so formally in her life. "Why aren't you speaking *Dietsch*?"

"I prefer English."

Odd. Then again, she already knew he was *seltsam*. But that didn't mean he was wrong to be offended by what she did. She had snuck up on him. She'd stared at him while he slept. She did peruse—what an interesting word—the cover of his book. He had the right to be upset with her, which made her hang her head a little. "I owe you an apology, then. I'm sorry I perused."

His lips twitched at the corners. "Apology accepted."

She turned and looked at the tree. "I can see why you like to come here," she said, touching the bark again. "This tree is beautiful, and the land around it is untouched. I imagine you get a lot of praying and reading done here."

"*Ya*," he said, putting on his yellow straw hat. "I do."

Ruby looked at him, puzzled. "Now you're speaking *Dietsch*?"

He shrugged. "Does it make you feel more comfortable when I do?"

"Did you learn that in *yer* book?"

"Page twenty-five. A man should always make a woman feel comfortable."

Strangely enough, she was feeling comfortable, but not because he was speaking *Dietsch*. It didn't matter to her which language of the two he spoke, since she was fluent in both. But for some reason she wasn't tripping over her words or feeling nervous around him, which sometimes happened when she talked to men. All right, it *always* happened when she talked to men, particularly ones her age. "What else did that book tell you?"

"I . . . I don't know." He scratched behind his ear. "I fell asleep."

"Must be scintillating reading, then."

His right brow arched. "Excellent vocabulary use."

"Thank you. I do know a word or three."

Chris frowned as if he didn't understand what she said. Then he straightened his hat. "If you'll excuse me, I'll be returning home." He started to walk away.

"Wait." She froze. Oh no, what was she doing? But her mouth ignored that question as she announced, "I can teach you more than a book can." *So much for thinking before speaking.*

Slowly he turned. "Are you offering to tutor me?"

"*Ya.*" *Nee.* Why couldn't she stop talking? She didn't owe Chris Ropp anything, much less a tutoring lesson. Yet it seemed a bit sad that he was going to a book for advice. "Don't you have a *schwester?*"

A shadow passed over his face. "I do, but I fail to see what she has to do with tutoring."

Ruby got the impression things weren't all that great between him and Selah, which explained why he needed the book. She drew in a breath. "If you want to learn about women, I'll help you."

Chris tilted his head. "And why would you do that?"

That was exactly the question running through her mind. "Because . . . because I'm a woman."

He looked her up and down, but not in a leering way. It was more like an intellectual observation. "Obviously."

Goodness, he was irritating. "You know, never mind." She turned and marched away from him. She should have never brought it up in the first place. "I try to do something nice—"

"Ruby."

She took a few more steps before she whirled around. "What?"

He touched his ear again. "I would be most appreciative if you would share your knowledge with me."

That brought her up short. Not only was he taking her up on her offer, but she saw something in his eyes that gave her pause. Desperation? No, that couldn't be it. She couldn't imagine this calm, cool, collected, and more than a little off-kilter man desperate about anything. He had a confidence about him that contradicted the entire idea. Still, she couldn't stop the thought that if he were desperate—and that was a big *if*—he would never show it. At least not in public.

"All right," she found herself saying in agreement. It was her idea, after all. "I'll tutor you."

"We need to set up a time to meet."

"Of course," she said. "I'll have to put you on my schedule. I am quite busy."

Chris smirked. "Of course. Next Saturday if—"

"The weather permits."

He nodded. "Do you think you can accommodate that?"

She tapped her finger on her chin, as if she were mentally checking her calendar. Which was untrue, since she didn't have a calendar. "I'll pencil you in." His expression remained impassive. She did have her work cut out for her. This would probably end in disaster, as most things in her life did, but she'd already given her word. She always kept her word. "One o'clock?"

"I'll be here."

"I'll see you then." She turned and started for home, remembering that she hadn't told Patience she was leaving. Her sister-in-law was probably wondering where she was. That wasn't good, since Ruby had promised not to cause any problems. She quickened her steps.

"Ruby," Chris called out.

"What?" she said, not turning around or slowing her gait.

"For the record, I don't think you're stupid."

She smiled as she kept walking.

CHAPTER 4

*C*hristian scratched his head, trying to figure out what had just happened. One minute he was reading the book he'd picked up from the library earlier this week—a rather silly book, and judging by the writing style and vocabulary, most likely written by a teenager—and the next he was looking into the blue-gray eyes of Ruby Glick. That was most unexpected, as was her offer to tutor him. He'd been stunned when she said she would help him learn about women, and more than a tad bit embarrassed. It was bad enough he had trouble talking to Martha. He didn't need Ruby knowing about it. *Too late for that.*

Why he took her up on her offer he had no idea. But maybe gaining insight directly from a woman would be a better investment of his time than to keep reading books about female psychology—or pseudo-psychology, as the case seemed to be.

He tucked the book under his arm and headed back to the house. He hadn't meant to fall asleep, but the nap had been sustaining. When he arrived home, he found a note on the kitchen table.

Went to Martha's.

No signature, but it was Selah's handwriting. *Hmm.* Maybe he should go over to Martha's, too, on the pretense that he needed to speak to Selah. Or he could tell Martha that his sister was needed at home. He could figure out something to say, perhaps even solicit an invitation to stay for coffee. Anything to put him in her proximity.

Before he could ponder the idea further, his palms grew damp. He grimaced. This happened every single time he thought about talking to Martha. He couldn't go over there, not when he was at risk of making a bumbling idiot of himself. Even he knew that wasn't the way to woo her. Then there was the added issue of Selah, who wouldn't appreciate Christian using her to get to her friend. Plus, he didn't want to see Martha under false pretenses.

He'd have to wait for the singing tomorrow. Hopefully Martha would be there. He expected her to be, since unlike him, she seemed to enjoy mingling with people. She was the only reason he was attending. He'd rather stay home than go through the excruciating process called socializing.

He spent the rest of the afternoon doing light housekeeping chores. The dishes from breakfast and lunch were still in the sink, and thick dust was on the furniture in the living room. Dusting needed to be done at regular intervals during the warmer weather months since the windows were open all the time. Selah knew this. She'd been a good housekeeper back home. At least he thought she was. In all honesty he hadn't paid much attention to what she did or didn't do. Maybe she'd always been this sloppy. Maybe their mother did all the cleaning. Yet that didn't sound right either.

He didn't mind doing chores, but since Selah didn't have a job and was at home most of the time, she had no excuse for not completing this work.

By the time he'd washed the dishes, dusted, swept the downstairs floors, and scrubbed away two spots he'd noticed on the floorboards, it was nearly six. When Selah still hadn't arrived home at six thirty, he decided to start making supper. By seven fifteen the casserole was done and cooling on the stove. At seven thirty he was a little concerned. Selah should have put a time when she was coming back on her note. That would have been the courteous thing to do. Did she enjoy making him worry? At eight o'clock he decided to go to Martha's. He had a legitimate reason now—to tell Selah it was time to come home.

He was marching toward the barn when he saw Selah walking up the driveway in the dusky sunlight. "Where have you been?" he said in *Dietsch* as he hurried over to her.

"Martha's. I left you a note." She pushed past him.

"For the whole afternoon and evening?"

"It's not that late, Christian." She stopped at the bottom of the porch steps and faced him. "I'm not a little *maedel* anymore. I don't need a curfew."

"You do if you continue to be irresponsible like this."

Her eyes narrowed. "You're not *mei vatter.*" She scowled. "And when did you start caring, anyway?" She whirled around and stormed into the house.

Christian flinched as the screen door bounced shut behind

her. Again, she was overreacting. He was the one who should be angry, not her. He was the one who'd been worried. And what did she mean about him not caring? He always cared about her. It was true that they didn't have much in common. She was two years younger than him and female. They had different interests and different goals. He'd worked for years studying to be a teacher, increasing his education not just for professional reasons but also personal ones. She had . . . well, he supposed she had spent time with her friends. That's what most women did, right?

He rubbed his left eyebrow. While he didn't know how she spent her time, he did care about her. They were siblings. What he couldn't do was understand her.

Christian went inside and headed for the kitchen. Selah was standing over the sink, slathering peanut butter and jelly on a piece of white bread.

"I made chicken and rice," he said. "It won't take long to warm up in the oven."

"I'm not that hungry." She slammed another piece of bread on the one she'd prepared and left the kitchen—without looking at him and without cleaning up her mess.

Should he go after her? He was tempted, but according to the adolescent psychology books he'd read, he should give her space. After she cooled off, he would express his expectations— whenever she left home she had to tell him both where she was going and when she would be back. He wasn't her father, but she was only nineteen, and he felt responsible for her. Besides, she always knew where he was—either at school, church, or under the tree near the empty pasture.

As he put the lids back on the peanut butter and jelly jars, he sighed. His relationship with his sister was deteriorating, and he didn't know why. All he'd wanted was a little courtesy tonight and in the future. That wasn't too much to ask. Selah apparently felt otherwise.

Ruby smoothed the sides of her *kapp* and licked her lips before she climbed the steps to the Yoders' front porch. Freemont and his wife, Mary, were hosting the singing in their basement, so she knew Seth would be there along with his brother Ira. Judah, their younger brother, was still school age and wouldn't be expected to attend. The beating of her heart sped up as she knocked on the door, wanting Seth to answer it, and then again, not wanting him to. She didn't feel prepared to see him or any of the other young men tonight, even though she'd been looking forward to this all day. A ball of nerves ping-ponged in her stomach.

Fortunately, Mary answered the door, giving her a few more seconds before she had to see Seth and everyone else. "Hello, Ruby." She smiled and opened the door wider. "Come in. I'm glad you could join us. Everyone is in the basement, and feel free to make *yourself* at home. There's plenty to eat, so don't hesitate to fill up a plate, or two." Her smile widened. "I knew we had to provide a lot of food for the *buwe* to agree to attend."

Ruby chuckled, Mary's good humor slightly relaxing her. "The way to a man's heart is through his stomach. Or so I've heard."

"You heard correctly. That's how I got Freemont. Now, *geh* on downstairs and enjoy *yourself.*"

She thanked Mary and headed down to the basement. She paused at the bottom of the stairs and surveyed the room. She almost clapped with glee. Eight young men were standing near a table laden with various snacks and several jugs of apple cider. But where were Martha and Selah? She didn't want to be the only girl in the room.

She hesitated, and then she seriously considered dashing back up the stairs to go home. She'd make up some excuse to tell Mary. Yes, she knew she was being a chicken and probably blowing a big chance to get Seth's attention, but she wasn't sure she could go through this alone. Just knowing other females were there would make her feel a little less outnumbered.

Then she saw Martha waving at her from across the room. *Thank goodness.* Selah stood next to her, her hand curled as she studied her fingernails, looking as if she'd rather be anywhere than the Yoders' basement.

"I'm glad you came," Martha said when Ruby reached them. "I thought you might be scared off by all the *buwe* here."

"Me?" Ruby scoffed. "I wouldn't let something like that bother me." She inwardly cringed at the fib, and then she twisted one string of her *kapp* as she looked around the room, pretending she hadn't scoped it out already. Great. She'd barely started her husband-hunting and she was already being deceptive.

"I wouldn't have blamed you if you had, but you don't have to worry." Martha gestured to one corner of the room, where Freemont kept a watchful eye on the group.

"It's not like any of these *buwe* would do anything wrong anyway," Selah said. "They're all so *nice.*"

"That's a *gut* thing, Selah," Martha insisted.

"If you say so."

Ruby didn't comment. She agreed with Martha, and it was obvious that Selah was in a bad mood. But Ruby wasn't going to let that bother her. She was on a mission. She turned around and searched for Seth. It didn't take long to find him. He was talking to another young man who was almost as tall as he was.

She brushed her palms over the skirt of her dress. Now was the time to make her move. "Here we *geh*," she whispered as she walked toward Seth and his friend.

"Where are you going?" Martha called out.

But Ruby didn't stop. She felt bad for ignoring Martha, but she had a goal to attain, and she'd put off pursuing it for long enough.

"Hi," she said when she reached Seth. "I'm Ruby." *Uh-oh.* Judging from his startled expression, she'd said that a little too loudly.

"Uh, hi." Seth regarded her for a minute. "Have we met before?"

"Oh *ya*," she said, slapping her knee. "But it was several years ago." She laughed. "You were much *shorter* back then."

He nodded slowly. "Okay." He gestured to the young man next to him. "This is Zeb Bontrager. I don't think you two know each other."

Zeb swallowed a bite out of the large chocolate chip cookie he was holding and looked straight at Ruby. "We don't. I would have remembered you, for sure," he said.

She didn't know if that was supposed to be a slight. Preferring to be optimistic, she looked at Zeb. Not bad. Black hair, blue eyes, nice smooth voice. Definitely a contender, although Seth still had the edge. She turned her attention back to him. "What are you two talking about?" she said, moving closer to him.

"Fishing." Seth took a step back.

"*Really?* I *love* fishing!" Good grief, why couldn't she keep her voice down? She glanced around the room and saw a few people looking at her, including the bishop. "I mean, I love fishing," she whispered. Oh, that was too much. Suddenly she let out a giggle and then hiccupped. *Oh nee.* Not the hiccups. Not now.

Seth and Zeb exchanged an amused look. "So you like fishing," Seth said, his lips twitching.

"*Ya.*" *Hiccup.* "Timothy"—*hiccup*—"and I used to"—*hiccup*—"fish all the"—*hiccup*—"time." *Hiccup!*

Seth and Zeb burst out laughing.

She wanted to crawl into a hole. This was awful. How could she make a good impression when she couldn't stop hiccupping? Or yelling? Or whispering? And of course the hiccups weren't delicate. They were more like a cross between a cough and a belch.

"Here." Chris Ropp appeared at her side, holding a red plastic cup.

Ruby looked up at him, a little surprised.

"It's been proven that quickly drinking water can extinguish hiccups. Of course, the evidence is anecdotal, but it's worth a try." He thrust the cup at her, giving her little choice but to take it.

Seth and Zeb were still chuckling, and she knew from experience that attempting any further conversation with them was a lost cause. She walked away, still hiccupping, her face as hot as a fire poker. Instead of going to Martha and Selah, she went to the basement door, grateful to find it unlocked. She escaped outside and drained the water in one gulp.

Please let this work . . . for once.

"Better?" Chris asked.

Hiccup. She turned and faced him, surprised he'd followed her. *"Nee." Hiccup.*

"Have you seen a doctor about those?"

She glared at him. *"Nee." Hiccup.* "They'll *geh"—hiccup—*"away soon." *Hiccup.*

"Perhaps some sugar would help."

"It won't." She looked down at the ground and hiccupped three more times. She didn't get these often, thank goodness, but when she did they were horrible. And embarrassing, as she'd already proved to everyone, including her husband prospects. "I have to"—*hiccup*—"wait for them to pass." *Hiccup.*

"All right." He didn't move, and the two of them stood in the Yoders' backyard, the sky streaked with beautiful shades of peach, lavender, and pale yellow as the sun set. Normally she would pause and enjoy the view, but her chest started to ache from the hiccups. She didn't know how long it took for them to subside, but they finally did. When the hiccups became softer and more spread out, she looked at him again. Why hadn't he gone back inside? "What are you doing?"

"Standing outside."

"I can see that. I was wondering why you're still here."

His expression remained emotionless. "I want to make sure you're all right."

Huh. She hadn't expected that from him. No one else had come out to check on her. Not Martha or Selah. Not even Seth. Not that she'd expected him to, but it would have been nice if he had. She frowned. "I don't need a babysitter." Then she bit her lip. "Sorry. That was rude of me."

"No offense taken."

He was so predictable. "At least you didn't say 'apology accepted.'"

"Why? Is there something wrong with the phrase I chose to use?"

"*Nee*, just . . . Oh, never mind. *Mei* point still stands, though. You don't have to stay out here with me."

He didn't say anything, and she glanced at him. He was looking at his shoes and made no move to go inside. He wiped the palms of his hands down the sides of his broadfall pants.

Understanding dawned, and she remembered the book he'd been reading. "Is the reason you were reading that book here tonight?"

His brow lifted, but he remained silent, which was the same as if he'd answered her.

She clasped her hands together. "You like Martha, don't you?"

"*Like* is a strong word."

"*Nee* it isn't. *Love* is a strong word. *Like* is a little above neutral."

His right brow arched higher. "I don't like her, per se. I don't really know her well enough to ascertain how I feel."

"But you'd like to get to know her." Now that she had her mind off her own ineptitude, she could smile. She leaned against the white wood siding of the house.

He paused again as his brow lowered. He looked out at the cornstalks that lined up on the Yoders' land. They'd been harvested already, leaving behind drying stubble. "Yes." He nodded. "Yes. I would like to get to know Martha better."

She moved to stand in front of him. "That's not going to happen if you're standing out here with me."

"I realize that." But he still didn't make a move toward the Yoders' house.

She hiccupped softly. The hiccups weren't completely gone, but at this point she could at least carry on a conversation. "I don't know her well either, but she's very nice and friendly. Just go inside and talk to her."

He peered down at her. "And shall I yell at her the way you yelled at Seth and Zeb?"

Her cheeks heated again. "I wasn't yelling."

"I'm sure you were heard all the way to the next district."

"I didn't realize there was another district nearby," she said, frowning.

He turned to her. "There isn't."

She faced him, putting her hands on her hips. "Are you always this direct?"

"I don't see any reason not to be."

"Well, here's lesson number one. Learn some tact."

"I fail to see what tact has to do with anything since I haven't offended you." He tilted his head and scrutinized her. Then he said, "However, if I have offended you, I apologize."

She sighed and shook her head. "You didn't offend me."

He rubbed his forehead. "But you just stated that I did."

"You were being blunt, not offensive." He was also accurate, which didn't offend her as much as annoy her. She did tend to raise her voice when she was nervous. The hiccups hadn't helped matters much.

He scowled, which was the first show of emotion she'd seen from him. "This is why I don't understand women. One of many reasons."

"We're really not that difficult."

Chris turned his head and lifted his brow again.

"*Nee* one likes their flaws pointed out to them," she said, letting go of some of her annoyance. "Even when it's the truth."

His brow lowered, and his face relaxed, but only slightly. He did have nice eyebrows, she had to admit. And they conveyed quite a bit of what he was thinking, even while the rest of his face was blank. She thought about explaining tact to him a little further, but decided to let what she told him sink in.

They both faced the sunset, not saying anything. The muffled sound of singing reached her ears, the men's voices drowning out Martha and Selah's. If Selah was even participating. Ruby suspected she wasn't. "The singing's started," she said. "We should probably go inside."

"Yes." He continued to stare at the setting sun. "We should."

But neither of them made a move to leave. Ruby fiddled with the ribbon of her *kapp*, while Chris stood there, his arms straight by his sides, staring at the cornfield and dusky sky above it.

Finally, he spoke. "I'm not all that enamored of singing," he said in a low voice.

She nodded. "Me neither."

He turned to her. "Then why did you come?"

She couldn't exactly admit she was scouting out potential husbands. But she could tell him part of the truth. "I came to meet people. I'm new here, and I want to make some friends."

"I thought you were friends with Selah and Martha already, since you were talking with them after church."

"True," she said, pressing her toe against the short, green grass.

"And if you wanted to cultivate those friendships, you could easily visit one of them, or invite them to visit you."

Why was he choosing to play detective now? "*Ya*, but I want to get to know some other people in the community too—"

"Usually one of the intentions of attending a singing is to sing. But you don't like singing."

She turned and put her hand on the doorknob of the basement door. "Chris, we should really *geh* inside—"

"The other intention is to . . ." His brow lifted again.

She met his gaze directly with one of her own. If he wanted her to admit she was here for romantic purposes, he could forget it. Even though he was right—again. *No one likes a know-it-all either.* She steeled herself for further questioning. Or teasing, although so far Chris hadn't shown any ability to tease. He would be more apt to point out his correct assumptions.

To her surprise, he turned from her and stared at the field again. After a pause, he said, "I noticed some apple cider on the table next to the snacks."

She resisted the urge to sigh with relief. No need to show him how tense she was. "I do like apple cider."

"It is delicious." He looked at her again as the song ended. "Shall we go inside?"

Ruby nodded and opened the door. Apple cider did sound yummy. Once inside, she went straight to a jug of cider to pour herself a cup, only to stop when she realized everyone was staring at her and Chris.

He was standing close behind her, and while she knew he wasn't doing it on purpose, she imagined it looked purposeful to the rest of the group. Martha's mouth dropped open. Ruby thought she saw a flash of surprise on Selah's face before it changed into a smirk. The boys' expressions ran from mild curiosity to disinterest.

"Uh, hi," Ruby said, giving the group a self-conscious wave. "Chris and I just stepped outside for some fresh air."

Martha's smile widened. Selah was still smirking. The rest of the group had already lost interest and was huddling around the snack table again.

Ruby glanced at Chris, who was rubbing his ear like it had frostbite.

"How about you sing another song?" Freemont said, shooing the young men away from the table. "I enjoyed the first one. Ruby, you and Chris can join in."

No one was going to defy the bishop. Chris joined the boys, who had moved away from the table and stood near a sofa and chair set that looked like it had seen better days, and Ruby joined Martha and Selah. As the song started, Martha leaned next to her and whispered, "I want details later."

"Details?"

"About you and Chris."

"There are *nee* details," she hissed. "He was checking on *mei* hiccups." Which had completely disappeared, by the way. At least something good had happened tonight.

"If you say so." Martha smiled and went back to singing.

Ruby opened her mouth to sing, but she sensed someone watching her. She glanced at Selah. Instead of the smirk that seemed to be permanently on her face, now Chris's sister looked confused. When she noticed Ruby looking at her, she gave her a glare, and then she went back to singing, although halfheartedly compared to Martha.

Well, wasn't this dandy? She hadn't been in Birch Creek for much more than a week and she was already in a jam. Now everyone thought there was something between her and Chris, which was ridiculous. Then there was the problem of getting Seth's interest. She'd embarrassed herself quite well tonight. And what about Chris and Martha? If Martha thought he was interested in Ruby, it would be harder for him to talk to her, which was a struggle for him to begin with. All because of some stupid hiccups.

She wasn't sure what she should do, so she started singing, a bit off-key. But that didn't matter since one of the boys—who she assumed was related to Zeb since they had the same black hair—had a loud enough voice for all of them. And unlike her singing voice, his sounded glorious. He was talented. She needed to find out who he was.

Stop getting sidetracked. She needed to figure out how to fix this. She didn't owe Chris anything—he'd made the decision to check on her outside. But it was a nice gesture, and she did feel a bit guilty that she'd made it harder on him when it came to Martha, not to mention harder on herself to find a husband. Somehow, she'd set everything to rights—for them both.

CHAPTER 5

*T*he evening had not turned out the way Christian planned. Then again, he wasn't exactly sure what should have happened, other than his making a connection with Martha. Instead, he was fielding questions from his sister about Ruby Glick.

"I didn't know you were interested in her," Selah said as they walked home from the Yoders'.

"I'm not." The sun had set by the time they left the singing. He had a small flashlight in his pocket, but it was a cloudless night with a full moon, giving them plenty of illumination.

"But you were outside with her. Alone. None of us even realized you'd left."

That was a bit disappointing to hear, considering there weren't that many people at the singing. Discovering he wasn't consequential enough to be missed didn't lift his spirits at all. "She had the hiccups. I was merely checking on her welfare."

Selah tugged her navy-blue sweater closer around her. The

temperature had dropped a little bit, and although it wasn't cold, a slight chill was in the air. "Hiccups aren't that serious."

"One never knows."

"Hmm."

He looked at Selah and saw her side-eyeing him in the silvery light. He wasn't in the mood to discuss any aspect of tonight with her, but since this was the most she'd engaged him in the past two weeks, he would humor her. "What do you mean, hmm?" he said in *Dietsch*.

"I think you might have some feelings for her."

That must be another thing women did—make assumptions about others' romantic concerns. His sister was reminding him of Ruby right now, although since she'd easily guessed the truth he'd had to admit to Ruby that he did indeed have an interest in Martha. He did not, however, have any interest in Ruby. "You're mistaken." He stared straight ahead, hoping his direct answer would appease her.

He supposed he shouldn't blame her for questioning him. Checking on Ruby had unintended consequences, one of which was people suspecting something was going on between them. His intentions toward her were purely platonic, and that was a stretch since he didn't even consider her a friend. Ruby Glick, while rather nice, wasn't the type of woman who would be suitable for a wife—at least not his wife. She was more than a tad perplexing. Martha had far more potential.

Martha's potential wouldn't matter, however, if he couldn't even talk to her.

He shoved his hands into his pockets. He could blame Ruby for his lack of progress tonight, but it was his own fault. He'd frozen up again once he saw Martha. Ruby even encouraged him to go inside and strike up a conversation with her, and he'd failed to do something as simple as that.

"Why don't you like Ruby?"

Christian glanced at Selah. Apparently, his sister wasn't ready to let the topic drop. "I didn't say I don't like her."

"Then you do like her."

"I . . ." Then he saw the teasing glint in Selah's eyes. She was having fun at his expense, and for once he was happy to see it. While he never really got the gist of teasing, Selah enjoyed it, and if she was able to tease, then perhaps her mood was changing for the better. He would greatly welcome that. "I don't dislike her. Ruby is a nice young *maedel*. I'll leave it at that."

"She's different, that's for sure."

He didn't want to talk about Ruby. He'd squandered tonight's opportunity, and he needed to figure out a way to approach Martha again. Although Ruby did say she would help him. He thought about what she'd said about him learning tact. "Do you think I'm rude?" he asked Selah.

"That came out of the blue." Then she hesitated before saying, "You are at times."

Another disappointing revelation.

"But I don't think you mean to be. You're not trying to hurt anyone's feelings."

"Yet I do."

"Sometimes." She touched him on the arm and they stopped. "But we're all rude sometimes. What brought this up?"

"It's come to *mei* attention that I need to learn tact." He started to walk again.

Selah followed him. "Ruby told you that?"

He paused and then nodded.

"How much time have you two been spending together?"

He blew out a breath. There was no point in being deceptive with Selah, especially since he'd asked for courtesy from her. This morning, after their argument last night, he'd asked her to leave more detailed notes whenever she left. To his surprise she'd agreed without protest. She had even joined him in the living room today while he was reading a book for pleasure, this time one on quadratic equations. He found math fascinating.

"Not much," he replied, finally answering her question. "We ran into each other at church last Sunday." No need to add that they had literally run into each other. "Then we talked for a few minutes the other day. Other than those two occasions and tonight, we haven't interacted."

Selah tapped her chin. "Seems like you've made an impression on her in a short time."

"Clearly an unfavorable one."

"Why do you say that? It sounds like she was trying to be helpful. It also sounds like she's got you pegged."

He was about to contradict her, but then he changed his mind when he realized she was right—at least when it came to his lack of tact. And Ruby telling him about that personality flaw would be beneficial.

They were nearing home when Selah said, "Why don't I invite her to visit this week?"

Christian turned to her, exasperated. Why wasn't Selah listening to him? "I already told you, I don't like her that way. There's *nee* need to invite Ruby over."

"I meant Martha. She *is* the one you like, *ya*?"

"Oh." He stopped and looked at her. "How did you know?"

She giggled. "Christian, you're acting like you did in seventh grade."

He frowned. "I am?"

"Remember, when you had a crush on Suzanna Miller?"

His face heated. "She was our teacher, Selah. I didn't have a crush on her."

"Everyone knew about it. You'd get tongue-tied whenever she asked you to recite anything."

Cringing, he turned and walked away, quickening his steps. He'd thought his feelings for Suzanna—immature and inappropriate, in retrospect—had been his secret. He'd been devastated the way only a thirteen-year-old boy who had suffered unrequited love could be when she moved away two months into the school year. The teacher who replaced her, Katherine Byler, had been acceptable as an educator, but she wasn't Suzanna.

"I know," Selah said as she caught up with him. "I could invite Martha *and* Ruby." She grinned. "That might be kind of fun."

"Selah—"

"We'll have *kaffee* and game night," she said. "We haven't played games in a long time. It might be easier for you to talk to Martha in the comfort of our home."

How did this get so out of his control? Then again, game night might not be a bad thing. If Ruby was there and saw how he failed to interact with Martha, she could pinpoint his problem. He was also excellent at all sorts of games, especially trivia ones. He could impress Martha with his knowledge, which would give him the confidence to talk to her.

"All right," he said. "Game night it is." He paused. "I have just one question."

"What?"

"Why are you doing this? Why are you helping me with Martha?"

She crossed her arms against the night chill as their house came into view. "I know I've been out of sorts lately, and I haven't been very nice to you at times. That isn't right of me, especially since you let me move here with you."

"Do you want to *geh* back home?"

Selah shook her head. "*Nee.* I definitely don't want to do that. I like it here, even though I haven't shown it much. I'm going to try to do better." She lifted her chin and looked at him. "Helping you with Martha is a start."

"*Danki,*" he said, stunned by her admission. And pleased. He was glad she was coming around. He made a note that they should talk more often. Just not about Ruby Glick.

After the supper dishes were washed Monday evening, Ruby sat at the kitchen table and for the first time ever wrote out her plans for the week. As someone who liked to keep her options open, using a calendar was a new experience. She wasn't too excited about working with a schedule, but she was willing to do what needed to be done. She was finished throwing caution to the wind and hoping it didn't blow back in her face. She was mature. Adult. And adults used a calendar.

She opened the small pocket calendar and wrote *Games at Selah's* in the Thursday square. She'd been surprised when Selah stopped by earlier in the day and invited her, considering she'd been rather cool to her the two times they'd interacted. Maybe she'd had to warm up to Ruby. Regardless, Ruby was glad for the chance to socialize, considering how disastrous last night had been. Selah hadn't mentioned anything about Chris attending, not that it mattered to Ruby if he did. Knowing him, he probably thought playing games was juvenile. Besides, she'd see him this Saturday for their first lesson. She marked that down on the calendar too. Although she told him he needed to learn tact, and she believed he did, it wouldn't hurt for her to brush up on that subject herself. She wrote down the words *Barton Library* on Tuesday's square.

Timothy walked into the kitchen and glanced at her. "What's this?" he said, coming to the table. "*Mei* little *schwester* is using a calendar? Must be a miracle."

"Very funny." She tucked her pencil under her *kapp* and behind her ear.

"Never thought I'd see the day." He gave her a teasing smile as he looked over her shoulder. "Looks like you're filling up the days. But what does *Lesson #1 Chris* mean?"

She snapped the calendar shut. "It means none of *yer* business."

"The only Chris I know is the teacher. Is he tutoring you in something?"

For a split second she was insulted. He'd assumed she was the student and not the teacher. Then she realized his assumption was common sense. What other reason would she have for meeting a teacher about a lesson? Still, she didn't appreciate his nosiness. "Like I said. None of *yer* business."

"Okay, okay." He headed straight for the chocolate cake she'd made earlier that day and cut himself a thick slice before placing it on a plate she'd just washed and dried.

"Didn't you already have some cake after supper?" she asked.

He grabbed a fork and took a bite. "None of *yer* business," he said around the mouthful. Then he swallowed. *"Sehr gut,* Ruby. You should think about helping Carolyn Shetler at her bakery."

"Are you saying you want me to get a job?"

Timothy licked some of the frosting off the fork. "Might not be a bad idea since *yer* visit here seems to be open-ended."

"I offered to help you with the farm, but you won't let me." She turned her chair so she could face him. "I can tell you're tired, Timothy."

He set his fork on the plate. "Everything's fine, Ruby. I know you don't care for farm work anyway. I'll leave you to *yer* calendar." Then he left the kitchen before she could respond.

Ruby frowned. She wished her brother would let her help him. She enjoyed watching her nephews and helping Patience, but sometimes during the day she was at loose ends, and she could fill those times with work. Maybe it wasn't a bad idea to consider checking out Carolyn's bakery. She did like to bake, after all.

She went outside. The sun had disappeared behind the horizon, but a bit of dusk was still left. She drew in a deep breath and listened to cicadas, crickets, and katydids play their night music. She really did like Birch Creek, and she felt at home here. Timothy might not like to hear that, but it was true. He wouldn't have to worry about her after she found a husband anyway. Despite her utter failure at the singing, she was more determined than ever to talk to Seth Yoder—without hiccupping.

She sat down on one of the wooden chairs on the back patio. Even though the world was calm around her, her mind was whirring. Her brain was always moving fast, sometimes too fast. Now would be an excellent time for her to quiet her mind and listen for God's voice. He might have some insight for her about Seth. All her life she'd known people who said they had heard his voice, but she'd never even experienced a whisper. Then again, had she really taken the time to listen?

Ruby closed her eyes and tried to keep her thoughts still. But it didn't take long for her to think about her calendar again. She hadn't put Seth in her calendar or come up with a good excuse to see him. She'd have to be casual about it. Being too direct when it came to men didn't get her anywhere. She learned that the hard way when she asked not one but three men to go with her to a Saturday frolic when she was seventeen. All three were shocked, and all three had said no. Granted, they were all standing next to each other when she asked. Perhaps that hadn't been the best way to get a date. Being covert was key. She was sure of that now.

She sighed and opened her eyes. The sun was gone, and unlike last night, fluffy clouds gathered in the darkened sky. Maybe she should just give up the whole husband thing. It was getting a little too complicated. She didn't have to go back to Lancaster, though. She could get a job and do it perfectly. Patience had already mentioned the midwife option, or she could work as a baker . . .

A baker. She popped up from the patio chair. Perfect! She could bake Seth a cake and take it to him. The way to a man's heart was always through his stomach, just like Mary said, and the young men of Birch Creek seemed far more interested in eating at Sunday night's singing than doing anything else. Besides, nothing about taking a cake to the neighbors was overt, even though these neighbors lived several streets away.

Ruby hurried back into the house, grabbed the pencil from

behind her ear, and opened her calendar. She squinted as she wrote *Seth* in the Wednesday block, resisting the urge to draw a heart around his name like the old Ruby would have done.

She closed the calendar and hugged it to her chest. For the first time in her life, she had a week of activities planned and recorded. Determined to follow through with every one, she wouldn't allow any diversions, distractions, or disasters. With her plans in order, this week would be flawless.

For the first part of the week, Christian put game night and Martha out of his mind. It was the last week of September, and his students were settling down and getting into the rhythm of school. He'd given a few extra assignments to Malachi he thought would challenge the boy's intellect. Although Malachi didn't seem excited about doing the work, to his credit he did complete the assignments, and most of them were one hundred percent correct.

On Wednesday he stayed after school to provide extra reading assistance to two of Thomas Bontrager's sons, Jesse and Perry. Like Malachi, they were difficult to engage when it came to their reading, as well as to their pencil and paper work. That was no excuse to be lax about their assignments. Christian had learned from an early age that disciplined learning led to increased knowledge, a concept he wanted to pass down to his students. Especially the reluctant ones.

They were seated at the same kidney-shaped table in the front of the classroom where Christian worked with the reading groups. He occupied his chair in the middle, with Perry and

Jesse across from him, the way they would be during their own reading group. Perry was already squirming in his chair.

"Jesse," Christian said, pointing to the reader open in front of him, "please read the first paragraph on page thirteen."

Jesse's legs swung back and forth as his stubby fingers turned the pages in his reader. Christian was tempted to tell him and Perry to stay still, but he knew that was practically impossible for children their age, particularly when they had already spent all day in school. There was no need to put extra restraint on Jesse while he was struggling with his reading. Just as Jesse found the correct page, Christian had an idea. "Before you read, Jesse, I'd like you to stand up."

"What?" the boy said, rubbing his finger under his nose.

"Stand up, please. Like this." Christian pushed back his chair and stood. "Perry, you may also stand up."

Perry followed suit, looking just as baffled as his brother.

"Now hop on one foot," Christian said.

Jesse's eyes widened. "Why do you want us to do that?"

"Because the movement allows the blood to circulate through your body, which will invigorate your mind. In turn, that will enable you to focus on your reading."

"What did you say?" Perry said.

Christian looked at him and then at Jesse. "Hop because I told you so."

The boys understood that simplified explanation, and they began hopping on one foot. Christian glanced out a classroom window to make sure no students were lingering outside, and then he joined them. Of course, the boys couldn't stay in one place for very long, and after about three hops they lost their balance, knocking into the chairs and tables, giggling all the while.

"Now switch feet."

They did, and then they hopped a few more times with the same results. Before the boys were completely out of control, Christian halted and held up his hand. "Stop."

The boys froze and looked at each other. Perry was on one foot, and Jesse was leaning to the side. They giggled again.

"Sit down, please."

They sat down in their small chairs, still grinning. Both of their readers had fallen closed.

"Open your readers." The boys followed his instruction. "Jesse, read the first paragraph on page thirteen." Christian pulled out his chair and sat down.

Although both brothers struggled with their reading during the next twenty minutes, they gave optimal effort. Christian was pleased. He had read that letting students release pent-up energy helped them concentrate, and he was glad it worked. "That's enough for today," he said, closing his book.

"I didn't read very well," Perry said, his eyes downcast.

"Me neither," Jesse added through pursed lips.

"But you both gave your best effort, and that's what's important. Reading will become easier with time."

Neither boy looked convinced, but Christian was confident they would be good readers in the future. They would have to work and practice a little harder, but in the end it would be worth it. He just wished he could give them more self-assurance. Sometimes he wondered if his words of encouragement to his students were getting through. At times they looked at him with blank expressions when he tried to give them a pep talk.

After Jesse and Perry left, Christian stuck to his schedule of grading the day's papers, reviewing the next day's lesson plans, and tidying up the schoolroom. He locked the schoolhouse and headed home. When he arrived, he found a note from Selah on the kitchen table.

Spending the night at Martha's. I'll be back tomorrow morning. Don't forget about game night. You can impress Martha with your skills.

He smiled and folded the note. So far Selah had kept her word about making a better effort. No dirty dishes sat in the sink, and on Monday she had left the house and driven Einstein and the buggy over to Ruby's to invite her for game night. She was more pleasant, and she'd even talked to him during supper, asking how he liked his job.

"I could never be a teacher," she said as she finished eating the small slice of meat loaf on her plate. The mashed potatoes and gravy she'd also made were delicious.

He picked up a scoopful of potatoes. "Why not?"

"I'd have to be around *kinner* all day, for one thing." She looked at him. "I'm surprised you have so much patience with them. I don't see you as the fatherly type."

He wasn't sure how to take that. "I'm not their father. I'm their educator."

"I know, but what about when they scrape their knees on the playground or one of them gets sick and throws up in the trash can? I'm sure *yer* paternal instincts will have to come out then."

"I have a first aid kit in my desk, and plenty of disinfectant in the closet."

She chuckled. "Why doesn't that surprise me?" Her humor

faded. "Really, I am surprised you're an Amish teacher. I thought you'd leave to go to college."

He shook his head. "I've never had intentions to leave our faith. It's more important than being a teacher, although that is what I've wanted to do ever since I can remember."

"Is that why you always had *yer* nose in a book? And why you spent so much time at the library?"

He nodded. That, and it was a reprieve from working with their father, who was a butcher and wanted Christian to go into the family business. As far as Christian knew, his father still wanted that. "I like to learn. And when I decided to attend a teaching workshop with some other Amish teachers, I also discovered I liked to teach."

"Then you're happy here?"

"*Ya*," he said, switching to *Dietsch*. "I am." And he'd be happier if he could mark *marriage* off his list. With Selah's help, he might be able to do that.

Christian set down the note and went to the barn to let Einstein out in the small pasture behind the barn. After purchasing the house, he had hired someone to build a fence around a large portion of the backyard for the horse to have a place to graze and exercise. He was still getting used to this horse, which he'd bought shortly after arriving in Birch Creek. Einstein was a fine animal, a former racer, and gentle. He'd sold his other horse and buggy back in New York, and while he was happy with his current animal, he missed Charlie.

He went inside and washed up before making himself a ham-and-cheese sandwich and pouring a glass of milk. Then he sat down at the table to eat his meager supper. After saying a silent prayer, he opened his eyes and stared at the sandwich.

The house was quiet. He liked quiet, especially after a busy and loud day with his students. That was why he was glad to find the large tree and empty pasture approximately a mile from his house. There was something calming about being outdoors where it was quiet yet still humming with natural activity in the background. He'd come to think of the land with the tree as his personal space, even though he had no idea who owned the property and had never seen anyone around. If the owner objected to him sitting under the tree, he would honor his or her wishes. Until then, he would continue to spend time there whenever possible. The setting gave him peace.

But he wasn't feeling peaceful right now. The house was too quiet. Too empty. He noticed he missed Selah's company, which he had enjoyed the past three days. Not only that, but he also realized he missed having company in general.

Odd that he was experiencing this now. He was usually fine with being alone, often immersed in books or his own thoughts. However, he couldn't deny that tonight he felt . . . lonely.

Christian shook his head at the foolish emotion. Less than three hours ago he'd been tutoring Perry and Jesse. He was surrounded by children all day long, so he definitely wasn't alone.

Still, that didn't stop him from taking his sandwich and glass of milk outside. He leaned against the fence and watched Einstein graze. If anyone had told him he would be seeking out a horse for camaraderie, he would have thought they were joking. But tonight, for some reason, Einstein's company was better than no company at all.

CHAPTER 6

*Y*ou're baking another chocolate cake?" Patience asked Ruby as she entered the kitchen, carrying Luke with Tobias toddling in behind her. "We still have plenty of the other one left."

Ruby opened the oven door and placed the Bundt cake pan inside. She shut the door and then set the kitchen timer on the counter next to the stove. She smiled. It hadn't taken her long to whip this together, and in thirty minutes she'd have a delicious, fresh cake to impress Seth Yoder with.

"Ruby?"

She turned to Patience, still smiling. *"Ya?"*

"I appreciate *yer* help in the kitchen, and you are a *gut* baker." She glanced at the oven. "But Timothy and I can't, and shouldn't, eat that much cake."

"Don't worry about that. This dessert isn't for you and Timothy."

"Oh, I'm glad to hear that."

Patience set Luke in his high chair and then picked up

Tobias and set him on his booster seat at the table. She went to the drawer where she kept a few items to keep the boys occupied while she worked in the kitchen. She pulled out a blank piece of white paper, red, blue, and yellow crayons, and a teething ring. She gave Luke the teether and put the paper and crayons in front of Tobias, who picked up the red crayon and started scribbling.

As Ruby watched all this, she was relieved her sister-in-law wasn't asking the next logical question. Thank goodness for the distraction of her nephews.

"Then who's the cake for?" Patience asked when she turned to look at her.

Ruby bit her bottom lip. She'd been caught. If she said Seth, then Patience would think something was going on between him and Ruby. That would be fine with her once she knew for sure that Seth liked her back. Unlike many young Amish couples, she wasn't concerned about keeping her relationship a secret—once she had a relationship. One thing was worse than unrequited feelings, though, and that was *public* unrequited feelings, even if the public was only her sister-in-law. "I thought I would take a cake over to the bishop's family, as a welcoming gesture," she said, pleased with her explanation.

"Don't you have that backward?" Patience pulled down a large metal bowl and walked over to the gas-powered refrigerator. "You realize you're the visitor who's welcome here, not the other way around."

"Oh." She hadn't thought about it that way. "Well, I'm just trying to be friendly."

Patience smiled at her before opening the fridge door. "That's sweet of you, Ruby. I'm sure the Yoders will appreciate the cake—and the gesture."

Ruby nodded, glad that she didn't have to come up with another excuse to take a cake to Seth. She walked over to the cabinet where Patience kept the spices. Her sister-in-law was highly organized and posted a weekly menu on the refrigerator each week. She was making meat loaf tonight. "I thought I would *geh* over there after supper," she said, reaching for a jar of garlic powder.

Patience pulled out a two-pound package of hamburger that had been defrosting in the refrigerator. "That sounds nice. Why doesn't Timothy go with you? He and Freemont are friends, and I'm sure he'd like to visit with him for a little while."

She dropped the jar. Fortunately, it was plastic, so it bounced instead of shattered when it hit the floor. The last thing she wanted was for her brother to accompany her to Seth's. He'd know what was going on in less than a minute after they got there. That would be worse than Patience knowing because he'd tease her mercilessly about it. "That's okay," she said, snatching the jar off the floor, grateful it hadn't exploded and made the kitchen smell like an Italian eatery. "I'm sure he'd rather spend time with you and the *kinner* without his little *schwester* around. I'm fine going by myself."

Patience looked at her for a moment and then nodded. "You're right. He's been so tired lately when he finishes with work."

Ruby set the powder on the counter next to the metal bowl. "Are you worried about him?"

Patience dumped the hamburger into the bowl. "*Nee.* Not too much. The farm is hard work. It always has been, but he enjoys it." She glanced at Ruby. "Sometimes I wish he'd hire a helper, though. I think that would make things a little easier on him."

Ruby nodded and walked to the oven. She didn't bother to

tell Patience about her offering to help Timothy. Sometimes her brother could be so stubborn.

She opened the oven door just a crack and peeked at the cake. It was starting to puff up a little. She straightened. Now, what kind of frosting should she make? Did Seth like all one flavor? If so, she should make chocolate frosting. Or perhaps he preferred the contrast of vanilla and chocolate. There was some cream cheese in the refrigerator, so she could add that to the frosting too. She spied some mint flavoring while she was getting the garlic powder from the spice cabinet. Mint and chocolate sounded good. Or maybe strawberry. She'd have to see if Patience had any strawberry flavoring—

"Ruby?"

She turned to Patience. "*Ya?*"

"The cake will take longer to bake if you leave the oven door open."

Ruby looked down and saw the oven door was indeed still partway open. She frowned and shut it. She had to keep her concentration, or she'd ruin the cake and all her effort would be for nothing. She made a quick decision—Seth was getting cream cheese frosting.

An hour later the cake was cooled and frosted, and the meat loaf was almost done. While Patience whipped up some potatoes and green beans, Ruby put Luke in his high chair again and started to set the table, letting Tobias help her. She lifted him up as he plopped a spoon near each place setting.

"*Gut* job." Ruby planted a kiss on his chubby cheek, and then she set him in his booster seat next to his brother. None of the spoons were straight, but that didn't matter. Tobias picked up his own small spoon and grinned.

Patience set a salad on the table. She'd used up the last of the fresh tomatoes from the garden. "Have you given any more thought to being *mei* midwife assistant?"

"Um, *nee.*" She'd been so busy thinking about Seth and preparing for her lesson with Chris that she'd forgotten about Patience's idea. Or rather shoved it out of her mind.

"I hope I'm not pressuring you," Patience said, taking the teething ring from Luke. "I think we really do work well together, though."

Patience was right about that, but Ruby liked helping out at home. She was comfortable with the boys and household chores. She'd even be comfortable working with the cows, but Timothy had made up his mind about that. She just wasn't sure she'd be comfortable with midwife duties. She'd never seen a baby's birth, and she didn't know a lot about pregnancy. While she knew she could learn, she was also a little nervous about it. But she did feel obliged to give it serious thought and prayer, for Patience's sake. "I promise I'll think about it," she said.

"*Danki.*"

Timothy walked into the kitchen wearing a fresh shirt and pants, his hair damp as if he'd just taken a shower, which he often did before supper. He sat down in his seat at the head of the table, looking drained. Patience put her hand on his shoulder as she set a glass of tea in front of him. He glanced up at her and gave her a weary smile.

After they finished supper, Ruby had started to clear the table when Patience said, "I'll take care of this. You *geh* on to the Yoders'."

"You're going to the Yoders'?" Timothy lifted Luke from his high chair. "Why? Did something happen?"

Ruby put her hands on her hips. "Why do you always assume something happened?"

"Because it usually does when you have to see the bishop."

"Oh." He was right about that. When she was younger Bishop Miller had stopped by a few times to give her what he called *a bit of extra learning* when it came to the *Ordnung*. The first time was when she was fifteen and at a salvage store, picking up a few bargains for *Mamm*. An English family had asked if they could have their picture taken in front of her horse and buggy, and they also wanted her to take it with their camera. She didn't see the harm in it. She wasn't in the picture, and the family seemed nice.

Later she found out Judith Esh, a woman in her district who really needed to learn how to mind her own business, had seen what happened and told Bishop Miller. She had stepped outside the bounds of the rules a few other times, and each time the bishop had been kind but firm with her.

"I realize you're not breaking the rules on purpose," he'd said on his last visit. She had just turned nineteen. "But they're in place for a reason, and everyone is expected to follow them. You're not a *kinn* anymore, and you said you want to join the church. That means knowing and respecting the *Ordnung*."

And she had respected the *Ordnung* ever since she joined the church almost two years ago. But she shouldn't be surprised that Timothy had jumped to his conclusion. "I'm not in trouble," she said defiantly. "I'm just paying the *familye* a visit."

"That's nice." He pulled his head back as Luke reached for a tuft of his hair. "I'm glad you're getting to know people here. Then again, I'm not surprised. You've always had a gift for being friendly." He and Luke left the kitchen.

Ruby was pleased and a bit surprised by the compliment. She'd never seen a reason not to be friendly, even to strangers who looked like they'd eaten a bag of lemons for breakfast.

Feeling a little guilty that she was leaving the cleanup for Patience, she asked, "Are you sure you don't need me to help?"

"I'll help," Timothy said, coming back to the kitchen. He carried the playpen from the living room and a bag of toys in one hand, while his other arm supported Luke.

"I can do it by myself," Patience said, going to Timothy.

He shook his head. "I don't mind helping. Let me get the *buwe* settled."

Patience looked like she wanted to say something else, but instead she turned and picked up the glasses from the table and put them in the sink. Timothy put both boys in the playpen, and they immediately busied themselves with the small toys he'd dropped inside. They really were well-behaved children who took after their father, not their aunt.

Ruby placed the cake in Patience's plastic cake carrier before putting on a blue sweater and slipping on her tennis shoes. She told her family good-bye, picked up the cake, and walked to the barn. She set the cake in the buggy and hitched up Timothy's horse, Harvey. Careful not to knock the cake as she got in the buggy, she moved it closer to her and away from the edge of the seat as she guided Harvey down the driveway. Reins in one hand and holding onto the cake with the other, she set out for Seth's.

A short while later she pulled into the Yoders' driveway, her heart pounding a little faster. There was no turning back now. She parked the buggy and tied the horse to the hitching rail near the barn, and then she cradled the cake in both her arms as she made her way to the house. The lowing of cows reached her ears, a sound she was used to while living at Timothy's. She breathed in the scent of freshly mown hay and saw several wire corncribs halfway full of field corncobs near a large barn. She had covertly learned from Patience that the Yoders lived near two other farms that belonged to the Bontragers and the Chupps. The three houses, fields, and barns looked like they belonged to one big compound.

Ruby climbed the porch steps and stopped at the front door. She drew in a breath, put a smile on her face, clutched the cake tightly with one arm, and knocked. The sound of dull footsteps reached her ears, and the door opened. Seth stood there. "Oh, hi, Ruby. I didn't know you were coming over."

She stumbled back a step. She'd assumed Mary would answer the door, not Seth. Which didn't make sense now that she thought about it. Then she realized he'd remembered her name. That sent the butterflies in her stomach flapping. *He remembered.* Either he was interested in her or she'd made such a fool of herself with the hiccups that he remembered her for the wrong reason. She hoped it was the former, even though she suspected the latter.

Anyway, she couldn't stand here not saying anything to him, so she opened her mouth to say hello. Not a single sound came out. She tried again, moving her lips up and down. Nope, nothing.

He squinted at her. "Are you okay?"

"I . . ." The cake. She'd brought a cake. She held it up in front of her face. "I made this."

Seth peered at her around the cake container. "That's, uh, nice. What is it?"

"Cake!" She shoved it at him. "I made cake. Chocolate cake.

With frosting. Cream cheese frosting. Do you like chocolate cake with cream cheese frosting?" Her heart sank. She sounded like a babbling fool. A loud, babbling fool.

"I like any kind of cake and frosting." He took the cake from her, smiling slightly. "Who's the cake for?"

"Definitely not for you." She bent over and laughed like she had told the funniest joke ever uttered. "Why would I bake a cake for you? It's for *yer familye,* silly." She froze, her giggles stuck in her throat. Oh no. She did *not* just call him silly.

His faint smile faded, and he took a step away from her. "Ah, well, that's really nice of you. I'm sure we'll all enjoy it."

She nodded and grinned, her cheeks stretching. She rocked back and forth on her heels, unable to speak or stop grinning or stop feeling like a fool. Right now, hiccups might be preferable.

Seth tilted his head, frowning slightly. "Would you like to come in? *Mamm* and *Daed* are in the kitchen. *Mei bruders* are over at the Bontragers'."

Wow, he was so polite. Few men would let someone acting as *seltsam* as she was in their house. As a bonus she might have Seth all to herself after she spent a few minutes visiting with his parents. Not that she would do anything untoward, but she needed to show him she wasn't *ab im kopp.* She felt her grin widen more than she thought possible. "I'd *love* to come in!" She started to step inside, reminding herself to keep her voice down.

At the same moment he pushed on the screen door. The wooden frame slammed into her face, and the blow made her stagger backward.

"Oh *nee.*" He set down the cake and went to her. "Are you okay?"

She held her throbbing nose. Good grief, that hurt. Were

those stars she saw twinkling over Seth's head? Or just spots dancing around. "I . . . think so."

"Let me see." He moved her hands away from her nose. "Great, it's bleeding. *Mamm!*"

Without thinking she looked at the blood on her fingers. *Uh-oh.* That was a mistake. She never could stand the sight of blood. The world suddenly tilted, and her vision filled with dark dots. "Oops," she said before everything went black.

Ruby looked at her bruised nose in the bathroom mirror. She'd hoped the swelling would have gone down by now, almost twenty-four hours since Seth had accidentally banged her face with the door. She winced, remembering how she had passed out in a lump at his feet. She came to right away, making sure she didn't look at the blood again. Then Seth lifted her in his strong arms, took her inside the house, and set her on the Yoders' living room couch.

That entire happenstance would have been amazing, except then Seth had disappeared and his mother, Mary, had taken care of her. She gently wiped off the blood and pressed a cold washcloth to Ruby's tender nose. "I don't think it's broken," she said. "I'm sure it hurts, though."

Ruby nodded. Mary was nice, and Ruby liked her a lot. But she had hoped Seth would return, thinking she might be able to salvage the evening with him. He never did, and Freemont had driven her home in Timothy's buggy, insisting he didn't mind walking back to his place. Project Impress Seth Yoder was in ruins—again—and her dignity was in shambles. Hopefully the cake had tasted good.

She shook her head at her reflection, but she stopped when her nose started to ache again. Patience had looked at it this morning and agreed with Mary that it wasn't broken. "I didn't realize you were so sensitive to seeing blood, Ruby," she said, handing her a few ice cubes wrapped in a clean washcloth.

"*Ya.*" She carefully touched the washcloth to her nose. "I don't know why. I see it, and then I faint."

"That would be a problem if you were a midwife."

Ruby looked at her. She hadn't thought about that. While she wasn't knowledgeable about childbirth, she did know it involved blood.

"I think I have *mei* answer about you becoming *mei* assistant."

Setting down the washcloth, Ruby said, "I'm sorry, Patience."

Patience waved her hand. "It's all right. I do think I'll have to find someone else, though. I'll make sure they don't mind blood."

Ruby washed her hands in the bathroom sink, dried them on the hand towel hanging nearby, and then glanced at her reflection one more time. Her nose was also a little scabbed up. Not enough for her to miss going over to Selah's, though, and she looked forward to the distraction. Only Selah and Martha would be there tonight, and she could put yesterday's embarrassing moment out of her mind for a little while. She'd decided to walk to Selah's just in case she had another mishap. She didn't want to depend on someone else for a ride home. Freemont had said he didn't mind taking her home, but she didn't like that she had to put him out.

She passed through the living room as she made her way to the front door. "I'll see you later," she said.

Patience paused in the middle of her game of patty-cake with Tobias. "Have a *gut* time."

"I will." She glanced at her brother and Luke, who were both dozing in a chair on the other side of the room. She put her hand up to her mouth. "I didn't realize they were sleeping," she whispered.

Patience chuckled. "You know *yer bruder.* He can sleep through anything. Luke takes after him."

Ruby nodded, but she made sure to open and close the front door quietly anyway. As she headed for Selah's, she touched the pocket of her light jacket where she kept her flashlight. She'd need it when she walked home later in the evening.

The day had been cool, and she anticipated it would be colder after the sun went down, but Patience told Ruby the walk to the Ropps' wasn't too far. It took her only half an hour to get there. The house was a little smaller than Patience and Timothy's. The yard was neat and trim, and the scent of freshly mown grass hung in the air. A gray barn stood on the other side of the driveway, a small fenced-in pasture behind it.

She knocked on the door, and a few moments later Selah answered it. "Hi, Ruby . . ." Her mouth dropped open. "My goodness, what happened to you?"

Ruby's cheeks heated, and she resisted the urge to touch her sore nose. Maybe it was worse than she'd thought. "I had a small accident, but I'm fine. *Nee* real harm done."

Selah's small, perfectly shaped, and bruise-free nose scrunched. "It looks awful."

Gee, thanks.

Selah took a step back. "Come on in."

Ruby cautiously waited until Selah held the door open for her, and then she crossed the threshold. She wasn't taking any chances when it came to doors. Suddenly she was having second thoughts. Did she really look that bad? *Maybe I should have stayed home tonight.*

"I've got some *kaffee* brewing," Selah said, motioning for Ruby to follow her. "Or would you rather have tea?"

"*Kaffee* is fine. Can I help you with anything?"

"*Nee.*" She set a plate of cookies on the kitchen table—peanut butter, and they were huge.

"Those look *appeditlich.*"

"Have one. Make *yerself* at home."

Ruby couldn't wait to taste them, and she reached for one.

"Martha and Chris should be here soon," Selah added.

Surprised, Ruby pulled back her hand. "Chris is coming?"

"Of course."

"You didn't mention him."

Selah looked at her. "He lives here. I didn't think I needed to."

"Oh." She was right, of course. Ruby shouldn't have questioned it in the first place. What did it matter that Chris was here? Knowing him, he probably wouldn't join them for something as fun as a game. He'd probably raise those skeptical eyebrows of his, scoff accordingly, and then go find a book to shove his nose into.

Still, she couldn't resist touching the tip of her own nose, wishing she looked a little bit better.

At the sound of someone knocking on the front door, Selah said, "That must be Martha. I'll be right back."

Ruby nodded and remained by the table. The percolator on the stove started to bubble. She looked over her shoulder, wondering if she should turn off the gas burner. Probably not, since Selah and Martha would be there any minute. She waited, the sound of coffee percolating behind her and filling the room with its rich aroma. Which made her want a cup. Surely Selah wouldn't mind if she helped herself to one. She'd told Ruby to make herself at home.

Next to the stove were four coffee cups, ready to be filled. Ruby turned off the stove, and then she glanced at the cups. She picked up the pot and started to pour.

The kitchen door opened, startling her. She turned and looked over her shoulder, thinking Selah and Martha must have gone outside for some reason. Oh, it was only Chris. "Hi," she said as he walked inside.

As she'd predicted, his eyebrows shot up. But what he said next surprised her. "Why are you pouring *kaffee* on the counter?"

"What? Oh!" She set down the percolator as coffee dripped onto the floor. "Sorry." Good grief, couldn't she do anything right?

Chris quickly grabbed the towel off the hook near the sink at the same time she reached for it. "I can clean it up," she said.

"It's all right," he replied in *Dietsch*. "I don't mind."

Before she messed up anything else, she stepped away and let him go to work. He ran the towel across the counter, catching the drips underneath the edge, and then knelt and wiped up the floor. When he was finished, he stood, his gaze taking her in.

She felt her cheeks flush with embarrassment. Or was it . . . She didn't know. Why was Chris looking at her so intently? So . . . personally? And why had her heartbeat doubled in time?

"You splashed *kaffee* on *yer* dress."

Ruby looked down and saw several brown spots. She cringed. Not only had she made a mess of her dress, but she'd also thought Chris was . . . She shook her head. He was being Chris and noticing a problem or a flaw. That was all, and she'd been irrational to think anything else. She'd had her mind so much on Seth and husband-hunting lately that she wasn't keeping her thoughts straight.

Chris wrung the coffee-soaked towel in the sink. Then he opened a drawer and pulled out another small towel. "Here," he said, handing it to her. "This should suffice. You didn't burn *yerself*, did you?"

"*Nee.*" She dabbed at the spilled coffee, but most of it had soaked through the fabric already. After a few fruitless attempts, she shrugged and handed the towel back to Chris. No use fretting over spilled coffee. "Oh well. Won't be the first time I stained a dress."

She expected him to say something about her remark, such as *I believe it* or *Of course you have.* But he remained silent as he turned on the tap, rinsed and wrung both towels, and then draped them neatly over each side of the sink. Then he went to the stove and started pouring coffee without spilling a drop.

As Ruby watched him, she appreciated that he hadn't made a sarcastic remark or cruelly edged joke, like some people had in the past when she made a mistake. Usually she made her own self-deprecating remarks to cover up her embarrassment. And although spilling coffee wasn't exactly high on the list of her humiliating achievements, she desperately wished she could get through at least one social event in Birch Creek without being inept or klutzy.

He handed her one of the cups as if nothing had happened and he was being the perfect host. "Where's Selah?"

"She went to let Martha in." Ruby glanced in the direction of the living room. "They've been gone a while. I don't know what's keeping them."

Chris took two of the cups over to the table and set them down. "I can't fathom a guess either."

Back to English again. The language flip-flopping didn't bother her, but she found his constant use of "proper" speech a bit *seltsam*. Yet it was also kind of charming, in a peculiar way.

He turned to her, his brow furrowed, a contrast to his normally composed expression. He opened his mouth, and then closed it, and then opened it again. This hesitancy was unlike him. "Ruby . . . I have a slight favor to ask, if I may."

"You may." She sipped her coffee, wondering what he could possibly need from her.

He rubbed the back of his neck. "I thought maybe you could . . . if the opportunity arises, that is . . ."

Well, this was painful to listen to. *Just spit it out.* "Maybe I could what?"

He dropped his arm to his side. "Tell me what I'm doing wrong?"

She almost laughed, but then realized he was serious. "About Martha?"

He nodded and then looked away.

She hid a smile. His determination to get Martha's attention was sweetly endearing. "You want a pre-lesson before our lesson?"

He nodded again, still not looking at her.

"Of course. I'm happy to help, if I can."

She saw Chris lean against the table, a contrast to his normally upright posture. He really was tense. Then he tilted his head and scrutinized her face. "You have a large contusion on your nose."

"Contusion?"

"Bruise."

She guessed she'd have to get used to everyone pointing out her injury until it healed a little more. "You're just noticing this now?"

"I was distracted by the coffee." He moved closer to her, focusing on her swollen nose. "Your proboscis is not seriously damaged, is it?"

"If you're asking if *mei* nose is broken, *nee*. It's not."

"I'm glad to hear that." He sat down and folded his hands on the table in front of him, looking straight ahead.

Ruby sat down in the opposite chair. Instead of following her instincts and engaging him in conversation, she simply looked at him. Unlike her, he sat very still. Stiff, almost. His folded hands were tight, the knuckles almost white. She could tell his mind was elsewhere, especially since he wasn't really meeting her gaze.

"Chris?"

He blinked and then seemed to focus. "Yes?"

"Are you nervous about seeing Martha tonight?"

He unfolded his hands and sat back in the chair, although it didn't look like a natural position for him either. "Of course not. There's nothing to be nervous about. We're going to play a game and enjoy each other's company."

"Right. But that will be hard to do if you can't relax."

His shoulders dropped, but then he put his arm awkwardly over the back of the chair next to him. He cocked his head until it looked like he would strain a neck muscle. "See? I'm relaxed."

At that moment Selah and Martha walked in. "Sorry we took so long," Selah said. "I was showing Martha a new book I got at the library."

"I read it last year, and it's really *gut*," Martha said. She turned to Ruby. "Hi. I'm glad you could come." Then her gaze moved to Chris, and she frowned. "Hello?"

"Hi." He lifted his hand in what Ruby realized was supposed to be a casual gesture but looked like he'd had a spasm. Not to mention his voice cracking on that one-syllable word. *Oh dear.* She had her work cut out for her.

Selah ignored her brother's strange behavior and gestured for Martha to have a seat. "*Danki* for setting out the *kaffee*," she said to Ruby.

"Chris did it."

When the three women looked at him, he jerked up his hand again. Ruby had to resist the urge to face palm.

Selah sat down and grabbed a cookie. "What game should we play?"

"How about horseshoes?" Martha suggested.

Ruby started to nod, but then she saw Chris almost pop out of his seat, all traces of his awkward posture disappearing. "I thought we were playing a trivia game tonight," he said in *Dietsch.*

"But I love horseshoes." Martha smiled. "I play with *mei schwester* all the time."

"That's nice, but there isn't enough daylight," Chris said in a strained voice.

"The sun doesn't *geh* down for another hour." Martha turned to Ruby. "Do you like horseshoes?"

"I do." She wasn't the most graceful player, but she was decent.

"Great! It's a pretty evening tonight. *Nee* need to stay inside when we can enjoy it. Cold weather will be here before we know it."

Selah glanced at Chris. "You're right, but maybe we should—"

Martha was already getting up from her chair, leaving her coffee behind. "Do you have a horseshoe set? If not, I can run home and get ours." She tapped her finger against her temple. "I should have thought of this before I came over, but the idea just occurred to me."

"We have a set," Chris said weakly. "It's in the shed."

Martha grinned and turned to Selah. "I can help you set it up."

Selah looked at Chris again. When he didn't say anything, she shrugged and picked up a cookie. "All right. Let's *geh*."

Ruby watched the girls walk through the mudroom and out the back door. Why hadn't Selah asked Ruby to help too? Not that it took a lot of people to set up horseshoes, but it would have been nice to be included, not only in that, but also when Selah was showing Martha the book. She'd hoped that tonight she would make some headway in her friendship with the girls, but that was looking more unlikely by the moment.

"This isn't *gut*."

She turned at Chris's harried whisper. She was stunned when she saw how pale he was. The contrast was so stark she could see the dark stubble on his chin. His eyes were wide as they darted back and forth. It was the most emotion she'd ever seen him reveal, which made her wonder if that was also a bad sign.

"Are you okay?" she asked.

He jumped up from his seat. "*Nee*. I am not okay." He started to pace back and forth. "I'm definitely not okay."

"Why? It's just a game of horseshoes."

Chris halted and looked at her, wild-eyed. "Exactly." He started to pace again.

"I don't understand."

But he ignored her as he paced, and then he stopped and gripped the back of his chair, his head down. She could see him breathing heavily. She hurried to him. "You're not going to pass out, are you?"

He lifted his head. "That is a distinct possibility."

"C'mon, you two." Selah poked her head into the kitchen. "We're ready to play." She looked at Chris, pity in her eyes. "Don't worry," she said. "I'm sure everything will be fine." The screen door bounced shut.

"It will not be fine," he muttered. "She knows that."

Ruby got up from the table. "It's just a game."

He shook his head. "It's *mei* doom."

Now he was being ridiculous. "Don't be so dramatic." She went into the mudroom and held the door open. When he didn't follow, she stepped back into the kitchen. "Do you want me to tell Martha you've chickened out?"

He straightened and shook his head. "I never chicken out." He stood from the table, back to his normal, emotionless self, and pushed past her.

She shook her head. "It's just horseshoes," she mumbled. "How bad can it be?"

Ten minutes later she saw exactly how bad.

Selah and Martha were on one team, which left Ruby with Chris. Since the players for each team stood on opposite ends, that meant Chris and Martha were standing next to each other—which would have been perfect except for one thing.

Chris Ropp was bad at horseshoes, and the word *bad* was too mild. He was horrendous. Not only did he throw the horseshoes everywhere but close to the stake, but he looked like a newborn colt doing it. As soon as he started to throw, his rigid and controlled body went haywire. To add insult to injury, the result was hilarious.

"Come on, Chris," Ruby said after Selah threw a perfect ringer. "You can do this."

Chris's dark eyebrows set in a straight line as his gaze locked on the stake. He yanked his arm backward and the shoe flew behind him.

"I'll get it." Martha picked up the horseshoe from a few feet away and then hurried to hand it to Chris. When he took it from her, he dropped it on his foot.

"Are you okay?" Ruby called out.

He nodded and picked up the horseshoe. Then he took aim again. This time the shoe flew straight but hit the ground only halfway to the stake.

Ruby heard Selah chuckle. She turned to her. "I don't think it's funny," she said.

Selah stopped chuckling, but she was still smiling. "It is. A little." She called out to Martha. "*Yer* turn."

"You sound like you want him to be embarrassed." Which he was. Anyone could plainly see that. She looked at Chris, who was standing as far as he could from Martha while she threw the first horseshoe, his face pinched into a miserable expression.

Selah faced her, all traces of humor gone. "You have *nee* idea what I want." As soon as Martha's second shoe landed—another ringer—Selah picked up the horseshoes. "*Yer* turn." She shoved them at Ruby.

Ruby took the horseshoes, nearly dropping them. But for

once it wasn't from clumsiness, but confusion. Obviously, she'd said the wrong thing. But why was Selah acting this way? She'd been friendly a few minutes before, and now she seemed to enjoy watching Chris struggle. Or was Ruby reading the situation wrong? She'd done that a time or two.

If she thought Chris was confusing, Selah was even more so. What a strange set of siblings.

She looked at Chris. Ruby didn't know or understand what Selah wanted. What she did know was she didn't want Chris to be humiliated. Not like this and not in front of Martha. She threw the horseshoe a few feet wide of the stake and followed with the second horseshoe the same way. "Ugh," she said in an exaggerated yell. "Stupid game!"

"I thought you liked horseshoes," Martha called out.

Time to backtrack. Ruby crossed her arms. "I do. But I never said I was *gut* at it." Which wasn't the complete truth. She wasn't that bad a player.

They finished the game, and the score was a blowout since she and Chris hadn't scored a single point. "That was, um, fun." Martha held out her hand to Chris. "*Gut* game. Better luck next time."

He stared at her hand as if she'd given him a rattlesnake to shake. When he didn't take it, she shrugged and went over to Selah, who was heading toward the house, ignoring both Ruby and Chris.

Ruby frowned, but not at Martha, who was a perfectly nice person and probably completely unaware of the tension between Ruby and Selah. She shook her head as she walked over to Chris. She might think twice before accepting another invitation from Selah Ropp.

She gave Chris an encouraging smile. "I guess we're left to pick up the—"

"Why did you do that?"

Ruby stepped back, stunned by his angry question. "Do what?"

He moved in front of her, his eyes stormy, which was not only out of character but also alarming. "Why did you make a fool of me in front of Martha?"

CHAPTER 7

*C*hristian knew his anger was misplaced. It wasn't Ruby's fault he had no athletic ability. He was terrible at all outdoor games and sports, including horseshoes, and he tried to avoid participating at all costs. But he couldn't refuse this time, not when Martha had suggested the game. Yet what he predicted came to fruition, and he'd embarrassed himself in spectacular fashion.

Although his atrocious performance had nothing to do with Ruby, she hadn't helped matters. "You didn't have to throw the game on my account," he snapped.

"I . . ." She looked down. "I thought I was helping."

Her contrite tone should have stopped him, but it didn't. "By making me look bad in front of Martha?"

Her head snapped up. "You did a *gut* job of that *yerself*."

He flung off his hat and tossed it aside. It landed perfectly on top of the horseshoe stake.

"See? You got a ringer after all."

Christian glared at her. Her smile was bright, her eyes cheery, her voice sweet. All of it grated on his nerves. He snatched his hat off the stake and charged toward the house.

She hurried after him. "I'm sorry, Chris. How can I make it up to you?"

That stopped him. Even after his poor behavior, she still wanted to make amends. *She's a better person than I.* He turned and faced her, his anger cooling.

"You said I embarrassed you. I didn't mean to." She clasped her hands. "You're upset, and I want to make it right."

He felt like a complete dolt. "I don't expect restitution for a horseshoe game," he said in a quiet voice. He paused and collected himself. This was what happened when he lost control of his emotions. "I made a grave error." He drew in a breath. "I'm upset with myself, and I took it out on you. It is I who owe you an apology."

"Accepted." She threaded her arm through his.

He raised an eyebrow and looked at her arm before meeting her gaze. "That's it?"

"What do you mean?"

"You've forgiven me that easily?"

"Of course. Taking the high road is always the wisest decision."

True. Although he hadn't expected her to travel that path so quickly.

"Let's *geh* inside," she said. "Hopefully we can salvage the rest of the evening with Martha."

He pulled her arm from his. "I don't believe that is possible."

"Why? Because you're not perfect? Here's a little tip—women like men with a few flaws."

Christian scoffed. "Martha didn't witness a mere flaw." More like an epic tragedy.

"So? She had fun anyway, *ya?* Isn't that what matters?" She tilted her head in the direction of his house. "I hope Selah made some fresh *kaffee.* I don't like to drink it cold." She headed for the back door.

Christian watched her. Logically he knew forgiveness was important. It was one of the most important tenets of their faith. But he also knew forgiveness didn't come instantaneously for most people. His family members were masters at employing the silent treatment, even after presumably offering forgiveness. He remembered a time when his mother didn't talk to his father for three days. Seeing Ruby brush off his insolence with genuine forgiveness was refreshing. And a little . . . touching.

Ruby was already in the kitchen by the time Christian arrived inside. She was standing near the door to the mudroom while Selah was emptying the pot of coffee in the sink. The cookies and cups were nowhere in sight. "Where's Martha?" Ruby asked.

"She had to leave early. She said to tell you good-bye." Selah kept her back to them as she turned on the tap.

Christian had to admit he was relieved. Despite Ruby being right about everything, he wasn't prepared to face Martha right now.

"I should *geh* home too," Ruby said, looking at her feet.

Christian might not be the best at reading body language, but he could tell she was uncomfortable. "Do you need a ride home?"

She shook her head. "I walked. And I brought *mei* flashlight." As she pulled it out of her pocket, she dropped it on the floor.

He bent to get it at the same time she did, and they bumped heads.

"Ow," she said, standing up and rubbing the top of her *kapp.*

Christian picked up the flashlight and handed it to her, his head smarting a little bit. Spilled coffee, a tragic game of horse-shoes, a lost chance with Martha, and now knocking heads with Ruby—the whole evening had turned into a calamity before sunset.

She took the flashlight, her blue-gray eyes above her bruised nose looking sheepish. "Bye," she said, and then she scurried out the back door, which was the quickest escape.

He placed his hat on the table and gripped the back of one of the kitchen chairs. "That went swimmingly," he mumbled.

"Shouldn't you walk Ruby out?"

Christian glanced up to see Selah rinsing off one of the coffee cups. She set it on the drying mat on the counter. "Why would I do that?"

"Why not?" Selah turned off the water and faced him.

"You invited her. Did you walk Martha out?"

"Of course not."

His hands tightened around the back of the chair. He wasn't in the mood to figure out what she was driving at. "I hope I pro-vided enough entertainment for you and Martha tonight."

Selah crossed her arms. "Don't blame me for what happened. You're the one who agreed to play horseshoes."

"You could have suggested something else."

She dropped her arms to her sides. "I was going to, but you were set on trying to be a show-off."

"A show-off?" His blood pressure seemed to rise, but he tempered his reaction. He'd already lashed out at Ruby unfairly. He didn't want to do the same to Selah. Like Ruby, she was right about tonight's disaster being his fault.

"Besides," she said with a smirk, "Martha enjoys horseshoes.

I also hear she's an excellent volleyball player. Shouldn't you learn how to do what Martha likes to do?"

She was right about that too. He'd have to ponder what that fully meant later, but something else was bothering him about tonight. "You were rather rude to Ruby."

Selah picked up a dish towel and wiped the already-clean counter. "That's *yer* opinion."

"*Nee*," he said. "That's a fact. You could have at least made her feel welcome to stay even after Martha left."

She whirled around. "I'm sorry *mei* behavior isn't up to *yer* standards, big *bruder*." She scowled and marched out of the kitchen.

He heard her bound up the stairs. Should he *geh* after her? He had *nee* idea. He was upset, she was upset, which he didn't understand. Because when it came to the way she treated Ruby, she was in the wrong. He suspected she knew it, too, since she was avoiding discussing it.

Maybe he should call their mother. She might have some advice, or at least some insight into Selah's behavior. Then again, he and Selah were adults, and they should be able to handle their own problems.

He jerked his hat off the table. When he came to Birch Creek, he assumed teaching would be the biggest challenge he'd face. He'd never imagined that educating a classroom full of children would be effortless compared to dealing with the women in his life.

Selah leaned against the back of her bedroom door, fighting the angry tears pooling in her eyes. Why was she crying—again?

All she'd wanted was to have a nice evening, and to possibly help Christian with Martha a little bit. If her feelings weren't on such a roller coaster, she might feel sorry for him. Right now, all she felt was anger—with herself. He was right. She had been rude to Ruby, and Ruby hadn't deserved it.

She closed her eyes, her emotions in turmoil. She didn't understand why she was behaving this way. Christian was annoying and oblivious and always had been. He was also generous and caring, in his own way. She'd been treating him poorly ever since they moved here. She had hoped tonight would be her peace offering.

Instead she'd infuriated him, but she could tell he was trying to keep his anger under wraps. Unlike her, he could contain his emotions, just as their parents could. They never raised their voices, never got into arguments—at least not the verbal kind— and she'd never seen either one of them cry. That made for a cold, isolating home.

"I thought life here would be different," she whispered, moving to the window. She looked out on the backyard. It was almost dark, but she could see Christian putting away the horseshoe set. She hadn't even thought about it after the game. She just wanted to go inside and get away from her brother. Because he was right—she had enjoyed seeing him fail. He was so smart, so successful in everything he did. To witness him make a complete idiot of himself in front of the girl he was trying to impress was so, so satisfying.

And liking it was very, very wrong.

She leaned her forehead against the window. There was something reprehensible about her. She was moody and spiteful, and Ruby Glick's cheerful personality chafed Selah's every nerve. She shouldn't feel like this. She shouldn't have this inner despondency and hopelessness inside her.

But she did. And she had no idea what to do about it.

Ruby almost didn't show up for her and Chris's lesson on Saturday. Even though he apologized for his outburst, she thought he might still be unhappy with her. She'd played horseshoes badly to try to make him feel better, but in retrospect, she understood why he'd been mad. Next time she wouldn't get involved. If there was a next time. Selah had seemed in a hurry for Ruby to leave once Martha was gone. So much for her and Selah becoming friends, which bothered her a little. What bothered her more was that she had no idea why.

But she was a woman of her word, and she showed up at the specified time. Chris wasn't under the tree. She didn't think she was late, and she was surprised he wasn't there. Considering how precise he was about everything except horseshoes, she expected him to be prompt.

Maybe he'd changed his mind. She'd give him some time before heading back to Timothy's.

The morning had started out clear, but now bands of clouds were gathering in the graying sky. She sat down under the tree and closed her eyes. It really was peaceful here, and she should take the opportunity to keep her mind still. She tried, but her thoughts kept going back to Chris. She hoped he was okay. The horseshoe game had been two days ago, but maybe he was holding a grudge after all. She frowned. She didn't like it when people held grudges. Being angry about something that in the end wasn't that big of a deal was a waste. So what if he couldn't play horseshoes? He had a lot of fine qualities to recommend him, and hopefully after Ruby tutored him, he could show those qualities to Martha.

"Ruby?"

She opened her eyes and saw Chris right in front of her. He must have moves like a cat, because she hadn't heard him approach. Chris wasn't wearing a hat, and a light breeze ruffled his thick hair into unruly waves as the leaves above them softly rustled. Seeing him a little disheveled was strange. Strange and somewhat . . . attractive.

Attractive? Chris Ropp? How could a stick-in-the-mud like him be attractive? She jumped to her feet and focused on the task at hand. "Ready for our lesson?"

"I'm always ready to learn." He pulled a small spiral note-book out of his pants pocket and removed the pen from inside the metal spiral. Then he opened the notebook and folded its cover back, pen poised above the paper. "We may commence."

If he was still upset about Thursday evening, he wasn't let-ting on. Then again, his expression was so serious all the time she couldn't tell what he was feeling—except when they played horseshoes, and especially after the game. He'd been angry with her, but he didn't seem to hold grudges. *Gut.* Another aspect of him Martha was sure to appreciate. "Let's sit down first."

He gave her a curt nod and sat down under the tree. She sat opposite him, folding her knees to the side and smoothing her skirt over them. "Lesson number one. Tact."

Chris bent his head and wrote the word down in neat, com-pact writing. No surprise there.

"According to the *Webster's Dictionary*," she began, using what she hoped was her best teaching voice, "tact means—"

"*Webster's Dictionary*," he said.

"What?"

"It's not *the Webster's Dictionary*. It's *Webster's Dictionary*."

She frowned. "I don't see the difference."

"Using the article *the* when referring to *Webster's Dictionary* is unnecessary."

She wished he wasn't so particular all the time. "Why?"

"Economy of words. You shouldn't use three words when two will do. Concise speech is essential to convey one's message succinctly."

"You should follow *yer* own rules occasionally," she mumbled.

"Pardon me?"

"Never mind. Can we get back to the lesson?"

He nodded, another breeze kicking up and ruffling his hair. "Of course."

She wished he'd worn a hat. His wavy hair was distracting. Why was she thinking about hair right now? *I need to focus.* "Now, according to *Webster's Dictionary*," she said, grinding the words out, "tact is . . . it's . . ."

His brow raised. "Is what?"

She knew she'd forget the exact definition, so she'd written it down. She pulled a piece of paper from her pocket and unfolded it. "Tact is a keen sense of what to do or say in order to maintain good relations with others to avoid offense." That didn't sound concise, but it got the message across. Chris started to write. She continued to read. "Or it can mean a sensitive mental or aesthetic perception."

He glanced up at her. "Which is?"

She'd hoped he wouldn't ask her that. "Why don't we focus on one definition at a time."

Nodding, he read over his notes. "I do appear to have a problem knowing what to say around Martha."

"But not around anyone else," Ruby said, pointing out what she'd just experienced.

He frowned slightly. "Perhaps not to Selah as well. And I seem to have said more than one off-putting thing to you of late."

She shrugged. "I don't hold that against you."

"I know," he said, looking directly at her. "I appreciate that." His words brought a smile to her face. It was nice to be appreciated.

"Is Selah *yer* younger or older *schwester*?"

"She's younger by two years."

"And how old are you?"

"Twenty-one."

She blinked and then blinked again. She'd thought he was at least twenty-five, if not older. "You're only twenty-one?" She could hardly believe they were so close in age. "But you act so old."

Now it was his turn to blink. "I don't think you meant that as a compliment."

"I, uh . . ." Might as well use this as a teaching moment. "That, Chris Ropp, was an example of being tactless."

"Yes, it was."

Had she hurt his feelings? She hadn't meant to blurt the words, but she'd been so surprised. "There's nothing wrong with acting old," she said. "I'm usually told to grow up."

"Why?"

She looked at him, and he seemed genuinely interested. "If you haven't noticed, I'm a bit of a disaster."

"I noticed."

"Tact, Chris. Tact."

He nodded. "I wouldn't say you're a disaster. Although you do seem to have a bit of a problem with refinement."

She sighed. If someone else had said that to her she would be insulted. But this was Chris, and he was nothing if not truthful. Painfully truthful. Teaching him tact was going to be tougher than she thought. "You're right. I do. But a better way to tell me that would be to compliment me first and then find a nice way to point out *mei* shortcomings—if that's even necessary."

"I should treat you the way I treat my students, then."

"Right."

He tilted his head and studied her for a few moments. But the longer he kept silent the more irritated she became. "It can't be that hard to come up with something nice to say about me," she mumbled, looking away from him. *Or maybe it was.*

"Ruby, I'm glad you took the time to consult the dictionary before our lesson."

She turned to him, smiling a little. That was some progress. "You're welcome."

"In addition, I think it would behoove you to read a book on exercise physiology. That might help with your clumsiness."

"I give up." She fell back on the grass. He just might be hopeless. Although maybe checking out an exercise book or two might be a good idea. She looked up at the canopy of leaves in the tree above her and felt the soft grass beneath her. Nice and comfortable. Her mood brightening, she placed her hands behind her head.

After a few moments he got up and stood above her. "Was that answer not satisfactory?"

She turned and looked at his shoes. Unlike most Amish men, they weren't scuffed or worn. They weren't fancy either—just a pair of serviceable shoes. She looked up at the tree again. *"Nee.* It wasn't."

"Where was my error?"

Ruby turned up her gaze. "You don't have any idea?"

After a pause, he shook his head, his thick eyebrows knitted in confusion.

She scooted over and patted the ground next to her. "Lie down here next to me."

"Why would I do that?"

"Because I'm the teacher and I said so." She put her hands on her waist and gave him what she hoped was her best teacherly expression.

She thought she saw his eyes roll before he lay down next to her, making sure to keep plenty of space between them. That was fine. She didn't want to be close to him and his unruly hair anyway.

"Now," she said, letting her eyes flutter closed, "close *yer* eyes."

"I fail to see—"

"Close *yer* eyes, Chris."

"Fine."

"Did you treat *yer* schoolteachers this way?" she asked.

"They didn't ask me to do nonsensical things, so no, I did not."

She opened her eyes and angled her head, checking to see if he'd followed her instruction. To her surprise, he had. Also surprising was his profile, which was unexpectedly attractive. Because of the short distance between them, she saw a bit of five o'clock shadow, even though it was only early afternoon. His eye-lashes were the same dark brown his hair was, and she noticed he had a tiny freckle near his temple.

"How long do you want me to lie here like this?" he asked.

She jerked her eyes closed, which she should have done as soon as she knew he had complied. "Not too much longer. Take a few deep breaths."

He breathed in and then out several times.

"Are you relaxed now?"

"I wasn't aware that I was tense."

She couldn't help but laugh, and she opened her eyes again. "You're the tensest person I've ever met."

His eyes flew open and he turned his head toward her. "I am?"

Ruby nodded.

He kept his gaze on hers. "I . . . I guess I am a little . . ."

"Uptight? High strung?"

"What happened to using a compliment first?"

She rolled onto her side and put her head in the crook of her arm. "You want some compliments? All right. Here are a few. You're smart, probably the smartest person I've ever met and definitely the smartest one close to *mei* age. And despite not being able to play horseshoes, you were a *gut* sport and finished the game. The fact that you want to learn how to improve so you can talk to Martha tells me you don't think too highly of *yerself.*" She paused. "Maybe you don't need any lessons at all. Other than just one."

He turned and rolled on his side, mimicking her position. "What's that?"

"Be *yerself* . . . the way you are with me."

Christian had to admit Ruby was a pretty good teacher. He'd never use her approach, and he still didn't quite understand the nuanced difference between straightforward honesty and tactfulness, but she had managed to make him feel something he hadn't felt in years . . . relaxed.

Even when sitting under this tree, some days he couldn't unwind, couldn't get his mind off his students or lesson plans, and lately off how to deal with Selah and how to talk to Martha. But with Ruby he didn't think about those things. He simply felt calm, albeit sometimes confused, in her presence. She was unquestionably a breath of fresh air in his life, which until now he hadn't realized had felt quite confined.

But feeling relaxed didn't mean he'd get a date with Martha when he was uncontrollably apprehensive around her. "I don't know how to be myself with her," he admitted.

She didn't say anything for a minute. She simply ran her palm over the green grass, still lush this time of the year. Uncharacteristic doubt entered her eyes, which for some reason looked particularly appealing at the moment. "I know what you mean," she said, looking down at the back of her hand. "I have the same problem when I talk to a *mann*."

"You talk to me adequately."

"You're different." Ruby looked at him, her expression rueful. "With you, I'm not trying to—" She slapped her hand over her mouth.

His brow raised. "Trying to what?"

"Never mind." She scrambled to a sitting position. "Today is about you, not me."

"Are you saying you're in need of instruction as well?"

She pulled up a strand of grass. "I'm quite capable of managing my own romantic life, thank you very much."

That insight made him smile a little. "Then you are trying to procure a husband."

"I never said that," she bit out. Her lack of eye contact said differently.

"Intriguing." He moved to a sitting position and crossed his legs at the ankles. "We both have the same goal."

She scoffed and flicked a piece of grass from her finger. "Hardly."

"Then you're denying that you're looking for a husband?"

Ruby met his gaze, and he saw the resignation there. "*Nee,*" she whispered, "I'm not denying it." She put her face in her hands. "This is so embarrassing."

"How so? We're both trying to achieve the same goal, and we both have similar problems. This symbiosis is quite remarkable, in my estimation."

"I'm not going to pretend to understand that last statement." She uncovered her face. "No one knows about this, Chris. I want to keep it that way."

"Shouldn't the object of *yer* affections be aware of *yer* intent?"

"Shouldn't *yers?*"

She had him there. "She will, if I get an opportunity to talk to her."

"Not if, Chris. When." She smiled. "Like I said, you have to be *yerself.*"

"And you should be *yerself*." He was starting to warm up to the idea of their mutually helping each other. It would alleviate the problem of showing his appreciation for her willingness to assist him. "What would it hurt for me to give you a little insight to the male psyche?"

"You're not exactly a common example."

He would take that as a compliment. "I mean when it comes to conversation. I could teach you how to be *yerself* around men while you teach me how to be myself around Martha."

She paused, averting her gaze again. "You don't think I'm hopeless?"

Even though she wasn't looking directly at him, he could see the sadness in her eyes. This subject was clearly painful for her, much more so than for him. His lack of finesse around Martha was an annoyance, but Ruby's issue with her own awkwardness seemed to cut deep, which brought out his sympathy. "*Nee*," he said, still speaking in *Dietsch*. "I don't think you're hopeless. Why do you?"

She chewed on the tip of the blade of grass. He doubted she realized she was even doing it. "It's been said once or twice."

"That doesn't mean it's true. Or that you have to believe it." He reached over and took the grass from her hand. "You just pointed out that I can act myself around you. You're doing the same with me."

"Are you saying we should get married?"

"Us?" He chuckled and shook his head. "We're ill suited, don't you think?"

She nodded, a twinkle of good humor back in her eyes. "I agree."

He was glad to see her resuming her usual joviality. "But I

do think there's a degree of friendship between us. And friends do help each other when required."

"Do you have any friends here?"

He thought about two of the men he grew up with back home. They would go fishing occasionally after they graduated from school, and that had always satisfied his friendly companionship needs. Otherwise, he was content to pursue his interests on his own. Yet somehow admitting that to Ruby seemed a bit pathetic. "Not in Birch Creek. I've been busy establishing myself with the school and getting a place for Selah and me to live. There's been little time to cultivate friendships."

She nodded, seemingly accepting his explanation. After a moment she said, "Okay. We can teach each other." She held out her hand and they shook on it. Then she lay back down.

He joined her. There was something tranquil about his back against the cool grass while he looked up at the majestic tree's branches and leaves. After a few moments of silence, he decided to get the ball rolling, so to speak. "Are you interested in anyone at the moment?"

She hesitated before answering. "Seth Yoder might be a possibility."

He didn't know Seth very well, but from what he'd observed, the Yoders were a fine family. He'd been spiritually challenged by some of Freemont's sermons, which he considered a mark of a good preacher. "A *gut* choice."

"I baked him a cake," she said, her speech speeding up.

"Did he like it?" A small flock of blackbirds flew above them.

"I don't know. I told him I made it for his *familye*. Then he accidentally knocked the door into *mei* nose, and then I saw the blood and passed out. His mother took care of me and Freemont took me home." She sighed. "See? I *am* a disaster."

Her mention of her nose made him realize he hadn't noticed it today. The dark coloration had faded, but it was still there. He was surprised it hadn't caught his attention. "More like a victim of unfortunate happenings," he said, trying to encourage her. "It wasn't *yer* fault he hit you with the door."

"It wasn't really his, either. What happened was accidental." She brushed a fly from her face. "That doesn't make me feel much better, though."

"Why didn't you tell Seth the cake was for him?"

"Because I was nervous." She grimaced and stared up at the tree. "That's why I need help."

Christian pondered that for a few moments. "You should bake him another," he said, deciding that her initial idea, while flawed in execution, was a good one.

"Right. I should show up at his door with another cake. That wouldn't be obvious at all."

"What about a pie, then? If you can bake a cake, you can bake a pie."

She sat up and gaped at him. "I'm having second thoughts about *yer* manly insight. Are you sure you can help me?"

He stared up at the branches and nodded. "I'll make a valiant attempt."

CHAPTER 8

*C*hristian spent the rest of Saturday afternoon pondering his lesson with Ruby. Despite her unorthodox manner, he had learned a few things. First, if he was able to be himself with a woman he wasn't romantically interested in, then there was hope that he could learn to be himself with Martha. Martha was sweet, pretty, kind, and generally not intimidating. With renewed confidence he decided to attend the next singing— whenever that would be—and ask to drive her home afterward.

The second thing he learned, which was more surprising, was that he could help Ruby the same way she was helping him. They had decided to continue their lessons, setting up another session for this upcoming Saturday, and he was already making plans. How could he help Ruby connect with Seth? He took the facts into consideration, writing them in the same notebook he had taken to the tree for his first lesson with Ruby.

1. Ruby and Seth are barely acquaintances.
2. Ruby has little hope that things will turn out in her favor.
3. Ruby has been foiled by hiccups and a screen door.

He regarded the list and then crossed out number two. He had high hopes for Ruby once she could get past her own barriers. Perhaps he could be a mediator between them, but he had to be stealthy about it. Walking up to Seth and informing him of Ruby's interest wouldn't work. Christian should probably get to know Seth at least a little. That would require him to extend the hand of friendship. Normally he didn't pursue such things, but in this case the result would be worth it.

He hoped. How unfortunate it would be to go to all this effort, only for Ruby and Seth to discover they were ill suited for each other—like Christian and Ruby were.

He attended church the next morning, intent on speaking with Seth after the service. Seth's sister Karen and her husband, Adam, were hosting today, thus Christian expected him to linger afterward. But once they all exited the Chupps' barn, Christian couldn't find him. He did spy Ruby. She was near the barn and talking to Martha, who had her back to him. Ruby tilted her head in Martha's direction, gesturing for him to join them. He shook his head. The idea of talking to Martha with a large group of people around them made him queasy. He wasn't eager to humiliate himself further. Better to approach her another time.

Ruby rolled her eyes and focused her attention back on Martha. Christian decided not to stay for the lunch meal and returned home. Selah hadn't gone with him to church, claiming to have a headache, but he wondered if she was being truthful.

He made a quick sandwich for himself, and after he finished eating it, he decided to pay Seth a visit.

When Christian arrived at the Yoders' and knocked on the door, Judah answered it. "Hi, *Herr* Ropp," he said, looking surprised and then concerned. "Did I do something wrong?"

Christian shook his head. "No. I'm here to see your brother Seth."

The young man blew out a breath of relief. "He went for a walk a little while ago. You'll probably find him over by the pond near Jalon's."

"And where is that?"

"Not too far from here." Judah gave him the directions, adding, "You can cut through our backyard to get there."

"I'd also have to pass through Jalon's yard, then."

"*Ya*, but he won't care. We all *geh* to that pond all the time. I like to fish and ice skate on it."

"Must be a special place."

Judah nodded. "I think so. I'd *geh* with you, but . . ." He hung his head. "I'm not allowed."

Christian was mildly curious as to what Judah had done to merit the restriction, but he didn't ask, and Judah didn't volunteer the information. "I'll see you tomorrow," Christian said.

"*Ya*." Judah didn't look too excited about the prospect.

As Christian walked away, he wondered how he could convince the boys in the district to have some enthusiasm about their education. A tall order for sure, but he wasn't giving up on the possibility. They didn't have to embrace education with the verve Christian did, but he did want them to get to the point where they didn't resent going to school.

He walked through the Yoders' backyard, musing on the

matter, and then crossed through Jalon's backyard. No one was outside. He approached the copse of trees Judah said Christian would have to walk through to get to the pond.

A strong breeze kicked up, and he heard a banging sound. He turned to the right and saw movement. Then he heard the banging sound again. Intrigued, he walked toward the source of the sound and found a small, decrepit shed that was well hidden.

Another gust of wind kicked up, and the door banged open. Seth came out and grabbed the door.

"Seth," Christian said, walking toward him. "Judah said you were at the pond."

Seth's eyes widened, obviously surprised to see Christian. No, surprised wasn't quite right. Stunned was more accurate. "I . . . uh, I was there earlier," he said, closing the door behind him and standing in front of it, almost as if he were deliberately blocking the entrance.

Christian looked at the shanty, which could use an improvement or two. Judah hadn't mentioned a shed.

"You were looking for me?" Seth said.

"Yes." He supposed here would be as good a place as any to converse. He pulled his notebook and pencil out of his pocket. "It's been brought to my attention that I should get to know the people in this district better."

Seth's stunned expression turned to confusion. "What do you mean?"

"You and I are in the same age cohort. It only makes sense that we would become friends." He positioned his pencil above his pad, ready to take notes about any pertinent information he could pass on to Ruby. "Your occupation is farming. Do you enjoy any recreational pursuits?"

"Recreational pursuits?"

"Hobbies." Christian looked at him, noticing for the first time that his black pants were covered in sawdust. A clear yellow plastic handle, the type on the end of a screwdriver, poked out of his pants pocket.

As if he realized what Christian was looking at, Seth quickly brushed off his pants and shoved his hand in his pocket, concealing the tool. "Don't have much time for hobbies. Farming is hard work."

Christian wrote *no hobbies* on his pad. "What are your favorite foods, then?"

Seth's bewilderment turned to wariness. "What's up with the notebook?"

"This?" Perhaps taking notes wasn't the wisest decision. He thrust the notebook and pen behind his back. "Nothing. Just, um, writing down a grocery list."

"In the middle of a conversation?"

"I don't want to forget the milk." Christian grimaced. This was almost as bad as trying to talk to Martha. If he couldn't strike up a normal conversation with Seth, he was beyond incompetent. "You missed some of the sawdust," he said, trying to detour their dialogue into something innocuous. He pointed to Seth's knee. "Right there."

Seth batted at it, and then he looked at Christian. "*Danki,*" he said, his voice tight. "Anything else?"

Christian rocked back on his heels, unsure what to say next since he suspected Seth might be annoyed with him.

"No?" Seth said. "Then if you're finished with the interview, I'll be going home now."

Christian nodded as Seth pushed past him. He glanced at

the shed with a passing curiosity about what was inside. That disappeared as soon as he realized he'd not only failed to get any meaningful information for Ruby, but he also might have come across as a little peculiar to Seth. *Oh well.* He shrugged and headed back home. It wouldn't be the first time someone considered him eccentric. He also saw no point in telling Ruby he'd even made this visit, and he hoped Seth wouldn't either.

Selah covered her pocket flashlight with her hand, muting the light as much as she could as she approached her house. It was past midnight, and the windows were completely dark. Selah knew Christian had gone to bed hours ago. Had he checked on her before then? No, because if he had, he would have seen that she was gone. The lights would still be on in the house and he'd be waiting for her. Not out of actual consideration, of course, but out of duty. Her brother had an abundance of that quality.

She felt a blurred mix of relief and disappointment. She'd managed to sneak out again without getting caught, but a part of her wished her brother would care enough to make sure she was all right. She'd told him this morning that she had a headache and couldn't go to church. He had accepted her explanation with his usual blank look.

As usual, her feelings didn't make sense. Nothing in her life made sense. She pulled the screen away from the basement window and climbed inside. She replaced the screen and shut the window, slipping off her shoes before she went upstairs. She didn't have to be too quiet, since Christian could sleep through anything.

Selah went into her room and turned on the battery-operated lamp on the side of her bed. She slipped out of her jeans and sweatshirt and put on a nightgown. She didn't bother putting up her hair, which she had kept down all day, and she didn't feel like taking off the makeup she'd applied before leaving the house. She tucked her English clothes into a suitcase at the bottom of her closet, turned off the lamp, and climbed into bed.

She knew she couldn't live like this anymore, having her foot in two worlds, not feeling like she belonged in either one. She'd have to make a decision . . . and she'd have to make it soon.

CHAPTER 9

*T*he next morning Christian walked to the schoolhouse, his mind shifting from Ruby, Seth, and Martha to teaching and lessons. He always arrived well before the students, and today was no exception. An hour later, with little fanfare, the school day began.

Christian handed out the morning's work to the students, giving them a short review activity to ease them into the school day. Since his classroom was almost all male, he understood the need to capture their interest and keep it, especially after a weekend.

As the students worked, he looked over his plans. He'd made a note last week to get Malachi's feedback on his new assignments. Now would be an appropriate time to bring that up. "Malachi," he said, glancing up from his desk. "Please come here."

Malachi didn't pop out of his seat as he usually did. Instead he stayed put, his eyes flittering back and forth. Finally, he slunk out from behind his desk.

Christian frowned as Malachi kept his head down, slowly approaching the front of the room. There was something off-kilter about his gait. Christian visually inspected him and noticed he was lopsided. One pocket of his pants was puffed out more than the other, and some lumpy objects seemed to be straining against the dark-blue denim fabric. In addition, an odd clattering noise accompanied each leg movement. The noise was loud enough to capture the other students' attention.

Christian folded his hands and placed them on top of the sixth-grade math teacher's guide. "Malachi."

The boy's eyes peered up at him. *"Ya?"*

"I presume there's something in your pocket. Am I correct?"

He started to shake his head, but then changed it to a nod. *"Ya.* There is."

"Please explain."

Malachi's head lifted, and his eyes were filled with remorse. "I got marbles in *mei* pocket. But I promise I won't play with them until recess. Double promise. I just needed a place to put them until then."

Christian wasn't unsympathetic to Malachi's eagerness to play with the marbles. However, the boy was violating school policy. "What are the rules about bringing items from home?"

"I have to get permission from the teacher first."

"And did you get permission?"

Malachi shook his head. *"Nee."*

Christian held out his hand. "The marbles, please. You'll get them back at the end of the school day."

Malachi dug into his pocket, brought out a few loose, colorful marbles, and handed them to Christian.

Christian opened the desk drawer and deposited the marbles,

which rolled off a package of number two pencils. "You may go back to your seat now." This had been enough of a distraction for the other students. He would discuss Malachi's schoolwork with him later. Right now he had to get the students back on track.

"That's not all." Malachi dug deeper into the pocket and pulled out another handful of marbles, handed them to Christian, and then stuck his hand in his pocket again. "I've got a few more."

How many marbles can one boy cram into his pocket? A lot, apparently. Christian held out his hand to collect the last of them.

As Malachi handed them to Christian, they slipped out of his grip and scattered all over Christian's desk. Several students snickered as the marbles clattered onto the floor. Emma Miller, who was a year younger than Malachi and also Martha's cousin, got up and started to help Malachi pick them up.

One of the marbles rolled past Nelson Bontrager, who bent down from his desk and flicked it away with his finger toward Judah Yoder. Judah then launched it toward Jesse Bontrager, who caught it in his hand.

"Enough," Christian said, his voice loud enough to capture their attention. "Jesse, the marble, please."

Jesse left his seat and handed Christian the marble.

"Return your attention to your assignments, everyone." Christian gave them a stern look. He was gratified when they immediately complied.

Malachi and Emma handed him the marbles. "I'm sorry," Malachi said meekly as Emma went back to her seat.

After tossing the marbles into his desk drawer, Christian said, "Keep them in a container next time. Not that there will be a next time."

"I will."

"Go back to your seat."

Malachi turned and took a few steps, but then he went back to Christian's desk. He searched his pocket again, revealing two more marbles in his palm.

"Are you sure that's all?" Christian asked, his patience ebbing. He took the marbles and stood.

"*Ya*. That's all." Christian heard a few more snickers and whispers as Malachi returned to his seat.

Christian placed the glass balls on his desk. He'd put them away later. Valuable education time had been wasted over Malachi's marbles. "Emma, Perry, and Jesse," he said, heading for the reading table, "come to the front, please. And bring your math books."

The rest of the morning went smoothly, as did lunchtime, and the marble escapade was forgotten. Christian escorted his students out to recess, following behind Judah, who was the last student out.

Christian was shutting the schoolhouse door when his heel landed on something hard and slippery. His right foot flew out from beneath him, and his other foot tripped over the threshold. Before he knew what was happening, he'd tumbled down the three steps and landed on the small concrete pad at the bottom.

"*Herr* Ropp, are you all right?" Judah hovered over him.

He shook his head, trying to get his bearings. His right ankle was strangely twisted underneath his left leg. "I'm fine," he said, brushing Judah away. What an inept way to start recess. But when he moved his ankle out from underneath his leg, a sharp pain sliced through it. He recoiled, trying not to cry out.

"Why aren't you getting up, *Herr* Ropp?" Jesse asked, joining Judah.

"Judah," Christian said through gritted teeth, "direct the students to the playground."

Judah looked up. "Too late. They must have seen what happened."

Christian swung his head in time to see a small stampede of students hurrying toward him. He reached for Judah. "Help me up."

With Nelson's help, Judah assisted him to his feet as the other students gathered around. Christian grabbed the rail and tried to put some weight on his right foot. More pain shot through it, and he lifted his foot, his stomach feeling queasy.

"I think he tripped on one of Malachi's marbles," Nelson said.

"I thought we picked them all up." Malachi sounded worried and upset.

"Did you break *yer* foot?" Emma asked, looking at Christian with round green eyes.

Christian shook his head, but he wasn't so sure he hadn't. He'd never broken a bone in his life, but he couldn't imagine what else could cause such intense, throbbing pain. Still, he had to keep it together for his students' sake. He turned and attempted to go up one step, only to yelp as soon as he put the slightest pressure on his foot.

"Yep, he broke it." Jesse looked up at him. "Do you want me to *geh* get help?"

Christian couldn't fathom how slipping on a marble and falling down three small steps could result in such an injury. "*Nee*—"

But Emma, who lived next door to the school, ran to her house while Christian held on to the bannister. The children were still huddled around him, most of them looking concerned, while a couple of the older boys looked faintly amused. Malachi stood off to the side, worrying his lip. Emma immediately returned with her mother and father.

"Let's get you inside." Hezekiah Miller grabbed Christian underneath his arm as Judah supported him on the other side. Christian had no choice but to allow them to assist him, aware that his students were watching everything unfold with rapt attention.

Emma's mother, Amanda, herded the students into the classroom as Hezekiah and Judah helped Christian to a nearby chair.

"You can't put any weight on it at all?" Hezekiah asked.

Christian shook his head and pulled up his pant leg. His ankle was already swelling, and now it hurt independent of any weight he put on it. He squeezed his eyes shut from the pain.

"Judah," Hezekiah said, turning to the boy, "bring over another chair so he can prop up his foot."

Judah returned with a child-size chair, and Christian put his foot on it. That didn't help much with the pain, but he felt a little bit of relief. He glanced at the classroom and saw all the children in their seats, quiet as they stared at him with concern. Through his haze he could still appreciate how well they were behaving.

"I think you should see a doctor," Hezekiah told him. "You might have a sprain or even a break."

"The students—"

"The students are going home." Hezekiah, a large man with a thick beard that grazed the top of his chest, gave him a look that brooked no argument. He walked over to Amanda, who was standing at the front of the classroom and surveying the students as if to see if anyone of them dared to step out of line. He talked to her for a few moments and then came back to

Christian. "Amanda agrees with me. I'm going to call a taxi and take you to the emergency room."

Christian knew Hezekiah ran a watch and binocular business from his house, and he was interrupting his work day. "I can *geh* by myself—" He saw Hezekiah grimace and leaned back against his chair. "*Danki.*"

Hezekiah used the school cell phone, given to Christian for emergencies, to call a taxi, and Amanda dismissed the students. Christian watched helplessly as they filed past him, each giving him an apprehensive look, even the ones who had at first thought his fall was funny. Malachi was the last to leave. He gave Christian a sorrowful look and then dashed out the door.

"I'll be right back," Amanda said as she followed the students. "I want to make sure they're all heading directly home."

Christian nodded, his side suddenly sore. That felt like nothing compared to his ankle. He rubbed his forehead with his fingertips. How was he going to teach a classroom full of active children with a broken ankle? *All because of one little marble.*

Monday evening after supper, Ruby began planning her week again. She'd discovered that planning her activities was useful, and with enthusiasm she wrote *Lesson #2 Chris* in Saturday's box. She added *No church* in Sunday's box and then backed up to look at the rest of the week. It was empty, other than helping Patience with her sons and whatever chores she needed Ruby to do. With the midwife assistant option out of the question and her brother still stubborn about not letting her help with the farm, she needed to find work elsewhere.

Maybe she'd visit Barton again this week. Working there wouldn't be too bad, except part of her pay would go toward hiring a taxi to and from work. It was a nice small town, and it had a yarn and craft shop she wanted to check out. She didn't do a lot of crafting, but she enjoyed looking at pretty yarns and ribbons and other craft supplies. While she was in the city she could ask around about any job opportunities. She wrote *Barton* on Wednesday's square.

Timothy passed through the kitchen to the mudroom, and then Ruby heard him slipping on his boots. She got up and reached him just as he was opening the back door. "I thought you finished the chores," she said.

"I did. There's an emergency school board meeting at Freemont's. Just got the call."

"Emergency?" Alarm went through her as she thought about Chris. "Did something happen to the school?"

"The school is fine." Timothy let the door shut behind him and spoke to her through the screen. "The teacher isn't. The news will get out soon enough. He sprained his ankle. Really serious, from what Freemont was telling me."

Ruby gasped. "How did he do that?"

"I don't know," Timothy said. "I'm sure I'll get more details at the meeting."

"May I come with you?" She couldn't sit around waiting to hear news about Chris. "Maybe there's some way I can help."

"How? You're not on the board, and you're not an employee of the school."

She couldn't exactly admit that she was that concerned about Chris. Her level of apprehension surprised her, but she didn't like the idea of him being in pain. "I promise I'll stay out of trouble. I'll just sit in a corner, quiet as a mouse. You won't even know I'm there."

"I doubt that."

"Timothy, that was a little rude." She frowned. "A little accurate," she added, "but still rude."

He rubbed the back of his neck. "You're right, and I'm sorry. I'm sure they won't mind if you visit with Mary while we have the meeting."

The mention of Mary's name made her think of Seth. She hadn't put two and two together to realize the meeting was at Seth's home. She should be figuring out a way to talk to him without scaring him off, yet for some reason she couldn't move her focus from concern about Chris. There would be time to think about Seth later.

After the short drive to the Yoders' and joining Mary in the kitchen, Ruby stood as close to the doorway leading to the living room as possible without being seen by the board members. She was trying to hear what they were saying, but the men's voices sounded like low rumbles to her, and she couldn't distinctly make out anything they said.

"It's *nee* use." Mary picked up an apple from the basket on the table and began peeling it with a paring knife. "More than one person has tried to overhear a conversation in our living room from the kitchen. It's too far to eavesdrop, and if you move any closer, you have a chance of getting caught. I think Freemont planned it like that when he built the house. Not that I would ever eavesdrop," she added, chuckling.

Ruby's face heated. "I shouldn't try to listen in." She sat down at the table, determined to make herself useful. She'd find out about Chris later. "May I help you with the apples?"

"Sure." Mary drew another paring knife from a drawer and handed it to Ruby before sitting back down. "I'm glad to see *yer* nose is looking better."

Ruby touched the top of it. It wasn't sore anymore, and the bruising was clearing up. "*Danki* again for taking care of me."

"*Nee* problem. Seth felt terrible about that, by the way. Too bad he's not here. He and Ira went to the Bontragers' tonight. I know he wants to apologize to you, having failed to do so that night. I think he was afraid it might upset you to see him then."

"That's not necessary." Ruby picked up an apple and looked back at the doorway to the living room. She wished she could find out if Chris was okay.

"You seem mighty interested in the board meeting." Mary set peeled apple slices in the large plastic bowl in front of her.

Ruby shrugged, hoping she looked nonchalant. "I've never been to one." A lame explanation, but she couldn't exactly ask how Chris was doing. Not without raising suspicions. Not that there were any suspicions to be raised. They were friends, and she was concerned for him as a friend.

"They're usually pretty quick since they expanded the schoolhouse and hired Chris. Although the last meeting was a little longer since they were talking about Phase Two."

"Phase Two?"

"Adding on to the *schoolhaus* again. Or maybe building a second one somewhere else. They haven't decided yet. They have time. Chris is doing a marvelous job running the school as it is." She shook her head. "Hard to believe he sprained his ankle so badly from stepping on a stray marble."

So that's what happened. She'd never suspected Chris would keep marbles in the school, though, or any other toys. School was serious business for him, and, she imagined, for his students. "How is he going to teach on crutches?"

"He can't. That's what the meeting is for. They need to discuss hiring a substitute."

Ruby slid the knife under her apple's red skin. "How long would they need one?"

"A week, maybe two. A sprain will heal quicker than a break, but they can sometimes be more painful than a break."

"That's true." She knew that firsthand. She'd sprained her wrist the first time she roller-skated. When she grabbed on to the side of the rink, her hand went one way and her feet went the other. Her wrist had been acutely painful for a few days, but it had healed quickly after that.

She tossed the apple peel into a smaller plastic bowl. "Do they have any candidates?"

Mary shrugged. "I don't know who could do it from our district. Martha, maybe, but she helps her *onkel* Hezekiah in his shop. Maybe Selah can do it."

For some reason she couldn't imagine Selah in a classroom full of kids. But there was someone she could imagine doing the job. She set down her apple and looked at Mary. "Or I could."

Mary stopped mid-peel. "You would be interested in teaching?"

"Substituting," she clarified. But as the word left her mouth, doubt already started to trickle in. She didn't think she was responsible enough to teach students year-round, but she could be accountable for the short-term Mary mentioned. "It sounds like fun," she said, smiling.

"I'm not sure I'd call it fun." Mary looked at her and then got up from the table. "I'll be right back."

Ruby had peeled and sliced two apples by the time she returned. "The board members want to talk to you."

Suddenly her palms felt damp. "Why?"

Mary grinned. "I think they want to interview you for the job."

"Interview?" Why would they do that? She was only offering to be a substitute. She hadn't known she'd have to be interviewed. She hesitated. Maybe this wasn't a good idea. Then again, she did like children, and they did need a teacher. Setting her misgivings aside, she wiped her hands on the towel on the table and walked into the living room.

Several men were there. She recognized a couple of them, and her brother, Timothy, of course. Then there was the bishop, and Jalon Chupp and Thomas Bontrager. Another man she didn't know was there, but she recognized him as the good-looking man who had sat next to Timothy during the last church service. Her gaze swung to one corner of the room. An elderly woman sat in a hickory rocking chair, crocheting what looked like a shawl. Or an afghan. She had no idea.

"Ruby," Freemont said, rising from his chair. He gestured to everyone else in the room. "I assume you know everyone here."

"I don't think we've met." The handsome dark-haired man stood and extended his hand. "Asa Bontrager. Nice to meet you."

She quickly shook his hand. He sat back down, and not knowing what to do with her hands, she thrust them behind her back.

"I'm Cevilla," the old woman said with a smile. "Welcome to the board meeting."

"Mary says you're interested in being a substitute," Freemont said, resuming his seat.

"Well, I, uh . . ." Where were her words? Panic squeezed her chest. *Please don't hiccup.* Then she remembered this wasn't about her. It was about the students . . . and Chris. "I thought it would be fun. "

"Fun?" Jalon lifted his brow.

Ruby saw her brother's head drop into his hand. *I guess that was the wrong thing to say.* "Educational fun, obviously," she continued. "I'm a firm believer that children need to learn, but it needs to be interesting and stimulating."

"Fun," Cevilla said, nodding. She peered at Ruby with an expression of approval. "Not a bad concept."

"Have you ever taught school before?" Asa asked.

She shook her head. *"Nee.* But I have extensive experience with *kinner.* I've been watching them, Amish and English, since I was twelve. I can also provide references if you need them. Timothy is one of them."

Timothy looked more relaxed now. "She is *gut* with *kinner.*"

"It's only for a few days," Jalon said. "A week at most. If you were to take the position, we wouldn't have to close school for that long."

Asa and Freemont nodded. "She can consult with Chris about lesson plans," Asa said, looking at Jalon.

That was a good idea. "I can do that," Ruby piped up, feeling hopeful. "He and I are friends, after all."

The men all turned and looked at her, as if trying to puzzle out exactly what she meant by *friends.* Cevilla merely chuckled.

"All right, Ruby," Freemont said. "As long as we're all in agreement, you're hired." He looked at the other board members. "Any objections?"

Ruby held her breath and looked at her brother. Would he

agree to this? Or would he be afraid that she'd burn down the school?

"None here," Timothy said, giving Ruby an encouraging smile.

She grinned back, grateful for his support.

"Then we have ourselves a substitute teacher." Freemont gave her one of his rare smiles. "How about you start the day after tomorrow? That will give you time to talk to Chris and learn about policies and procedures. I'm sure the *kinner* wouldn't mind another day off from school."

The school board members adjourned the meeting, and Ruby stood there, unable to stop grinning. She probably looked ridiculous, if not downright strange. But she didn't care. She had a job. Even better, she would be teaching children. She never would have been hired for such an important job back home. They knew her too well. But in Birch Creek she was different. Responsible. Mature. She was determined to do a good job. She'd make sure the school board didn't regret hiring her.

CHAPTER 10

*T*hey hired *you?*"

Ruby put her hands on her hips as she glared at Chris, although now she was wondering why she'd told the school board she'd be glad to inform him about their decision. After all, she had to talk with him anyway. "Don't sound so shocked."

He leaned on his crutches. "You're telling me this before *kaffee.*"

"I didn't realize *kaffee* was that important to you."

"It is when I'm awakened before sunrise."

Oh. Ruby bit her bottom lip. Perhaps she should have waited until after breakfast. She'd been up for more than an hour, excited to get started on her new job. She'd talked so nonstop on the way home from Freemont's house that Timothy had to tell her to be silent for a few minutes. He'd said it good-naturedly, though, and she had thanked him for giving her his vote.

"I won't let you down," she'd insisted. He only nodded in response, and she knew he had some reservations. She didn't blame him since she'd had some herself, but she was going to make sure this job went well for her and the students.

"I wanted to get a head start," she said, her smile hopeful. A man as dedicated to his job as Chris Ropp would understand that. "I'm ready and reporting for duty."

He gave her a bleary-eyed look. His hair stood up on end, even more untamed than during their lesson on Saturday. He also needed a shave. He was wearing a T-shirt and jeans and looked nothing like a buttoned-up, stick-in-the-mud teacher. Standing this close to him, she realized he smelled nice—like fresh laundry hanging on the line.

"Come on in," he said, his voice weary. He turned, his crutches thumping on the floor as he headed for the kitchen. "I'll get the *kaffee* started."

She eyed his crutches. He looked tired and unsteady on them. "Let me do it for you," she said.

He glanced at her over his shoulder. "I can handle it," he said, his tone sharp.

"Fine," she muttered, following him into the kitchen.

Chris hobbled to the stove and picked up the percolator. The coffeepot dangled from his fingers as he gripped the crutch handles, and he nearly lost his balance taking the few steps to the sink.

Ruby took the pot from his hand. "You should sit down," she said. "You don't want to make *yer* injury worse."

He nodded and hobbled to the table. She filled the pot with water, saw the coffee container near the sink, and put three scoops in the metal basket before she placed it back in the pot. She glanced at Chris as she set the percolator on the stove. He was hunched over in his chair, an unusual posture for him, and his face was twisted with pain. She turned on the gas burner and then went to him.

"*Yer* ankle must hurt a lot."

He started to shake his head, but then stopped. "No use in lying," he mumbled, switching to English. "It does hurt."

"Did they tell you to prop it up?"

"Yes."

"Then why aren't you doing it?" She moved one of the kitchen chairs closer to him, lifted his leg, and gently put it on the chair. Then she stepped back and looked at the arrangement. "You need a pillow," she decided.

"It's fine like this, Ruby—"

"I'll be right back." She went to the living room, remembering that Chris's couch had two small accent pillows on it. She picked up one, returned to the kitchen, and carefully lifted his leg and slid the pillow underneath his ankle. "Better?"

"Yes." He leaned back in the chair and closed his eyes.

She glanced around the kitchen, wondering what to do next. It might be early, but it was close to breakfast time. "Where is Selah?"

"Sleeping in, I suppose." He opened one eye. "I fell asleep as soon as I got home from the emergency room yesterday afternoon. I haven't seen her since then."

"Should I wake her?"

He shook his head, closing his eye again. "Let her sleep."

"Then who's going to make you breakfast?"

"I'm not really hungry." He crossed his arms over his chest. "I'll probably have some bread and peanut butter later."

"That won't do. You need *yer* strength." She moved closer to him, and he must have sensed her nearness because he opened

his eyes. They were rather handsome, too, now that she was seeing him this close. As she already knew, they were blue, but each
one had a thin circle of light green around them so faint she
hadn't noticed them before. Kind of unusual . . . just like him. "I'll
make you something to eat."

"Ruby—"

"I can cook, you know. Now, where's the pantry?"

"I suppose any protest will fall on deaf ears?"

"You suppose correctly."

He lifted his arm, pointing to a tall cabinet in the corner.
"Over there. Since it's just Selah and me here, it's not very full."

She walked over and opened the door. He was right about
the pantry being close to empty. She did find a loaf of bread and
the peanut butter, but he needed something more substantial.
"Do you have any eggs?"

He pointed to a small cooler in another corner of the kitchen.
"There might be some ham in there too."

Ruby found what she needed, and a short time later she had
whipped up ham, egg, and cheese sandwiches to go with the coffee. She sat down, closed her eyes, and prayed for her food. When
she opened them Chris was looking at her. "What?" she asked,
taking a sandwich and cutting it in half.

"I . . . I didn't expect all this."

"It's just a little breakfast. Emphasis on little." She took a
bite.

"It's adequate." He sipped his coffee, looking a little more
awake now. "More than adequate."

Ruby smiled. As they continued to eat, she studied him.
Now that he was more coherent, he was sitting straighter, at
least the best he could considering he still had his leg propped

on the chair. He cut his sandwich in half diagonally, and took small, even bites. She wasn't surprised that even his eating patterns were precise.

As he took another sip of coffee, she blurted, "You don't look like a Chris."

His brow raised, and he set the mug down on the table. "Pardon?"

"Selah called you Christian when I first met her. Is that *yer* given name?"

"Yes." He pushed away his plate with the half-eaten sandwich in front of him.

"Is something wrong with the food?" She wasn't a great cook like her mother and Patience were, but she was decent. Besides, even she couldn't ruin a breakfast sandwich.

Chris shook his head. "It's fine. As I stated before, I'm not very hungry."

"Are you still in pain?" At his slight nod she got up from the table and looked at his ankle. He was barefoot, and his pant leg was scrunched up. He had a half-cast of some kind on the back of his foot that didn't look very comfortable. "I'm sorry. I shouldn't have come over so early."

He motioned for her to sit back down. "It's okay. I appreciate your enthusiasm for the job. I didn't know they were planning to offer it to you."

"They didn't offer it, exactly." She straightened her shoulders. "I volunteered."

Surprise entered his eyes. "Have you taught school before?"

She shook her head. "But I'm willing to learn."

He gave her a half-smile, although she could tell he was hurting.

Ruby leaned forward, concerned. "Did the doctor give you anything for *yer* pain?"

"Yes, but I prefer not to take pain medication."

"For a smart *mann*, you're making a dumb decision."

His smile widened. "According to you, women don't like perfect men."

She started to nod, but she became distracted again, this time by his smile. He really was attractive, more than she realized the first time she saw him. She also appreciated that he hadn't questioned her substitute teaching ability. Then again, he did have personal experience when it came to her tutoring methods.

Selah appeared, her long hair a wild mess, wearing a plain sweatshirt over a nightgown. Ruby didn't think it was possible to look more disheveled than Chris, but Selah had accomplished it. She looked like she'd had a fight with her bedclothes—and the bedclothes had won.

Without looking at either Ruby or Chris, she yawned, took a mug from a cabinet, went to the stove, and poured coffee. She took a sip and then turned around and leaned against the counter, her eyes closed. When she opened them, her gaze seemed to finally take in the entire kitchen. Then her brow shot up as she focused on Ruby. "What are you doing here?" she said, frowning.

"She's substituting for me at the school until I'm back on my feet." Chris gestured to his leg resting on the chair. "Literally. She also made the coffee you're consuming right now."

"Oh." She took another sip of the coffee and yawned again.

"There's an extra breakfast sandwich." Ruby had made three of them, in case Selah would want one later.

"I'm not hungry." She topped off her coffee and left the room. Ruby could hear her footsteps going up the stairs.

She shot up from the table, angry. "She didn't even ask you how you were feeling." She grabbed her empty plate off the table.

"Neither one of us are early morning people, in case you hadn't noticed. Although I do whatever necessary to make sure I arrive at the schoolhouse well before my students do."

"That's *nee* excuse."

Chris sighed. "Selah's . . . complicated."

"She's rude." Ruby picked up Chris's dish and took the plates to the sink. She searched beneath the sink for the dish soap, found it, squeezed some into the sink, and turned on the water. "She should have risen early and made *yer* breakfast this morning."

"Then I wouldn't have had one of your delicious sandwiches."

Ruby turned around and looked at him, stunned by the compliment since Chris had difficulty giving them. He wobbled as he tried to get up from the chair. He shouldn't be doing that alone. She hurried over to help. "Here," she said, handing him his crutches. "And take it slowly. Do you need me to walk with you?"

"To the bathroom? Absolutely not."

That made her laugh, which made him smile again. So he wasn't as stuffy as she'd thought he was. Her laugh faded as she looked up at him and her gaze locked with his. Something happened inside her—a warm, fuzzy feeling that made her stomach seem to do a little backflip. That sounded terrible, but it felt nice. Very—

Selah came back into the room. "What are you trying to do, flood the kitchen?"

Ruby jumped away from Chris, who fell against the table, one crutch landing on the floor. "Ow!" he yelped.

Ruby turned from him to see Selah shutting off the tap.

Soapy, bubbly water overflowed from the sink and onto the floor. "Sorry!" *Not again.* This was worse than when she spilled the coffee, though, because this time she'd made a huge mess. Ruby grabbed a towel off the counter, crouched down, and started to sop water from the floor.

"Pay attention, next time," Selah snapped.

"That's enough, Selah!"

Ruby stopped her work and looked at Chris. He looked angry. Really angry.

"Ruby is a guest in this *haus* and you will treat her as such." He gripped the handles of his crutches. "*Geh* get dressed. You've lollygagged long enough this morning."

Selah's stunned expression turned sheepish. She nodded and then left the room.

Normally Ruby could shrug off hurt feelings, but she was finding it difficult. Not only was she embarrassed by yet another mess she'd made, but she was also upset by Selah's behavior toward her. She'd never been actively disliked before. People had been annoyed with her, even her friends. They'd had good reason to be at those times. But she was still well liked in her community, if not completely trusted not to make a mess of things. Yet Selah, whom she didn't know well at all, acted like she couldn't stand her.

"Don't take her behavior to heart, Ruby."

She rose from the floor and wrung the wet towel in the sink. "I'm not." That was a lie, but she wasn't about to admit she was letting his sister get to her.

"You asked me about my name earlier."

Ruby turned and looked at him. He was still leaning on the

crutches, still seemed in pain. He was also changing the subject, and she was glad to let him.

"I've wanted to be a teacher ever since I was in seventh grade. I loved school, loved learning, loved reading anything I could get my hands on. I was interested in every subject, and as I got older the idea of imparting knowledge to children appealed to me. However, that occupation didn't appeal to my parents."

Although the dishes still needed to be washed, she went to him and held out his chair. He sat down, and she sat down across from him.

"Like most fathers, mine wanted me to go into business with him."

"What does he do?"

"He's a butcher. Exceptionally skilled. He worked in a meat-packaging shop, but he also assisted other Amish with their butchering." Chris looked away. "The first time I saw him work I vomited. The second time I fell unconscious."

She nodded, sympathizing with him. "I have the same issue with blood."

"Eventually I learned how to manage my gag reflex, and I could get through a butchering session without heaving. My father continually telling me to 'be a man' also had something to do with it. He insisted that only little boys 'tossed their cookies.' Boys and females."

"He sounds a little mean."

Chris shook his head. "He's not. But he very much believes in the division of gender roles. There is men's work, and then there is women's work. Guess where teaching falls on his continuum."

"But that's not right. Some Amish teachers are male."

"I know. When I was studying and training I met several.

They were the ones who inspired me. They enjoyed what they did and found it fulfilling. I shadowed one of them, saw how he handled his classroom. From that point on I knew teaching was what God wanted me to do. I just couldn't do it in my district."

"Because of *yer vatter?*"

"Not only because of him, but because I knew the school board wouldn't hire me."

That didn't make sense to Ruby. "Why not?"

"Because my father was on the school board." He gave her a weak smile. "I refused to let that hinder me, and I searched for other teaching opportunities. That's when I looked for other offers and heard about the one in Birch Creek."

Ruby tilted her head. "This is all very interesting, Chris. But what does it all have to do with *yer* name?"

His cheeks slightly reddened, and she listened as he explained how Freemont had asked to call him Chris. "I wanted to impress him and the rest of the board, and I didn't want to contradict something as simple as what the bishop preferred to call me. That's why everyone calls me Chris."

He looked at her. "I'm still not used to it."

"You'd rather be called Christian?"

He nodded. "I'd rather not tell anyone that. I'll get used to Chris, and it's a little discomfiting to explain the story."

"But not to me."

His gaze met hers. "No . . . not to you."

That little flip-floppy feeling in her stomach happened again. He'd trusted her with a secret, one he thought was embarrassing. Ruby could definitely top him when it came to humiliating occurrences, but that didn't matter. What mattered was that he found his secret hard to admit, but he trusted her. *"Christian,"* she said with a smile. "You don't have to worry. *Yer* secret's safe with me." She had one other question, but she was hesitant to ask it since she was rather liking this little *moment* between them—if it could be called that. But her curiosity won out. "Why is Selah here with you?"

He frowned. "I often wonder that myself. The night before I left for Birch Creek, she asked to come with me. Begged would be a more precise term, because I at first told her no. I didn't understand why she would want to leave home and live in a district where she didn't know anyone. She persisted, and finally, I gave in."

He paused. "I'm still not sure what catalyst made her want to leave home. We're close in age, but not in any other way." He glanced at the table. "She doesn't seem any happier here, although she's managed to make a friend in Martha." When Ruby frowned he added, "But she's the only person Selah talks to. Granted, she's the only woman in her age group besides you, so that makes sense. Otherwise, she's been very much to herself."

Ruby thought that might be a family trait. Both Ropp siblings isolated themselves, which was unusual among the Amish. Part of the appeal of joining the church was to keep community ties. From what she could tell, Chris was as separate from Birch Creek as Selah was.

"We should get started on the lesson plans," he said. "I have a substitute folder in my room that has all the information you'll need for teaching and managing the classroom." He glanced down at his white T-shirt. "I will also put on more appropriate clothing."

She almost laughed at that. She didn't mind the T-shirt and jeans, but she knew he minded.

"Is *yer* room upstairs? The bathroom? Do you need help going up?" she asked.

"No. When we moved in, Selah insisted I occupy the master bedroom down here because she likes to look out at the trees. The downstairs bathroom is next to it. I'll be fine."

"I'll finish up the dishes."

He rose from the chair, this time without needing assistance. She expected him to say something about her not flooding the kitchen this time, but he just left the room.

That was one thing she liked about him. He wasn't the most tactful person, but he also wasn't sarcastic. She also appreciated his honesty. Chris—or Christian, rather, which really did suit him better—was a nice man.

The water in the sink had cooled, so she pulled the plug and refilled the sink, only halfway this time. She washed the breakfast dishes and had just started to dry them when he limped back into the room, holding a bright-red folder between the fingers on his right hand. "I'm nearly done," she said. "Do you want more *kaffee*?"

He shook his head and sat down. He looked tired. Spent. She quickly dried the dishes and wiped down the counters. Then she sat down next to him.

They spent the next hour going over the students' names and needs, the classroom rules and procedures, emergency practices, and assignments for the next four days. "I never expected to be out longer than that," he said. "I never expected to be out at all."

She looked over the paperwork. Everything was neat and self-explanatory. He'd even fashioned a small pocket taped inside the folder's larger pocket to hold a key to the schoolhouse. His meticulous preparation gave her confidence. "Don't worry. *Yer* students are in *gut* hands," she said.

When he looked at her, he didn't seem as confident as she was. She could be offended by that, but in the short time they'd known each other, she hadn't exactly been accident-free. Still, when it came to children, she was self-assured. "You can trust me," she said. "Everything will be fine."

He hesitated before nodding.

"Now, why don't you *geh* lie down? Better yet, you should take some of those pain pills. The doctor gave them to you for a reason."

"I just might do that." He didn't move. Neither did she. "I hope you'll excuse me if I don't walk you out," he said.

"You're excused." Still, she stayed seated.

"You can leave now," he said.

"Not until you *geh* lie down."

He arched his brow. "You don't trust me?"

She looked at him. "*Ya,*" she said softly. "I do." She picked up the folder and stood. "Take care of *yerself,* Christian."

He nodded, his eyes softening. "*Danki,* Ruby."

She let herself out the front door and thought about Selah as she walked down the porch steps and toward the road. Now that Christian had explained how unhappy his sister seemed to be, she wondered if she should reach out to her. People weren't miserable unless they had a reason, and maybe Selah would want to talk about it.

Then she shook her head. This was a situation that required prudence, and for once Ruby was going to employ it. But that didn't stop her from saying a silent prayer for Christian and Selah. They both needed God's healing presence right now.

CHAPTER 11

By Wednesday, Christian fully comprehended the term *cabin fever*. It didn't help that Selah wasn't speaking to him. At this point he was tired of her immaturity. She was nineteen, yet she insisted on acting like a seventh grader. He didn't want her waiting on him hand and foot, but it would be nice if she showed a little compassion. Right now, she was treating him as if he were a wad of gum on the bottom of her shoe.

Then there was the problem of his ankle. The swelling had diminished, but he was still in pain when he put weight on it. He used the pain pills once after Ruby left, but only because she told him to. He had to admit they'd helped. He'd gone back to bed and managed to sleep for the rest of the morning.

But sleep and lessened pain increased his eagerness to get back to the classroom. His students needed him. And now that he was incapacitated, he realized how much he needed the interaction with his students. It wasn't an easy revelation to accept.

He hadn't known how dependent he was emotionally on his job until now.

Christian thumped his crutches from his room to the kitchen, the school still on his mind. He poured himself a glass of milk. It wasn't that he didn't trust Ruby. All right, he trusted her mostly. But her penchant for accidents was a concern. He set the glass on the table and leaned against his crutches. He wasn't prone to fretting, but his stomach was in knots right now. Was she following all the procedures? Were the students behaving? Did he remember to tell her about Malachi's enrichment activities? What about Perry and Jesse's tutoring? He was supposed to meet with them tomorrow. Had he made a note of that in the folder?

Then there was the baffling issue that he might have been, for a moment and in his pain-induced haze, attracted to Ruby. Yesterday, before Selah barged into the kitchen and turned off the running water—which he hadn't realized was overflowing—he couldn't pull his gaze from Ruby. They'd been standing close, and he was noticing how one eyebrow was slightly higher than the other when it struck him how pretty she was. But she wasn't just pretty. She was kind, generous, and above all, eternally optimistic. In that moment, he simply wished to be near her.

Looking back on it, as angry as he'd been with Selah—and he was still upset with her—he was glad she'd interrupted them. Clearly his injury had disquieted his emotions, something he wasn't used to.

His ankle started to throb. He sat down at the table and closed his eyes. A verse from Philippians ran through is mind. *Do not be anxious about anything.* He'd always insisted on being in control to the best of his ability—at all times. Right now, though, he was struggling to find his bearings.

Selah sauntered into the kitchen. As had been her habit the past two days, she was still dressed in her nightgown. Again, she ignored him, getting coffee without even looking at him. Coffee that he'd managed to make. She turned to leave the room.

"Selah."

She paused and looked at him. Her hair was a mess, her nightgown askew, her expression weary. "What?" she said in a flat tone.

Now that he had her attention, he wasn't sure what to say. He recalled what he'd read about adolescent behavior and discipline to be prepared for the older students in his class. One recommendation was to avoid being confrontational. "I was wondering how you're doing."

"I'm fine." She turned away and left the room.

Christian clenched his hands into fists. Since his accident, she hadn't inquired about his physical state even once. She hadn't offered to do anything to help him either. She was mostly holed up in her bedroom upstairs. Very well. If that's what she wanted to do, fine. He wasn't about to navigate the stairs to check on her if she didn't care enough about him to ask if he was okay.

He brushed aside the hurt as immediately as it appeared. It was folly to dwell on it. Musing on situations he couldn't control wasn't productive. Instead he prepared his breakfast—two pieces of bread with butter—and sat back down at the table. He hadn't had much of an appetite, and he could only choke down three-fourths of his meager meal. He'd also noticed their food supplies were low. Selah needed to go to the grocery store. Or would he end up doing that too? Normally he didn't mind going shopping, but he didn't relish the thought of dealing with a shopping cart while on crutches, let alone hoisting himself into their buggy or even a taxi.

Perhaps some leisurely reading was in order. He went to the living room, settled on the sofa, and opened one of his favorite novels, *Of Mice and Men*. He tried to focus and failed. He even dozed off a couple times, something that never happened when he read Steinbeck. He'd been nodding off again when he heard a knock on the door. He sat up and waited for Selah to come downstairs and answer it. When she didn't, he struggled until he was upright and answered it himself.

He was surprised to see Phoebe Chupp standing there, holding a shallow box in one hand. One quick glance revealed what looked to be a casserole in a covered dish. She also carried a small white plastic bag that looked full. Then Christian noticed Malachi standing slightly behind his mother, holding a similar plastic bag, his gaze not meeting Christian's eyes.

"*Gute morgen*," Christian said, opening the door wider. A cool fall breeze filtered in.

"You mean afternoon." Phoebe smiled, her blue eyes sparkling.

"Already?" Had he slept on the sofa that long?

"It's almost three."

Surprised, he said, "I had no idea. Come in, please." He hopped away a few steps and let his guests in before pushing the door shut. He looked at Malachi. "Hello."

Malachi stared at the floor. "Hello," he said, his voice barely above a whisper.

Phoebe nodded at the covered dish in the box. "We brought you a hamburger-and-noodle casserole. Plus a few other things I thought you might like."

"*Danki*," he said. "Selah's upstairs. I'll call her to come down. You can set those things on the kitchen counter, if you don't mind."

As Phoebe and Malachi left the room, he limped to the bottom of the stairs. "Selah," he called out. "We have company." He waited but heard no response. "Selah!" All right, he'd had enough. He was about to go upstairs, crutches or not, when Phoebe came back into the living room.

"We found a note." Phoebe handed it to him.

Went out. Be back later.

He folded the note and shoved it into his pocket. No explanation, no return time. He should give her credit for even leaving him a note, but he wasn't inclined to. He gripped his crutches and comported himself. He wouldn't lose his temper in front of Phoebe and Malachi.

Phoebe gestured for him to follow her into the kitchen. "I put the casserole in the oven. It's still warm, but you can heat it up again whenever you like. There's also fresh bread, some butter, pickles, and chocolate chip cookies."

"I appreciate this," he said, calming down a bit as he focused on Phoebe's generosity. "You didn't have to *geh* to so much trouble."

"I didn't mind." Phoebe walked back to the doorway, where Malachi was standing just outside the kitchen. "Come in here," she said through gritted teeth.

He dragged his feet as he walked toward her. She placed her hand on his shoulder. "Malachi has something to say to you. I'll be in the living room while you two talk."

Malachi didn't move, his eyes still downcast. He didn't say a word.

Christian hopped to a chair and sat down, leaning his

crutches against the table. "Have a seat, Malachi," he said with a smile. The young boy looked miserable enough. He didn't want him to think Christian held any ill will toward him.

Malachi perched on the edge of a chair. "I'm sorry," he whispered. "It's *mei* fault you're hurt."

"That's true."

For the first time since he arrived, Malachi looked up. "I thought we'd picked up all the marbles." His lower lip started to quiver a little bit. "I won't ever bring them to school again. I promise."

Christian leaned forward. "You can bring marbles to school, Malachi. But you have to follow the rules. They're in place for a reason. You need to ask permission first. Also, make sure you have them in a pouch or bag. Understand?"

Malachi nodded.

Christian straightened. "I accept *yer* apology."

His small shoulders slumping with relief, Malachi settled further back in the chair.

"*Yer mamm* said she brought some cookies."

"*Ya*," Malachi said, perking up a bit. "Her cookies are the best."

"Would you like one?"

Malachi nodded. "I can get them."

Christian smiled as Malachi dashed to the counter and took a wrapped plate of cookies from one of the bags. "There's some milk in the cooler," Christian said. "The glasses are to the right of the sink."

A few minutes later Malachi and Christian each had a cookie in one hand and a glass of milk in front of them. Christian broke his cookie in half and dunked part of it in the milk. "This is the only way to eat a chocolate chip cookie."

Malachi followed suit, and they took a bite at the same time. Christian hadn't submerged a cookie in milk since he was a small child, but it had the desired effect on Malachi. He was much more relaxed now. Christian wanted to put the unpleasant business of spilled marbles and his sprained ankle in the past. "How is school progressing?"

"*Gut.*" His face brightened further. "I like Miss Ruby."

"Miss Ruby?"

"She asked us to call her that. She says *Frau* Glick is too formal. She's really fun, too, and today we learned all about clouds."

Clouds? His mouth tightened. He didn't recall that being in his lesson plans.

"*Ya.* She took us outside and we laid on the grass on the playground. There were a bunch of clouds in the sky and we all tried to guess what the shapes were. I saw a dinosaur."

Christian stiffened. "Anything else?"

"There was a bear, a flower, and Judah thought he saw an ice cream cone, but I think he was just hungry for lunch."

Phoebe came back into the kitchen. "Everything all right in here?"

"*Ya.*" Malachi jumped from his chair. "I was just telling *Herr* Ropp that school is fun." He looked up at his mother. "Can I *geh* home now?"

"As long as you apologized to *yer* teacher."

"I did."

Phoebe met Christian's gaze and he nodded.

"Then you may *geh* home."

Malachi gave Christian a small wave and ran out of the kitchen. Seconds later he heard the front door shut.

Phoebe walked to the table and sat down, placing her hands in her lap. "I'm sorry for what happened," she said, her chin tilting down. "I had *nee* idea Malachi had taken marbles to school. Jalon brought them home for him the day before, and they had fun playing with them. Then his little *schwester* wasn't feeling well that morning, so I was tending to her. That's when he must have slipped out the door with them."

"I understand." And he did. But Malachi wasn't his concern right now. Shapes of clouds? Not even the scientific names for them? That would be fine for preschool and kindergarten children, but a waste of time for the older students. In addition, clouds and the water cycle were topics for next semester. What else was she teaching—or *not* teaching?

"*Danki*, Chris," Phoebe said. "Rest assured, Malachi was disciplined at home for his actions." Her gaze softened. "Although he really feels bad that you were hurt. I think that's harder on him than his consequences."

"He's a fine young man," Christian answered absently. Was Ruby following anything on his plans? Why had she bothered to get them from him if she had no intention of implementing his lessons?

"And you don't have to worry about school. Ruby is doing a fine job. *Mei* little *bruders* can't say enough *gut* things about her, and they've never done that for any teacher before." Her lips formed an *O* shape. "I mean—"

"It's all right." He didn't go into teaching to be liked or have his praises sung. He wanted to educate, not play. "I'm . . . I'm glad the students are adjusting to the change."

"They are." Phoebe stood. "Enjoy the casserole, and if you need anything, just let Jalon and me know. We pray *yer* ankle heals quickly."

"*Danki.*"

"I'll see myself out."

He nodded as she left the kitchen, and then he grabbed his crutches and stood, intending to pace but remembering he couldn't, which further frustrated him. He gripped his crutches until his hands ached. He didn't spend all that time and effort getting the Birch Creek school to run like a well-oiled machine only to have Ruby dismantle it in one day.

The pain in his knuckles reined in his thoughts. He relaxed his hands, still holding onto the crutches.

Then he settled down. Why was he getting worked up? A wasted lesson on clouds wasn't the end of the world. And he did have only Malachi's word to go on. A seven-year-old wasn't the most reliable source. He should also be glad the students were accepting of Ruby. If they weren't, this would be a difficult situation for everyone.

He blew out a breath. Maybe it was the residual effect of the pain pills that made him jump to conclusions. Still, he couldn't let this go. Only one thing would give him peace of mind. He had to see what was going on himself. He wouldn't do anything in the classroom. Just observe. Maybe give her a few pointers after the lesson, if necessary.

His shoulders relaxed. Knowing he would be in school tomorrow to see firsthand what Ruby was doing relieved his tension. Realizing he'd missed lunch completely, he limped to the stove, opened the oven door, and touched the casserole dish. It was lukewarm. He turned the oven on and went back to the living room. This time when he picked up his book he was able to concentrate.

Selah didn't return home for her supper. Christian thought about waiting up for her, but he needed his strength for tomorrow. Besides, he may be responsible for her overall well-being, but he wasn't her keeper. He was having a hard enough time managing himself lately.

Ruby whistled on her way to school. The sun was shining, and a cool but not too cold breeze was blowing. The leaves were falling, the crisp scent of fall was in the air—and she was going to teach another day.

This would be only her second day subbing for Christian, but she knew after five minutes in the classroom that it was the place for her. She loved being surrounded by the kids, working with them, seeing their rapt attention when she talked to them or told them a story. She should have pursued teaching a long time ago, but she would have been afraid of the responsibility.

Not that it was an easy job—she was exhausted, but it was a good kind of tired. She did have to assert her authority on the first day, especially with two of the Bontrager boys who thought it would be funny to put a chewed wad of gum on her chair. She saw it before she sat down, fortunately. She didn't make a big deal about it. She just picked up the gum with a tissue and put it in the waste can. Perry and Jesse had given themselves away by giggling, and she had made them clean all the desks and tables after school as their consequence, which Christian had in his substitute folder. He had really thought of everything.

THE TEACHER'S BRIDE —⟡ 171

Except for fun. They had recess, but no time was scheduled for anything spontaneous. Even rest and silent reading time were planned. That spurred her decision to deviate from Christian's plans a tad. She'd taken the kids outside in the afternoon to look at the clouds. They were fidgety, and they needed the fresh air. Cold weather would arrive soon enough, and it had always been her personal policy to enjoy the warm sunshine whenever possible. Even the older students enjoyed it, although she could tell that, at first, they felt kind of silly lying on the grass with the younger ones.

She smiled. Speaking of spontaneous, yesterday morning she'd had a great idea. One of the students, Emma, mentioned her pet kitten and asked if she could bring it to school. Ruby was initially going to say no, but she changed her mind. She'd loved show-and-tell when she was in school, and how fun would it be to have an adorable kitten in the classroom for a day? Then she extended the idea and decided to have Bring Your Pet to School Day today. No, it wasn't in Christian's lesson plans, but she would adjust for that later. She imagined the dogs would lie at the students' feet and the cats in their laps. She'd never had pets growing up—her mother was allergic to animal fur—and she would have loved to do her schoolwork with a furry friend or two.

She unlocked the schoolhouse door, put Christian's folder on his desk, and then wrote the date and day on the board. She checked over the schoolroom and saw that everything was neat and orderly, just like Christian kept it. He would be pleased to see what good care she was taking of his school while he was gone. She wondered how he was doing. Hopefully his ankle felt better. Maybe she would pay him a visit after school.

Right before school was to begin she opened the door to let the children inside. *"Gute morgen—"* Her mouth dropped open at what she saw.

Emma had brought her kitty, which was more like the size of a medium dog. But that wasn't what surprised her. She hadn't expected every student to bring in a pet, but almost all of them had.

As the students filed in, she saw a gerbil in a clear globe, two dogs that weren't on leashes, three cats that were already hissing at each other, one pig—wait, a pig? At least it was on a leash. Two students were carrying boxes—she could only imagine what was inside. Then there was Fanny Beachy, a young girl whose family had just moved here last week, according to Christian. She was holding—oh dear—a chicken.

"Hi, Miss Ruby," Fanny said, holding up the fowl. "This is Feathers. She's *mei* chicken."

"You have a chicken for a pet?" she said faintly.

"Ya. And she lays one egg every day. She hasn't laid one yet today, though." Fanny came inside, cradling her chicken like a baby.

Malachi Chupp walked in last, looking forlorn. "What's wrong?" Ruby asked.

"Mei daed wouldn't let me bring Blue."

"Who's Blue?"

"Mei cat. He said it wasn't a *gut* idea to bring a cat to school." Malachi shoved his hands into his pockets and trudged in.

Ruby quickly shut the door and leaned against it. Malachi's father was possibly right. The students were in their seats, but they were also trying to control their animals. They were not successful. Two cats roamed the classroom, and Emma's kitty was feasting on the plant in one corner of the room. The gerbil was rolling around in his ball on the floor while a dog barked at him. At least Feathers was still in Fanny's arms, and the small pig was seated under Judah's feet. Who knew the farm animals would be the best behaved?

Ruby felt like her stomach had tumbled to her feet. This wasn't going to work at all. She hurried to the front of the classroom. "*Buwe* and *maedel*," she said above the ruckus. "Please get *yer* animals under control."

Perry retrieved his cat, who was now batting the pig's nose. Fortunately, the pig seemed oblivious.

"Kitty doesn't like dogs," Emma said, trying to coax her kitten from underneath the reading table. "She's scared."

At least Kitty had stopped eating the plant.

"Dumb cat." Samuel Beachy whistled for his dog, who was now chasing the gerbil.

"Miss Ruby, Jesse put a frog down *mei* shirt."

She turned to see Nelson wiggling and pulling his shirttails out of his pants. A small frog fell to the ground and sat there, stunned.

"Jesse, keep *yer* frog in its box," Ruby yelled.

"Miss Ruby, do you want to hold Snuggles?"

She turned, expecting to see a sweet fuzzy rabbit or one of the cats. Instead Caleb Beachy held out a black snake. She screamed—which was exactly the wrong thing to do.

Her screech disturbed the pig, who started to squeal and run around the classroom. Judah chased it, which made the dogs run and bark and the cats hiss and meow while the gerbil's ball zipped around the room, dodging the desks and chairs the other animals had tipped over.

Ruby heard a cry and turned to see Fanny standing next to her.

"Miss Ruby, Feathers got away." Tears ran down the little girl's face.

Ruby couldn't worry about the chicken now. She scooped up the gerbil, which had probably lost a few years off its little life by now. "*Kinner!* Get *yer* pets under control!"

"We're trying!" Judah called out. Even the students who didn't have pets were trying to corral the animals.

Suddenly the front door opened. The dogs dashed out, followed by three boys and then by three cats and one squealing pig. The rest of the students ran out the door too.

"*Kinner!*" She ran after them, holding the gerbil ball under her arm like a football. "Come back here." She skidded to a stop when she saw Christian, his back against the porch railing, a crutch in one hand, the most bewildered expression she'd ever seen on his face.

He got his bearings, put two fingers in his mouth, and let out a long whistle. The children stopped running. Even the dogs and the pig froze, while the cats ran off, ignoring Christian completely. The owners of the dogs and pig quickly corralled their pets. The rest of the students stood still.

"What is going on here?" Christian said, turning to her.

"Bring *Yer* Pet to School Day?" Ruby whispered.

Feathers suddenly landed on Christian's head. He looked up as she roosted on his hat. Then he glared at Ruby.

She shrank back, cuddling the gerbil ball. *Oh dear.* She'd definitely made a mess this time.

CHAPTER 12

*R*uby sat on her hands in the teacher's chair as the school board members examined the schoolroom—or what used to be the schoolroom. After Christian had corralled all the students—and Feathers had flown back to her owner—he sent them and their pets home for the day. "Tell your parents there was a problem at school," he said, glancing at Ruby.

Ruby had handed the gerbil ball back to Mahlon Bontrager. By some miracle Nelson had found his frog in the grass, and Caleb had put Snuggles the snake back in its box. The students were more than happy to have another day off.

Once the students left, Christian had limped up the steps, using only one crutch, and she followed him. Of all the times for him to pay a surprise visit. When she saw the schoolroom, she knew without a doubt she was fired.

Christian slowly turned around to face her. He didn't yell. He didn't say a word. But his face was red, the anger he was obviously trying so hard to control burning in his eyes.

She wanted to say she was sorry, but how could she apologize for this? Instead she started picking up one of the chairs.

"Leave it," he said. "I want the board members to see this." Then he limped past her, found the cell phone in his desk drawer, and went outside. Through one of the open windows she could hear him calling Freemont.

All the school board members were able to come within an hour since they worked nearby. All she could do was wait for her fate as they shook their heads and talked in low voices. Freemont barely avoided a patch of chicken poo near the front door. The pig had tracked in mud, and the animal hadn't been that clean to begin with. Christian's neatly organized small bookcase had been toppled over. On top of one of the books sat a pristine white egg.

"It could have been worse," Thomas Bontrager said, in a calm way only the father of twelve boys could say.

"How?" Jalon asked.

"Mose could have brought his pony. He treats that animal better than his *bruders.*"

But Jalon didn't find that amusing. None of them did— especially Christian, who was standing in a corner of the room, leaning against his crutch, looking at the disaster that once had been his neat and tidy classroom.

"I'm really sorry," Ruby said. Timothy looked at her and shook his head, his signal for her to shut up, but she couldn't stop talking. "I thought it would be fun for the *kinner* to bring in their pets."

"Why didn't you send a note home to the parents about that?" Freemont asked.

"And why have them all bring pets on the same day?" Asa

shook his head. "Anyone could see this was a disaster waiting to happen."

But she hadn't foreseen it. She'd thought it was a genius idea. An idea she hadn't thought through. She looked down at her lap. She'd never been this embarrassed or discouraged in her entire life, and that included the barn burnings. "I'll clean everything up," she said. Then she raised her head, afraid to ask her next question but needing to know the answer. "Am I fired?"

The men looked at each other, no one giving an answer. Christian looked at her, his angry expression now replaced with his normal impassive one.

"I see." She pulled her hands out from under her thighs and stood up. She shouldn't be surprised. She'd wrecked the school-house in a matter of minutes and had cost the children another day of education. She deserved to be fired.

"I'll be back in the classroom by Monday." Christian limped to the center of the room where the men were gathered. "The students are already used to Ruby," he said. "From what I've heard she's worked well with them. Today being the exception."

"Then you recommend she continue subbing for you?" Freemont asked.

Christian nodded. "I don't see any reason for the students' school to be upended any more than it already has. Ruby has already agreed to clean the mess, which will take less than a day to accomplish. Tomorrow, school will be back in session and will carry on as normal, *if*"—he gave Ruby a hard look—"she agrees to strictly stick to the lesson plans I've outlined."

"Ruby?" Timothy looked at her. "Do you think you can do that?"

She nodded vigorously. "I've learned *mei* lesson. I promise I won't do anything that isn't written down."

Freemont rubbed his beard and looked at the other school board members. They all nodded. "All right," he said. "You can finish out the week, Ruby."

She nearly melted with relief. "*Danki*. I'll get started cleaning right now." She began picking up the chairs and righting desks as the men filed out of the schoolhouse.

"Cleaning supplies are in the closet." Christian's expression was still unreadable, his tone flat. "You'll find a bucket and some new sponges there as well. You can get the water from the pump in the back."

She nodded, looking at him. "Why did you stick up for me? Aren't you angry?"

He didn't say anything for a moment. He just looked at her. "It was a logical decision," he finally said. Then he turned around and picked up the egg. "Don't forget this." He laid it on his desk and then left.

Ruby spent the rest of the day cleaning the schoolroom until it shone. Fortunately, the plant had only a couple of bites taken out of it, so she gave it some fresh water and put it in the windowsill to take in the afternoon sun. She moved all the desks to the side and washed the floor on her hands and knees. Then she put the desks and chairs back, wiping them down as well. She checked for any other surprises left by the animals, and fortunately didn't find anything. She put Christian's books back on the bookshelf, but she couldn't remember the order they were supposed to be in. Knowing how much he liked to be organized, she alphabetized them.

By the time she locked the schoolhouse, she was exhausted

and starving. She hadn't taken time to eat her lunch, which was probably inedible by now. It was a long walk back to Timothy's, and by the time she reached the house, all she wanted was a sandwich and to fall into bed.

But she would be expected to eat supper with the family, so she joined them at the table. After prayer, Timothy asked, "Did you get everything done?"

She nodded wearily. *"Ya."*

He reached for a roll. "You didn't have a terrible idea, Ruby. Just poorly thought out."

She shrugged. "What a surprise."

"I would have loved to have brought *mei* pet to school when I was a *kinner,*" Patience said.

Ruby nodded, appreciating their wanting to cheer her up. But she didn't deserve it. She had made a huge mistake, and ultimately the children missed a day of instruction. She felt the worst about that. "If you'll excuse me," she said, looking at her brother and his wife, "I'd like to *geh* upstairs to *mei* room."

"I'll help with the dishes," Timothy said. "You *geh* on."

She trudged up the stairs and plopped onto her bed. She'd wanted so badly to make a fresh start with her life, to show that she was mature and levelheaded. Instead she'd done the opposite. She had no business being a schoolteacher. That was clear. It also made her think she had no business being a wife and mother either. What if she made a bad mistake with her own children? Even then she was jumping ahead—once everyone heard what she'd done, no man would be interested in her anyway. She was nothing but trouble . . . and she'd proven that today.

Patience watched Ruby leave the kitchen. The poor girl was so dejected. She turned to her husband, hoping he wasn't going to use this opportunity to point out Ruby's shortcomings. Timothy was always fair-minded, but since Ruby's arrival, she'd learned that when it came to his sister, he was different. And now Ruby had shown why.

But Timothy continued to clear the table without a word, and he yawned as he put a stack of plates next to the sink.

Patience looked at him, taking in the dark circles under his eyes and the weariness in his voice. She set Ruby's plight aside and focused on Timothy. Patience couldn't hold her tongue any longer. "Why won't you hire someone to help you with the farm?"

He looked at her, bleary-eyed. "I don't need any help."

"You're exhausted." She got up from the table and went to him. "Lately you've been getting up two hours earlier than you used to."

"I need to take care of the cows."

"That early? If you have that much work, the district has plenty of young men with farming experience you can hire."

"Like I said, I don't need the help."

But he wasn't looking at her, which meant something was wrong. "Timothy?"

"*Mamm*, more milk." Tobias raised his cup.

She turned to her son. "In a minute." Then she looked back at Timothy. "There's something you're not telling me."

"These dishes aren't going to wash themselves—"

"Timothy Glick, you're not leaving here until you tell me what's going on." Patience rarely raised her voice with her children, and never with her husband. But she couldn't let him continue like this, so tired that he dozed off every evening and fell asleep as soon as his head touched the pillow.

He paused, and then looked at her. "First get Tobias his milk," he said, pulling out the chair he'd just vacated. "Then I'll explain everything."

She filled Tobias's sippy cup, handed it to him, and then sat down next to Timothy. She waited for him to speak.

"You haven't wondered why I haven't preached any sermons since I became a minister?"

She frowned. "*Nee.* I hadn't thought about it."

Timothy met her gaze. "I guess you wouldn't, because when he was the bishop Emmanuel preached all the sermons himself."

Patience nodded. She had lived in Birch Creek since she was a small child, and Emmanuel Troyer, the former bishop, was the only church official she had known before Freemont. Emmanuel had founded Birch Creek and said since the district was a small one, they had no need for a minister or deacon. Now she knew it was because he had kept secrets from the congregation, leading to his departure from their community in disgrace. No one knew where he was, although his wife, Rhoda, was sure he was coming back. His sons, Aden and Solomon, weren't so optimistic. Patience didn't know anything more than that.

What she did know, what she realized now, was that Timothy hadn't been himself since he'd been chosen minister. They hadn't talked much about that, though. Ruby arrived shortly after it happened, and Patience had been busy with the boys and her midwife clients.

"The main duty of the minister is to preach sermons on Sunday," Timothy said. "I should have preached soon after I was chosen."

"Why didn't you?"

He tugged on his beard. "Because I don't know what I'm doing. I asked Freemont to give me a little time to prepare, and he kindly did. That was almost a month ago, though."

Patience touched his arm. "I'm sure the Lord will be with you when you speak, Timothy. He is with Freemont. Everyone can tell that."

"But Freemont is a *gut* speaker. I'm . . . not."

"How do you know? Have you ever preached before?"

He shook his head, his gray eyes filling with doubt, which was unusual for him. "I haven't preached, but remember when Noah asked me to finish the school building auction back in March?"

"*Ya.*" Noah Schlabach, a professional auctioneer and Cevilla's nephew, had agreed to run the benefit auction the district held so they could build on to the schoolhouse. Near the end of the auction he'd become ill. Later everyone found out it was because of Meniere's disease, which caused severe vertigo and deafness. He'd since moved in with Cevilla and was dating Ivy Yoder, Freemont's daughter. Patience was sure the two would marry soon.

"I couldn't exactly tell him *nee,* not when he was in such bad shape. But the truth was, I nearly passed out from nerves."

She frowned. "But you did a great job auctioning off those last items." He didn't have the cadence of Noah, but no one in the district did. She thought her husband did well, considering he'd been put on the spot.

"I was trying to hold it together." He shook his head. "I got through it, but I promised myself I would never get up and speak in front of a crowd again." He pressed his thumb against the table again, so hard his thumbnail turned white. "God's got a sense of humor, doesn't he?"

"You've been so worried you haven't been able to sleep? That's why you're up so early?"

"Oh, I don't have a problem sleeping. I get up so I can study." Luke began to whimper in his high chair. Timothy stood and went to pick him up. "I've been going out in the barn with *mei* Bible and concordance and learning as much as I can." He sat down again and settled Luke in his lap. "That's why I've been so tired."

"Why didn't you say anything?"

He touched Luke's light-brown hair. "Because I didn't want to admit that I hadn't always listened carefully during the sermon. Or that I'd rarely opened a Bible. I thought I knew enough without having to do either of those things. But now that I have to preach . . . I realized I don't know much at all. And at the next Sunday service I *will* preach, for better or worse. I can't keep letting Freemont carry that load."

Patience's heart filled. "I'm sure you'll be fine."

"I get sick to *mei* stomach every time I think about it."

She took his hand. "Then I'll help you. We'll pray together for you to be calm. I can help you study too. You don't have to get up extra early anymore. We can study after the *kinner geh* to bed."

"I don't want to burden you with this."

"You're not." She leaned over and kissed him. "I'd be honored to study the Bible with you. And if you get nervous during *yer* sermon, just look at me. I'll be cheering you on. Silently, of course." She grinned.

He smiled. *"Danki, lieb."*

Tobias started to bang his sippy cup against the table. She rose from her chair and went to him.

"You're right about hiring some help." Timothy stood. "I've been thinking about that too. Ruby's offered a couple of times, but I turned her down."

"Are you thinking about hiring her now?" Patience asked, but she'd be surprised if he was considering it, especially after today.

"*Nee*. And not because of what happened at the *schoolhaus*, although that would give me pause if I was inclined to hire her." Luke leaned his head on Timothy's shoulder. "Farming isn't for Ruby."

"Neither is midwifing." Or teaching? But Patience wasn't so sure about that. Yesterday, after her first day of teaching, Ruby had been the happiest she'd seen her. She'd come home with stories about the students, telling them while she helped Patience make supper. Then right after doing the dishes, she studied the lessons for today. There was an enthusiasm in Ruby Patience hadn't seen before, and that was saying something considering how Ruby approached even the most mundane task with energy and optimism. Her teaching career in Birch Creek might be over soon, but that didn't mean she couldn't find a teaching job in another district—if she wanted to, and if she learned how to properly manage a classroom.

"But I know God has something in store for her, in his time," Timothy said. "I thought it might be teaching, but . . ." He shrugged. "I trust he knows what he's doing when it comes to Ruby."

Patience smiled as Timothy leaned down and whispered something to Luke, who then buried his face in his father's shirt.

Her husband looked more relaxed than she'd seen him in weeks, and she was glad. Whatever she had to do to help him, she would. Timothy would be an excellent minister—she knew that. And with her help and God's, he would believe it too.

On Friday morning Christian's ankle felt good enough that he could put all his weight on it. He still needed the crutch, but he wasn't as dependent on it. He could make good on his promise to the school board to be back on Monday.

He couldn't keep his mind off school, and especially Ruby. He knew she had meant well, and the idea of a show-and-tell day with a favorite pet had merit—if handled correctly. Which she hadn't. He had no idea what had been going through her head when she told the kids to bring their pets all at once. Not to mention that was another deviation from his lesson plans. And while she had promised to him and the school board that she would follow those plans from now on, he didn't trust that she would.

Unable to stand it, he decided he would pay the school another visit that afternoon, right after lunch. He was already dressed to go out and eating a scrambled egg and toast when Selah came downstairs. To his surprise she was fully dressed, wearing a green dress and blue cardigan sweater, her hair bound up and covered with a white kerchief.

"*Gute morgen,*" she said as she headed for coffee.

She still didn't look at him, but at least she greeted him. "*Gute morgen.*"

Selah turned and leaned against the counter. "You look like you're ready to *geh* somewhere."

"To school, after lunch."

"To check up on Ruby?" She smirked. "I heard all about Bring *Yer* Pet to School Day. That must have been a sight."

"It was. But she's learned from that mistake."

Selah huffed. "I wonder."

Christian frowned. "Why don't you like her?" he asked. Now wasn't the best time to broach the subject, but since Selah was in a talkative mood, he took the opportunity. Besides, he was baffled and irritated by her attitude toward Ruby.

"She's *too* happy. Too perky. No one's that upbeat all the time."

But Selah hadn't seen Ruby's face at the schoolhouse when she thought she was fired. It was as if the weight of the world had been thrust on her, as if she had let everyone down. Christian couldn't bear to see her like that, even if she'd brought it on herself. Everyone made mistakes, and everyone deserved a second chance.

"She isn't normal." Selah set down her coffee mug.

"And you are?" Christian turned in his chair and faced her. "Because *yer* behavior lately has been anything but normal."

She shrugged. "You're not *mei vatter.*"

"But I'm responsible for you."

"Why? Because you're older?" She rolled her eyes.

"*Ya,* because I'm *yer* older *bruder.* I care about you—"

"Don't give me that." She glared at him. "You don't care about anyone. You're not capable of it."

"That's not true—"

She'd turned away from him, and now she was storming out of the room. He grabbed his crutch and hurried after her as fast as he could. "We need to talk about this, Selah."

But she had already run upstairs. The door to her room slammed shut.

He swung his crutch and banged the wall, but then stilled, shocked. What had he done? He'd never lashed out at anything in his life, especially physically. He could have knocked something over, and that wouldn't have solved a thing.

But what would solve his problems when it came to Selah?

Ruby looked at the line of apples on her desk and smiled. Several of the students had brought them along with their apologies for what happened with their pets. At the very end of the line was a small chicken feather—clearly a token of apology from Feathers.

She was touched. She explained to the students that it wasn't their fault, that she should have thought the idea through. "Let this be a lesson to all of us," she said. "It's important not to be impulsive."

"What does impulsive mean?" Malachi asked.

"It means doing something without thinking it through first."

"Like the time Perry threw Jell-O up on the kitchen ceiling?" Jesse said.

"I didn't know it would stick," Perry said, giving his brother a side eye.

"Because you didn't think it through!" Jesse said.

Ruby's smile widened at the boys' story as she looked at the class. They had been model students today, and as she promised the school board and Christian she wouldn't, she hadn't strayed from his lesson plans. Right now they were doing their guided reading time, even the older boys, whom she knew didn't enjoy reading. She wasn't foolish enough to think their good behavior was because of her. They all had been shocked by what happened. Someday they would be able to look back and see the humor in it, but right now it wasn't funny at all.

The door opened, and to her surprise Christian limped in. He looked better today than he had just the day before, and he was putting some weight on his foot, even though he was still using his crutch. The children turned around and saw him and then whispered to their neighbors.

"Students," she said, rising from her chair. "Settle down, please. You still have five minutes left of *yer* guided reading time."

They nodded and went back to their reading. She saw the impressed look on Christian's face, and she had to admit it made her feel good. She was happy that he at least had a chance to see his classroom was still in good shape.

She walked over to him. "Another unexpected visit this afternoon?"

He nodded. "I'm merely making sure that you're following through on your word."

She deflated. "You don't trust me."

To her surprise he looked slightly contrite. "It's not that," he said in *Dietsch*. "It's just that . . ."

"It's okay." She looked at him. "After what happened yesterday, you shouldn't trust me. I have to earn that back." She gestured to the bench in the back of the classroom. "Why don't you have a seat? May I get you some water?" She pointed to his desk. "Or an apple?"

His brow lifted at the apples on the desk. "I'm fine, *danki*." He went to the bench, sat down, and leaned his crutch against the wall.

She turned and went to the front of the classroom. "Put

away *yer* books, please. According to the schedule, sixth through eighth graders will do their science lesson now. Chapter 10, Section 2. Third and fifth graders, pair up for *yer* vocabulary practice. And kindergarten through second graders, meet me at the table for *yer* art lesson."

The children shifted to their next assignment smoothly and with little chatter. She had to give Christian a lot of credit for that. His schedule and strict running of the classroom did give the school a lot of structure, necessary with so many students of varying ages, grades, and abilities. She put the art supplies on the table and asked Fanny to pass them out while she circulated around the room to make sure everyone was on task.

A few minutes after she began cutting out pumpkins to decorate the bulletin board for October, Judah raised his hand. "I don't understand question number five."

"Me neither," Samuel said.

She rose to go to them, but then Christian got up and limped over. Leaning on his crutch, he began explaining what the boys hadn't understood. They nodded and continued to work.

Ruby smiled as she sat down and picked up her scissors. In a few minutes Christian went to the students doing their vocabulary work to help them. He seemed able to move back and forth between the two groups easily enough, so she let him do that while she helped Mose and Mahlon with their pumpkins.

Once those lessons were over, the school day ended. The students gathered their sweaters, lunch boxes, and coolers and headed out the door. "Are you coming back on Monday, *Herr* Ropp?" one of them asked.

He nodded. "Everything will return to normal."

Emma ran up to him and threw her arms around his legs.

"I missed you." Then she hurried out the door with the rest of the students.

A lump formed in Ruby's throat as she saw Christian's expression. It was if he'd never been hugged before. A tiny smile formed on his face before disappearing as he walked toward her.

She steeled herself for his criticism. While she thought the afternoon had gone smoothly, she was certainly no expert. She'd probably done a number of things wrong or could have done some things better, and she was open to hearing about them. She folded her hands and waited.

He set the crutch aside. "I'm ready to get rid of this thing. My arm is tender and uncomfortable," he explained.

"How is *yer* ankle?"

"Better. I shouldn't need the crutch on Monday."

She looked out a window. "I'm sure you're glad to get back to *yer* classroom."

"I am. I've missed teaching." He paused. "You've done an excellent job, Ruby."

Stunned, she looked up. "I have?"

"Other than the mishap yesterday—"

"Mishap? You mean disaster."

"I see no reason to dwell on that, especially since it's clear you've followed correct procedure today. I was impressed to see that. You looked like an experienced teacher."

"I did?"

"*Ya.*" He paused again, this time glancing away before looking back at her. "I'm gratified to know *mei* students were in *gut* hands."

Without thinking, she clapped her hands together. "That's the nicest thing anyone has ever said to me!" She grinned. "I really liked being a teacher too. Well, other than the pet thing, but that will never happen again."

"It wasn't a terrible idea." He brushed his fingers over his chin. "I might instate something similar in the future, but with defined parameters."

She couldn't believe it. Not only was he complimenting her, but he might use one of her ideas. Smiling, she started picking up scraps of paper and throwing them into the trash can. While she put away the art project supplies, Christian sat at his desk and studied his lesson plans. They worked in silence for the next few minutes.

She put the small stack of crooked paper pumpkins on the table. "Is there anything else you want me to do?" she asked.

He kept his focus on his plan book. "I'll take it from here."

"All right." But she didn't move. "Christian?"

He looked up at her. *"Ya?"*

"Danki for the second chance. I didn't deserve it, but I'm glad you gave it to me."

He nodded. "Everyone deserves a second chance, Ruby. Especially when it comes to teaching. There are rules and guidelines and educational theory, but also trial and error. Some things we do in the classroom don't always work out the way we planned."

She noticed his use of the word *we*, but she didn't point it out. "I bet everything you've done has been perfect."

To her surprise he laughed. A genuine, deep-throated laugh. "Hardly true." Then he sobered. "Just ask Selah." He turned back to his review.

"Is something wrong?"

He shrugged, back to his unemotional self. "I don't know. She doesn't talk to me."

"But you're worried about her."

He hesitated and then nodded. "However, she is an adult. What she does isn't *mei* business."

"She is *yer schwester* and you care, so it is *yer* business, in a way."

"She doesn't agree."

Ruby didn't say anything. She wished she could do something to help them both, but since Selah clearly didn't like her and it wasn't her business to poke into their family affairs, she kept quiet. She was going to think things through from now on, and she wouldn't get in the middle of other people's problems impulsively.

"I guess I'll *geh* home now." She retrieved her purse and lunch bag from the floor next to his desk. Then she remembered what had been in the back of her mind ever since he'd come. "Will we meet by the tree tomorrow for our next lesson?"

Christian raised his head and seemed to be wrestling with the idea. "I'd like to, but would you mind if we wait another week? I'd like to ensure I'm prepared for my return on Monday."

"Of course. I understand."

"Aren't you forgetting something?" he said as she headed for the door.

"What?"

"These." He pointed to the apples with his pen.

"Oh." She went back and picked up a couple. "Why don't you take the rest? Except for this." She grabbed the feather. "Feathers' feather is mine."

He smiled. "You can have it."

For the next week Ruby didn't see Christian. She took care of the boys while Patience visited three pregnant women and then delivered Sadie Troyer's baby girl, who had come a week early but was in excellent health. When she came back that evening, Patience was exhausted. Ruby had made supper, bathed the kids, and put them to bed before she arrived.

While Ruby heated up Patience's supper, Timothy brought her a cup of tea. "I think this job is becoming more than one person can handle," he said.

Patience took the tea. "I have to agree with you. If I hadn't had Ruby here to take care of the *kinner* this week, I don't know what I would have done."

"Do you think you can find someone to help you?"

"In the district? *Nee*, not right now."

Ruby brought over the ham steak and mashed sweet potatoes. "I'm sorry I can't be of more help to you."

"It's all right. Besides, I think you might have found something you truly enjoy."

Ruby didn't answer right away. Patience was right. The only things she'd thought about this week were teaching, her former students, and, for some reason, Christian. She'd especially missed meeting him at the tree last week, and she was looking forward to seeing him there tomorrow. "I'll do whatever you need me to do here at home."

"Taking care of the *kinner* and the *haus* is exactly what I need. And next week I'll be visiting Sadie and her baby, but otherwise the rest of the women are doing well. And no one else is pregnant—as far as I know. Things should slow down for a while now."

Ruby smiled, glad to hear that not only was she a big help

to Patience, but that her sister-in-law would have a bit of a break.

Patience finished her supper and went to check on the children. As Ruby was doing the dishes, Timothy came into the kitchen, back from doing evening chores. "*Danki*, Ruby," he said, standing next to her. She could tell he'd already washed up by the fresh soapy scent she smelled.

She wiped her hands on a dish towel. "For what?"

"For being here for Patience." He leaned against the counter, looking tired himself. "She loves being a midwife, but we're having a population explosion around here. A blessed one, of course, but it takes a lot out of her to travel around the district. I know she misses being with the *buwe* too. I'm glad you're here to help her . . . to help us."

She swallowed. She'd made a bit of a mess of things lately, but her brother still trusted her, and with what was most important to him—his family. "I'd do anything for you and *yer familye*," she said, tears in her eyes.

He nodded. "I know." Then he smiled. "I should let *Mamm* and *Daed* know how responsible you are now."

She laughed and turned back to the dishes. "They wouldn't believe you."

"Oh," he said, suddenly turning serious. "I think they would. You've changed, Ruby. You said you were going to prove you're mature and responsible now, and you have."

"I wrecked the *schoolhaus*, Timothy."

"And you cleaned it up afterward. You learned a lesson, and you're using what you learned. That's maturity. *Mamm* and *Daed* would be glad to see it." He took a blueberry muffin out of the breadbox and left the room.

Ruby stared at the soapy water. She didn't feel that different inside. But she did have some confidence, especially after Christian's compliment. Maybe she had changed, sooner than she'd thought thanks to Christian and his trust in her.

CHAPTER 13

*B*y the Saturday following Christian's first week back at school, his ankle was completely healed. The school week had also gone well. He'd already started making plans for the Christmas program, even though it wouldn't be December for a couple of months. Christmas programs were important in the Amish communities, and Birch Creek was no exception. Since he was planning his first program by himself, he wanted to make sure he had a thorough road map to follow.

But as he was working through his plans, he kept thinking about Ruby. She had been so good with the younger students, having patience he usually had to pray for when working with them on things he wasn't that good at or interested in, like art projects. But art was an important outlet, especially for the younger ones. He imagined she would have some good ideas about the program, and he decided he would ask her at his next lesson—if she remembered they had one.

It was the first Saturday in October, and fall was in the air. He'd brought a book with him, and as he sat next to the tree, which was quickly losing its leaves, he leaned against its sturdy trunk, opened the book, and started to read. But he couldn't concentrate. After spending most of his life easily escaping into a book, no matter how dry the material, he was having difficulty doing it lately. He set down the book and looked at the pasture land in front of him.

More than once he'd looked up from his desk during quiet times in school this week and wondered—or maybe hoped—Ruby would walk in and pay a surprise visit. To the students, of course. He surmised she'd formed a bond with them, and that had been proven correct when Emma said she missed Miss Ruby. "When will she be back?" she had asked him.

"There is no plan for her to return," he said.

Emma frowned.

He bent down. "But you will see her at church, ya? You can always say hello to her there."

That pacified his student, but for some reason it didn't sit well with him, and he had no idea why. He knew Ruby's primary reason for visiting Birch Creek—to find a husband. Possibly Seth Yoder. And he had promised to help her, although that talk he'd had with Seth hadn't been fruitful. He frowned. Offering to help her had seemed like a good idea at the time. Now he wasn't so sure—and he wasn't sure why he wasn't sure.

His frown deepened. For someone who had always considered himself straightforward, his thoughts were taking a winding path.

"Christian!"

He turned his head to see Ruby waving at him from down

the road. He scrambled to his feet and brushed stray grass off his pants. He checked to see if his hat was on straight. Good, it was. "Greetings," he said, waving back.

She hurried to him, her steps quick until she practically bounced to a stop in front of him. "I thought for sure you'd forget about our lesson."

He smiled. "I thought the same about you."

"I didn't forget because I wrote it down." She lifted her chin and grinned. "I'm using a calendar now."

That almost made him laugh. "You sound as if you've never used one."

"I haven't."

His brow furrowed. "Ever?"

"In school our teacher liked for us to use a planner once we got to sixth grade, but I never could stick with it. I often lost it the following week anyway, and *mei* parents got tired of replacing them. But this time I'm determined to keep a schedule."

"It's not that difficult."

She scoffed. "Easy for you to say. You probably plan every single minute of *yer* day."

"Not every single minute." He put his hands in his pockets. "That would be extreme."

"Then every hour." When he paused she said, "I think you also schedule when you sleep."

"Now, that's going a bit far." He wasn't about to admit he used to do that up until recently. Recently as in a few months ago. "Speaking of plans, what do you have planned for lesson number two?"

"Topical conversation."

"I can converse on a variety of topics," he said.

"Ah, but can you converse on interesting topics?" She put her hands behind her back. "Topics a woman would want to engage in?"

He frowned. He wasn't sure how to answer that question.

"Just as I thought." She grabbed his hand and they sat down by the tree. Her knee bumped the book he'd brought earlier. She picked it up. "*Critical Thinking and Strategic Intelligence: An Analysis*. Doing a little light reading, I see."

Christian tried to grab the book, but she held it out of his reach. He leaned forward on his knees, but then he lost his balance and toppled on her.

"Oof," she said. Then she laughed. "At least it wasn't me falling on you this time."

Her laugh was contagious, and he started to chuckle. That made her giggle and her eyes sparkle. Their faces were a few inches apart, and he could smell the sweet scent of her fresh skin, see the three freckles on her left cheek he hadn't noticed before, the way her eyes started to darken . . .

"Christian?"

"*Ya?*"

"This isn't part of the lesson."

"Oh." *Oh.* He scrambled away until he bumped into the tree. "Sorry," he mumbled.

She handed him his book. "*Nee* problem. I'm used to being in awkward situations."

But it hadn't felt all that awkward to him. Being close to her had felt . . . good.

"Let's brainstorm a list of topics you can talk about with Martha."

Martha . . . he hadn't thought about Martha all week. He

hadn't even thought about her today while he was waiting for Ruby. He definitely wasn't thinking about her now.

He had to get his focus back on target. "All right."

She looked at him expectantly. "Where's *yer* notepad?"

He paused. How had he forgotten his notepad? He always took notes when he was learning something new. "I didn't bring it with me."

She nodded. "I was so busy this week I forgot to remind myself to bring a pad and pencil."

He listened as she told him about watching the boys while Patience visited her expectant mothers, plus delivered Sadie Troyer's baby. "I was glad I could be there to help. And of course, my nephews are the greatest little *buwe*."

He raised his right brow. "A little biased, are we?"

"*Nee*." She leaned forward. "I'm a lot biased."

Christian relaxed. It was good to see her like this—amusing, confident, at ease. He never wanted to see her as upset as she'd been on Bring Your Pet to School Day. "Emma missed you this week. So did the other students."

"They did?" She looked genuinely surprised. "That's so sweet." She paused. "Speaking of sweet . . . how is Selah?"

"*Mei schwester* isn't one of the topics of conversation," he said.

"Oh. I'm sorry. I didn't mean to pry."

He glanced away. "It's not *yer* fault. Things are at an impasse between us, and I don't see that changing."

"Maybe she needs something more to do than taking care of you and *yer* home."

"I know she does, but she doesn't seem interested in looking for a job. When we first moved here, I even asked her if she wanted to be *mei* assistant."

"And she didn't jump at the chance?"

He eyed her. "*Yer* sarcasm is noted."

She scooted a little closer to him, the movement so natural he wondered if she realized she was doing it. "Christian, maybe you should—"

"Like I said." He held up his hand. "Selah isn't a talking point."

"Got it." She shrank back a bit. "Then let's talk about Martha."

Martha. Right. That's why they were there.

"And I'll just trust that *yer* fantastic brain will remember this conversation later." She smiled. "Now, what does Martha like?"

"Like?"

"You know. Her favorite foods, hobbies. What does she like to do? What are her hopes and dreams?"

"I have *nee* idea." He realized he still didn't know much about her. "Isn't that the whole point of this lesson? So I can talk to her and learn those things?"

"*Ya*, but . . . if you don't know anything about her, then why do you think she'll be a *gut* spouse for you?"

"I could ask you the same thing about Seth Yoder."

"I know some things about Seth," she said, crossing her arms.

"Such as?"

"He likes cake."

Christian scoffed. "Doesn't everyone?"

"I don't."

That surprised him. "Why not?"

"Usually it's too sweet. There's so much sugar in the cake, and then you pile on the frosting, which is also full of sugar." She grimaced. "I prefer pie."

"What kind?"

"Any kind." She folded her knees, tucking her legs underneath her. "Raspberry, peach, blueberry, strawberry, rhubarb . . . I really haven't met a pie I didn't like. What about you?"

"I also like pie. And cake. I've never found either of them too sweet."

"Now we're making progress." She pushed up to her knees. "We just had a conversation where we found out something about each other. That wasn't so hard, was it?"

No, it wasn't. In fact, it was easy to talk to Ruby. It always had been, ever since the moment they met. Natural. As if they were meant to—

"Now you just have to do it with Martha."

He paused, tilted his head, and looked at her. A sudden thought came to him. "What if I don't want to?"

"I don't understand."

He knelt in front of her. "What if I don't want to get to know Martha anymore?"

She scoffed. "That's silly. How are you going to marry her if you don't get to know her?"

"I'll marry someone else, then." His mind warmed to the idea. Yes, this could work out . . . for them both.

Ruby rolled her eyes. "Who would that be?"

He leaned forward. "You."

Ruby fell back on her behind. "What did you just say?"

"I'll marry you."

This had to be a joke. But she wasn't sure Christian knew how to make a joke, and right now his expression was as serious as she'd ever seen it. "You're joking, *ya?*"

"I would never joke about something as serious as this."

"But . . ." She had no idea how to respond. She'd imagined what it would be like to be proposed to, and it was nothing like this. "What makes you think I would marry you?" The question flew out of her mouth, and she was about to apologize when she saw that he didn't seem offended at all.

"A logical inquiry. Obviously, I will need to convince you to agree."

"Obviously," she muttered. She wasn't sure how to handle this. A moment ago they were talking about Martha, and a little bit about Seth—she had to admit she hadn't thought about him at all until ten minutes before their lesson started—and now she was being proposed to. Sort of. More like commanded. In proper English. "You can't just tell someone you'll marry them."

"Why not?"

"Because it doesn't work that way." She got to her feet.

He followed suit." Why not?"

"Because . . . because . . . Well, I'm not exactly sure, other than it's not *romantic*."

"Does marriage have to be romantic?"

"Of course!"

"I beg to differ. Many marriages have been born out of convenience and have worked quite well. It's even a practice that's still continued in some cultures."

"Not in *our* culture."

"That you know of. Ruby, let's look at the facts. The first one—we are both ready to get married. The second—we both have limited prospects."

"You have limited prospects," she said. "I have quite a few."

"And yet you are unable to speak to one of them without hiccupping or getting injured."

He was being truthful. And annoying. "I only tried twice."

"And that leads me to number three. With me, you don't have to try."

She froze as something tingled inside her, which was weird because this was Christian. Mr. Logical. Mr. Non-Emotional. Mr. Feelings Are Immaterial. And yet for some strange reason she was feeling . . . something.

"We're friends, correct?"

She nodded, even though this was the strangest friendship she'd ever had.

"We can talk to each other. Confide in each other, even. We both have the same goal—marriage. Other couples who married for convenience have had less to go on."

"Since when did you become an expert on the subject?"

He frowned. "I read a lot."

She drew in a breath and turned from him. She had to admit he was making some sense, logically speaking. "But what about love?" she said, turning to him.

He arched a brow. "Love?"

"You've heard of it, I'm sure. You know, that emotion that makes you tingle inside with excitement when you think about another person. Or how you would do anything to make them safe and happy."

"Yes, I am aware of the emotion."

"And?"

"A solid marriage doesn't have to be based on love. Mutual respect, yes. Treating the other person well, absolutely. But love isn't a requirement." He paused. "Do you love Seth?"

His question took her off guard. "Well, *nee*—"

"Yet you saw him as a viable candidate for a husband?"

"*Ya*, but I wasn't ready to marry him right away. I assumed we would fall in love."

"And if you didn't?"

"Then I would find someone else."

He moved closer to her. "What if that someone else is standing right in front of you?"

Again, the tingle went through her. But when she searched his face, she saw no emotion there. "How long have you been thinking about this?"

"Approximately ten minutes."

"A whole ten minutes?" She backed away from him. "And yet you're so sure this is the right thing for you to do? For both of us to do?"

"It's the logical thing."

Ruby had never done anything logical in her life, at least not on purpose. She lived by her emotions and impulses. But wasn't that a trait she was trying to change? To become more responsible, to make decisions not with her heart but with her head?

"I do realize this is a lot to take in," Christian said. "It would behoove both of us to pray about it."

"*Ya*," she said. "It would behoove."

"And"—he glanced down—"I apologize if I've offended you or if you feel coerced at all. That's not my intention." He looked off into the distance. "Perhaps I should have thought about this more before speaking to you about it."

"Perhaps." For the first time since he'd brought up marriage he looked unsure. Concerned, and obviously he didn't want to hurt her feelings, which did touch her. "I will pray about it," she said. "You did bring up some *gut* points."

He nodded. "And I will pray too."

They both stood there, the breeze kicking up around them. She pulled her sweater closer. "I guess we can end today's lesson, then."

"Yes." After another pause he said, "What do you think is a good timetable for us to get together and discuss this again?"

"Later this week?"

"Wednesday, then?"

She nodded. "Wednesday."

"At a neutral location?"

Logical to the end. "Here will be fine."

"At three o'clock?"

She nodded.

"Good. I'll see you then."

Now it was awkward, which it hadn't been between them since she'd bumped into him the first time they'd met. He looked at her for a moment and she tried to figure out what he was thinking. He walked away before she could discover anything.

She plopped down on the grass, regretting that she'd even agreed to consider Christian's proposal. It didn't make any sense. The fact that he'd asked her so impulsively should have the warning bells going off in her head. And they were . . . They just weren't as loud as she'd thought they should be.

Ruby shook her head, trying to force some sense into her brain. No, she couldn't marry Christian. She couldn't imagine being married to someone she didn't love, even if everything else was logical. But she told him she would pray about it, and she would. Yet her mind was made up, almost one hundred percent. Yes, marriage was in her future, but definitely not with Christian Ropp.

Christian went home, pondering about his proposal the whole way. Doubts had crept in as soon as he was several yards down the road. It wasn't as if his reasoning was wrong, but he had blindsided Ruby. He had blindsided himself.

He sat down at the top of the front-porch steps. His ankle ached now after all the walking he had done. But that pain didn't compare to the confusion in his head. *What in the world was I thinking?*

The screen door closed behind him, but he didn't turn around. He knew it was Selah, and he wasn't in the right frame of mind to deal with her right now.

"What's wrong with you?" she said as she went down the steps. She turned around and faced him.

"An ironic question, coming from you," he mumbled.

"You look like you've seen a ghost."

That wasn't a good sign. He shouldn't be terrified at the prospect of marrying Ruby. And he wasn't. He was . . . perplexed.

Selah crossed her arms and looked down at him. "Tell me about it."

His brow went up. "You want to converse? With me?"

"I want to know what's going on. You have me curious. Does this have to do with Martha?"

He shook his head.

She tilted her head and looked at him. "Interesting."

"What?"

"I mentioned her name and you're not blushing or looking away or stammering. Which means you've given up on her."

He supposed he had. And without much fanfare. Not only that, but he didn't have any second doubts about it either.

"So it's not about Martha. And today is Saturday . . ." A smile crept across her face. "You met with Ruby today."

He didn't recall telling her about his meeting with Ruby. "How did you know that?"

"I'm not oblivious like you are. And never mind about me. What about you and Ruby?"

This was the most animated and interested he'd seen her in weeks. But this wasn't a conversation he wanted to have. He tugged on his shirt collar and didn't say anything.

"Are you two going out?"

He wasn't sure how to answer that. He swallowed and looked away. "I don't believe that's any of your business."

"It isn't. But I already have *mei* answer." She uncrossed her arms. "I'm going to the store today. What do you want for supper this week?"

That got his attention. "You're shopping? And cooking?"

"*Ya.* I'm sorry I've been so hard to live with lately."

"It's all right."

"*Nee*, it isn't." A shadow passed over her face, but then she smiled. "I'm going to do better."

"You sound like Ruby." He hadn't meant to say those words out loud.

"So there is something going on between the two of you." She looked at him thoughtfully. "I never thought of you two together."

"Because you don't like her."

She looked sheepish. "That hasn't been fair of me either." A brown oak leaf fluttered to the ground behind her. "Have you already asked her on a date?"

He realized Selah wouldn't stop questioning him until she got the answers she wanted. Truthfully, he was glad to see her like this instead of surly and secretive. Against his better judgment he said, "Not exactly."

"What do you mean, not exactly?" She smirked. "You either asked her out or you didn't."

"I, uh, asked her something."

"You're acting *seltsam* again. You must really like her."

He took off his hat and thrust his hand through his hair. He needed a haircut. Maybe Ruby could give him one. His hand froze halfway through his hair. He *did* like Ruby. Which was why getting married made sense. Yes, he understood love was a factor. But not the most important one, in his mind. Love came with companionship and meeting challenges head-on. And he wanted to do that with someone he at least liked. He started to place his hat back on his head.

"You don't have to be a scaredy-cat, Christian. It's just a date. It's not like you've asked her to marry you."

His hat slipped from his hands and landed on the ground.

She froze. "Christian . . . you didn't ask her to marry you, did you?" All trace of teasing humor disappeared from her tone. "Oh *nee*. What were you thinking? That's a terrible idea!"

Panic suddenly gripped him. Seeing the look of utter shock on Selah's face had snapped him back to reality. He couldn't marry Ruby Glick. What had he done? He snatched his hat from the ground and stalked away.

Selah hurried up behind him. "You can't drop a bombshell like that and then run off, Christian."

Fighting to catch his wits, he turned and cleared his throat, even though it felt like a noose was tightening around his neck. "I didn't drop anything. You assumed."

"Correctly." She frowned. "Okay, now you look like you're going to faint." She touched his arm. "Do you need to *geh* inside?"

He shook his head. This was turning into a nightmare. An embarrassing nightmare. He had to fix this. He had to tell Ruby he'd changed his mind. That he'd lost his sanity for a short time, and that marriage was undoubtedly out of the question. He'd go back to his original plan. He'd get to know Martha, and then, if the time was right and the feelings were right, he would ask her to marry him—

"Christian!"

He opened his eyes, unaware he'd closed them. "What?"

Selah's eyes were wild with worry. "I haven't seen you like this since we were *kinner.*" She squeezed his arm. "Whatever it is, it will be okay."

He looked at her hand and felt a calming comfort, barely registering that this was the same Selah who couldn't be bothered to talk to him for the past couple of weeks. She was right. It would be okay, because he was going to resolve this preposterous problem he'd created. He took in a deep breath. "*Danki,* Selah. I feel better now."

She nodded, dropping her arm. "Now, tell me everything."

He blew out a breath. "I asked Ruby to marry me."

"What did you do that for?"

"Because it seemed like a *gut* idea at the time."

"At the time? Christian, you never do anything spur-of-the-moment."

"I know." He rubbed the back of his neck. "Upon further reflection, I'm not sure why I did this time."

"What did she say?"

"What?"

"When you asked her to marry you?"

"She said she'd think about it."

Selah looked surprised. "She's seriously considering it?"

"Prayerfully, to be accurate."

His sister tapped her fingertip against her chin. "I suppose weirder things have happened—although I can't think of anything right now. But here's the important thing, Christian. Do you love her?"

"We both know love isn't required for a *gut* marriage."

Selah rolled her eyes. "If you're referring to *Mamm* and *Daed*, they aren't exactly a shining example."

"They're an excellent example of a partnership."

"Marriage is more than a partnership." She looked away. "At least it should be." She faced him. "If you really believe you and Ruby should be married, then you should be willing to court her. Slow things down. Take her a gift and tell her that you blew it and you want to start over."

He nodded. She was making sense. And he deserved a little dent in his pride for making such a foolish suggestion. He remembered their earlier conversation, before his sanity had escaped and he'd proposed. "I'll take her a pie."

"I was thinking more like a small candle or—"

"Raspberry pie. She'd like that. There's still time to get one from Carolyn Yoder's bakery and take it over to her." He turned to Selah. "Thank you. You've helped me immensely."

She smiled, the first genuine smile he'd seen from her in a long time. "Glad I could be of use—"

But he was already heading to the barn to hitch Einstein to the buggy, brimming with optimism. A pie, a proposal retraction, and the suggestion that they take things slow and court, if that was even something they should do. That would set everything to rights, and he and Ruby would get back to their normal, comfortable, relationship . . . friendship . . . whatever it was they had.

CHAPTER 14

*R*uby didn't know how long she sat under the tree before she went home, her mind still on Christian and his marriage proposal. She had prayed about it, but she knew it would take more than a few whispered prayers on a fall breeze to understand what God wanted her to do. At least she didn't have to make her decision today.

Once home, she found a note from Timothy and Patience. They had taken the kids to Sadie and Aden's for the afternoon and would be back by suppertime. Ruby was a little disappointed. She'd hoped to spend some time with her nephews to keep her mind off Christian. Now she was alone in the house. At least she could start making supper. Chicken stew sounded good.

She gathered the ingredients and had just put the chicken in the oven to bake when she heard a knock on the front door. She washed and dried her hands and went to answer it. When she opened the door, her mouth dropped open.

"Hi, Ruby." Seth Yoder stood in front of her.

She took a step back, her heel catching the edge of the throw rug. Fortunately, she regained her balance before falling. "What are you doing here?"

"I never apologized for hitting you with that door." He shifted his feet. "And *Mamm* sent this." He handed her a small basket.

She accepted it and peeked inside. Chocolate chip cookies. "*Mei* nephews will love these."

"Be glad it's not donuts," he muttered. He looked at her. "*Yer* nose seems better."

She touched it. "It is. Doesn't even hurt anymore. Would you like to come in?"

"Uh, sure." She opened the door wider and he walked through. "Something smells *gut*."

"I just put some chicken on to bake. We're having chicken stew for supper tonight. I'll put these cookies in the kitchen." She gestured for him to follow her.

In the kitchen she set the basket on the table and turned to him. "Tell *yer* mother I appreciate the cookies."

He tilted his head and looked at her. "You seem different today."

"I do?"

He nodded. "I can't quite put *mei* finger on it."

She shrugged. "I'm the same Ruby. Klutzy, nervous—"

"That's it." He snapped his fingers. "You're neither of those right now."

She frowned. He was right. She hadn't hiccupped, she'd managed not to fall, she was holding a decent conversation with the object of her affections . . . and she felt nothing. Not a butterfly or a damp palm or anything. "That's weird."

His gaze softened. "I wouldn't call it weird."

"Oh? What would you call it?"

Seth smiled. "Nice. I'd say it's nice."

Another knock sounded on the door. "Now, who could that be? I'll be right back, Seth."

She went to answer the door. When she did, her mouth dropped open for a second time. "Christian?"

He stood there, a square-shaped box in his hand and a strange expression on his face as if the neck of his shirt was too tight. He opened his mouth, but nothing came out. Then he thrust the box toward her. "Here."

She looked at it. "What is it?"

"Pie."

"You brought me pie?"

He nodded and opened the box. "Raspberry. Fresh made today."

How thoughtful. And unexpected. *"Danki."*

"It's a gift."

"Do you want to come in?"

"Yes. Yes, I do."

She moved so he could come inside, and then she shut the door behind her. "You didn't have to bring me a gift."

Christian swallowed. "We need to converse about what happened today."

"You said you'd give me time."

"I know I did. But I think we need to discuss some things more in depth."

"Like what?"

"Is everything all right?" Seth had walked into the living room. His eyes suddenly turned cool. "Hello, Chris."

"Seth."

Gone was the bumbling of a moment before. Christian's expression was inscrutable. "I didn't realize you had company, Ruby."

She glanced at both men, who seemed to be appraising each other. Why, she had no idea.

"I didn't realize she was expecting you," said Seth.

"I wasn't," she said.

"I don't see that it's any business of yours that I've dropped by unannounced." Christian's grip tightened on the pie box.

"He really does always talk like that, *ya?*" Seth asked Ruby.

With a sigh she nodded. "Usually."

Christian suddenly stiffened, which surprised her since he was already inflexible. "I see I've made an error," he said, his voice low. "About several things."

Now he was confusing her. "Christian, give me the pie and we can talk." She started to take it from him, but he held on to it.

"I should probably be on *mei* way too," Seth said, scooting past them both and out the door.

But Ruby barely heard him. Why wouldn't Christian let go of the pie? "Christian, why are you acting like this?" She tugged at the box.

"I'm being perfectly normal under the circumstances." He held on.

"You are being anything but normal." She tugged again. "Now give me the—"

He let go of the box and the pie went flying—right into her face.

Christian hadn't thought the day would go from bad to worse, but it had in an instant. His gaped as he looked at the raspberry pie covering Ruby's face. Pieces of crust were attached to her white *kapp*, while the bright-red filling dripped down her face and onto her neck.

"Oh *nee*," he said, going to her. He started to wipe off her face with his fingers, but that made a bigger mess.

"Just . . . stop." She pushed him away. "Christian . . ." She let out a cross between a growl and a squeal and marched to the kitchen.

He followed her. "I'm sorry."

She went to the sink and turned on the water, which she started splashing on her face. "What is wrong with you?" she said as she tried to get the destroyed confection off her cheeks.

"I . . . I have *nee* idea."

Ruby turned and looked at him, squinting between chunks of red raspberries. Then she sighed. "Let me get cleaned up upstairs."

"I'll leave now—"

"Oh *nee* you won't." She lifted her chin and managed to look defiant even while coated in pie filling. "You owe me an explanation, Christian Ropp."

Without another word he sat down at the kitchen table.

It wasn't long before she came back downstairs, her face freshly scrubbed, her dress changed, and her *kapp* replaced. She looked rather pretty. Very pretty. He drummed his fingers on the table.

She sat down across from him. "Now, what did you want to talk about?"

He opened his mouth to speak, but no sound came out. Why

was he acting like this with Ruby? She wasn't Martha. Until now he'd never had any trouble talking to her.

"Christian?"

He liked the way she said his given name. And she'd done it without him asking her to.

She leaned forward and tilted her head, looking at him. "Hello? Anyone in that big brain of *yers?*" She smiled . . . but soon her smile faded as her eyes locked with his.

A warm current ran through him. He knew it was merely his emotions firing the synapses in his brain, which accelerated his heart rate. Attraction. A simple chemical reaction that wasn't so simple. With her sitting so close to him, he had the tempting urge to touch her face . . . and he gave in to the temptation.

Her skin was soft. Warm, which probably explained the light shade of pink on her cheeks. He ran his finger lightly over the top of her cheek and heard her breath catch. That made his brain shut down completely. Logic, rational thought, and an appreciation for consequences flew right out of his head as he leaned forward and kissed her lightly on the mouth.

When he pulled away, her eyes were wide open. "What did you do that for?"

Her question, coupled with the shock on her face, and the very real possibility that she did *not* appreciate him kissing her, brought him to his senses. His chest tightened, and not in a good way. He jumped up from the chair and turned his back to her. "I . . . I . . ." It was official. He'd lost his mind, and as of five seconds ago, his dignity. "I apologize," he said, still unable to look at her. Then he felt her tap his shoulder.

"It's okay, Christian."

He slowly turned, her kindness sparking those foreign

emotions again, the ones he had no idea what to do with. "I have made an error—more than one since our lesson today." He fought to sound emotionless, and he hoped he was successful, because inside he felt the exact opposite. "I said I would give you time. Instead I push a pie in your face and then . . . and then—"

"Then you kissed me." She smiled. "And here I thought I was the awkward one when it came to romance."

That didn't improve his ego one bit. "Just forget I said—and did—anything." He started to move past her when she put her hand on his arm.

"How can I forget a kiss?"

"A mistake," he said.

That wiped the smile off her face. "A mistake."

He nodded. "Yes. One of several I made today."

"Like the pie."

"*Ya.*"

Her face pinched. "And the proposal."

He gulped. "Yes. It was a foolish idea made on the spur of the moment. Which is why it's important to think things through." He squared his shoulders, feeling on more level ground, until he saw the hurt in her eyes. He was still making a mess of things, but he couldn't turn back. "Now that we've settled everything, I'll return home." This time when he began to leave, she didn't stop him . . . until he got to the front door.

"What if I'd said yes?"

Christian turned. She'd followed him from the kitchen. "Yes to what?"

"What if I'd said I'd marry you?"

As usual, Ruby couldn't leave well enough alone. Christian had given her an out—not to mention a sweet kiss. And that kiss was why she couldn't just let him walk away as if nothing had happened between them. She had seen something in his eyes— something different from his typical impassivity. Even more important, she had felt something in her heart. Which was why she couldn't stop herself from blurting the question.

His left eyebrow arched. "A moot point, isn't it, since I've retracted my proposal?"

His words were blunt, but for some reason they weren't as sharp as she expected. "But if you hadn't, and I had said I would marry you, what would you do?"

"I . . . I suppose we would get married."

"Just like that?"

He nodded, and she saw his Adam's apple bobbing up and down. "But that's not going to happen."

"Because you changed *yer* mind."

"Right. I changed my mind."

"Then why did you kiss me?"

He blew out a breath and averted his gaze, but he didn't say anything.

The back door opened, and Timothy walked in, carrying her youngest nephew. He paused when he saw Christian. "Hello." He gave Ruby a questioning look.

Christian nodded to Timothy. "I was just leaving." He spun on his heel and hurried out of the kitchen. They heard the front door close.

Timothy frowned and set Luke in his chair. "Did something happen?" he asked Ruby.

She started to nod, but then slowly shook her head. How could she explain what occurred between her and Christian when she didn't understand it herself? He said it was a mistake to propose, but when she met his eyes she felt there was something between them. And the kiss? How could he act like it was nothing? Didn't he have any feelings? Or was she only wishing he had?

"Is something burning?" Timothy asked as Patience walked into the kitchen holding Tobias's hand.

"Oh *nee*, the chicken!" Ruby ran to the oven and opened it. Smoke billowed as she pulled out the roasting pan. She looked at the chicken, now charred black. She tossed the potholders on the counter. "It's ruined."

"Maybe we can just peel back the skin—"

"I'm sorry." Tears sprang to her eyes, unbidden. Great, now she was crying over burnt chicken. "Excuse me."

Ruby ran upstairs and shut her bedroom door. She wiped her eyes. Why was she letting Christian hurt her feelings like this? Obviously, he was fickle. One minute he liked Martha and the next minute he was proposing—and kissing—her. What kind of man did that? Not a nice one. Not one who would be a good husband.

She should have never offered to help him. That was her first mistake. Her second one was taking her focus off Seth. Maybe he'd come over to ask her out on a date. Christian had ruined that too. Everything was ruined . . . and all she could do was think about that stupid kiss.

Two weeks had passed since the day Christian kissed her and then walked out, and during that time she'd kept her distance from him. She saw him at church the next day, of course, but she ignored him, which was easy to do since he was ignoring her too. That was fine by her, since that made disregarding him that much easier, except for the quick glance she'd given him right before Timothy gave the sermon. Even though she was proud of her brother as he preached for the first time, knowing he'd been preparing for this every evening for almost two weeks, she couldn't stop herself from looking at Christian. She also couldn't stop herself from thinking how handsome he was today. Then she shoved him out of her mind, engaged her brain, and focused on what Timothy was saying. But her mind kept wandering.

She was exactly where she'd been almost two months ago—no job, no husband prospects. She couldn't bring herself to think about pursuing Seth. It didn't feel right, not after she and Christian kissed. She also accepted that she didn't have feelings for him, so there wasn't a point in chasing him . . . or anybody else. And now that she knew how Christian felt about her—that she was a mistake—her prospects for marriage in Birch Creek had dwindled to nothing.

Still, she didn't want to go home. She liked being in Birch Creek, and she was still helpful to Timothy and Patience. She needed time to figure out what she really wanted before she went back to Lancaster. She had to come up with another plan for her future.

The following week, she helped prepare food for a barn raising. The community was erecting two buildings—not only a barn for Solomon Troyer, who was expanding his carpentry business, but also a large workshop for him. Ruby had baked several dozen cookies the day before—chocolate chip, peanut butter, and, of course, her favorite, monster cookies, with an extra handful of coated chocolate candies thrown into the batter. She knew the kids in the community would enjoy those too.

On Saturday morning she arrived at the Troyers'. She now knew everyone. Some she was closer to—like Martha. Others she knew by name. She and Patience pitched in to set up tables and food while the men worked on the buildings. Patience's mother was watching Tobias and Luke at her parents' house.

As she set a platter of cookies near the rest of the desserts, Ruby paused, watching the men work. She was always amazed by how quickly many hands could put together a large barn or other outbuilding. She'd seen it often in her community back home. It was no different here. A mix of men—old, young, and teens—worked without a hitch.

Then she saw Christian. He was standing to the side holding a hammer, looking unsure what to do. She sighed.

"Is everything okay?"

She turned to see Martha setting a plate of brownies next to her cookies. Ruby nodded. "*Ya*. Everything's peachy."

"Oh. I'm surprised to hear that, because that was a big sigh you just let out."

Ruby pressed her lips together. Why couldn't she get her mind off Christian? She hadn't expected him to be here, much less pitching in to build the barn. As far as she knew, he was still holding himself separate from the community, and Selah had all but disappeared lately.

Ruby watched as Malachi Chupp walked over to him. Christian bent down, listening intently to what the boy was saying. Then he nodded and followed him to one of the corners of the barn. Christian hunkered down beside him and they both started nailing two boards together.

"That's so cute," Martha said. "Chris is really *gut* with *kinner, ya?*"

Ruby nodded, still watching him, and realizing she'd been wrong about him not knowing what to do with a hammer. In fact, he corrected Malachi's grip on the tool. Jesse and Nelson Bontrager joined them, and Christian easily slipped into teaching mode. Something seemed to squeeze inside her heart.

"He'll be a *gut vatter* someday." Martha straightened the plate of brownies.

"Do you like him?" Ruby asked.

"Chris?" Martha laughed. "He's a nice *mann*, but *nee*." She leaned over and whispered, "I have *mei* eye on someone else."

Ruby blew out a breath she hadn't known she was holding.

"And there he is," Martha said.

Zeb Bontrager passed by, carrying three two-by-fours on his shoulder. Now it was Martha's turn to sigh.

At least she wasn't interested in Seth Yoder. Ruby searched the area until she saw him, up high and helping several men secure the trusses on the roof. But she only glanced at him and went back to looking at Christian. Should she tell him about Martha being interested in Zeb? She was sure he was back to figuring out a way to ask her out. With the exception of his impromptu proposal, Christian didn't stray from plan. But there wouldn't be any point in approaching Martha now. Then again, what business was it of hers?

"Have you talked to Selah lately?" Martha asked, interrupting Ruby's thoughts.

She shook her head. "I don't usually talk to her." She refrained from saying that Selah didn't like her. That was embarrassing to admit.

"She's been acting strange lately. When she first came to Birch Creek, she was friendly and sweet. And she still tries to be, at least around me. But I can tell something's wrong. I was hoping I would see her today. It's been almost two weeks since we last visited."

Ruby didn't say anything. Again, it was none of her business. The last thing she wanted was to get between Christian and Selah. Whatever was going on with the two of them—and with Selah herself—was their problem.

"I should *geh* help *Mamm* with the sandwiches." Martha turned to her and smiled. "Would you like to join us?"

After one last glance at Christian, Ruby nodded. "I'd love to."

By lunchtime the tables were set and the food was prepared. The men and boys lined up to be served after everyone said a silent prayer of thanks. Ruby spooned out baked beans to each hungry worker.

"I don't like beans," Malachi said.

"Me neither," Jesse said.

"I do." Judah Yoder shoved his plate in front of Ruby. "I'll take their share."

Ruby chuckled and gave him one spoonful. "If there's any extra you can have seconds later."

Judah frowned a bit, but then he shrugged and moved down the line. Ruby stirred the beans in the large metal pan, and when she looked up, Christian stood in front of her, holding out his plate.

"Would you like some beans?" she said. Her voice was steady, but for some reason her insides weren't. *It's just Christian. No one special.*

"Please."

Despite her efforts to ignore him, she met his eyes. Blue and soft, and filled with . . . apology? Regret? Definitely not with interest, right?

"Ruby, you're holding up the line."

She looked at her brother, who was two men back. "Sorry." She quickly shoved the spoon into the beans and the sauce splashed on her apron. Of course. She knew she wouldn't get through the day with a clean apron. Carefully she put the beans on Christian's plate.

"*Danki.*" His voice was low, and he gave her a small nod. Then he moved down the line.

Ruby was still looking at him when she heard, "Hi." She blinked and then turned. Seth stood in front of her, holding out his plate.

"Oh. Hi."

"Beans, please."

She glanced at Christian again, who was getting a spoonful of broccoli salad from Martha. They started to talk, and Ruby strained to hear what they were saying.

"Uh, Ruby?"

She turned in time to see her miss Seth's plate completely. The spoonful of beans plopped onto the white plastic tablecloth. "Great!" she said, louder than intended. "Here." She scooped up another serving and slapped it onto his plate, annoyed with herself not only for spilling the beans but also for paying so much attention to Christian and Martha.

"*Danki?*" Seth looked at the beans, which were dripping off the side of the plate.

Ruby was about to apologize when she heard Martha laugh. She looked to see Christian smile at her before he moved away.

Something twisted inside her as she continued serving the men. If Martha didn't like Christian, what was she doing laughing and flirting with him?

"Ruby," Timothy said.

"What?" she snapped, looking at him.

"You're making a mess."

She glanced down and saw that in addition to the beans she'd spilled before, two more small piles sat around the pan. "I wanted to serve potato salad," she muttered as she gave her brother a spoonful.

"Pay attention to what you're doing." He gave her a hard look before moving on.

He was right, and she focused on being careful until all the men were served.

After the men finished eating, the women filled their plates and sat down. Ruby looked for Martha. She saw her near a table, talking to Christian again.

Ruby walked over to them and set down her plate. "Am I interrupting anything?"

"*Nee*," Martha said. "Chris was telling me about the new ice cream shop on Clarendon Road, just outside Birch Creek."

"Oh really." Ruby crossed her arms over her chest. "Ice cream, huh?"

Christian looked at her. "*Ya*. Ice cream."

"I didn't know you liked ice cream," Ruby said.

"I do."

They looked at each other for a long moment. Again, something was there in his eyes, and she couldn't figure out what it was. She only knew she didn't want Martha going with him to get ice cream.

"Maybe you two should *geh* sometime," Martha said.

They both looked at her. "What?" they said at the same time.

"You should both try out the new ice cream place." She smiled. "I would *geh* with you, but I'm lactose intolerant." She turned to Ruby. "What day are you free?"

"Uh, next Saturday?" she said. That was the first day that came to mind. She never did well when being put on the spot like this.

"And you, Chris? Are you free on Saturday?"

He leveled his gaze at her. "Saturday is fine," he said without hesitation.

Ruby gaped. Did they just agree to go out on a date?

Martha's smile grew. "I'll expect a full report about the ice cream shop. *Mei* parents really enjoy their banana splits."

Christian nodded slowly, and then he looked at Martha. "I better get back to work." He gave Ruby one last look, and then he left.

Martha giggled and turned to Ruby. "You're welcome."

"For what?"

"Fixing you up with Chris."

Ruby's jaw dropped. "You did that on purpose?"

"Of course." She gave her a sly grin. "You two look cute together."

Nothing could be further from the truth, but Ruby just nodded. It didn't matter, because she and Christian wouldn't be going to the ice cream shop or anywhere else together. She and Martha sat down and ate their lunch. Ruby avoided the subject of Christian.

The barn and workshop were completed by evening. Everyone was tired yet pleased with the results. Ruby was loading pans in

Timothy's buggy when she felt someone tap her on the shoulder. She turned to see Christian standing there.

When he didn't say anything, she started talking despite her better judgment. Nothing went well when she talked because of nerves. "That Martha," Ruby said with a laugh that sounded like a horse being strangled. "Always joking around."

"I never got that impression of Martha."

Ruby leaned against the buggy. "She was joking this afternoon about the ice cream shop."

He lifted a brow. "She said that?"

"Uh, *nee*. Not exactly."

"Then exactly what did she say?"

She opened her mouth, but then she closed it. How was she supposed to admit they'd been fixed up by the woman Christian truly liked? Who didn't like him back. How did all this get so unmanageable?

"What time should I pick you up on Saturday?" he asked, as if he were inquiring about the weather instead of confirming a date.

Her eyes grew wide. "Pick me up?"

"To take you to the ice cream shop."

"We're actually going?"

He nodded. "I agreed to take you to the ice cream shop. I'm a man of my word."

"Except when it comes to marriage proposals." *Uh-oh.* She shouldn't have said that out loud.

His gaze cooled. "I already explained that."

"Not really."

He blew out a breath. "Are you going with me or not?"

She did like ice cream. And they had agreed to go in front

of a witness. Those were the only reasons she was going along with this nonsense. "*Ya*. But it's not a date."

"Absolutely not."

"Fine. Just wanted to make that clear."

"Crystal clear." Without another word he turned and started to walk away.

"Six o'clock," she called out after him.

He nodded without looking back.

She watched him leave. At least she'd get some ice cream out of the deal. But a part of her—a tiny part she tried to ignore but couldn't—was looking forward to Saturday night, and not because she loved Rocky Road.

CHAPTER 15

The next Saturday, Ruby waited for Christian to show up. She stood by the front window and peeked out. Anytime his buggy would be coming up the driveway to get her. Anytime now.

She turned and looked at the battery-operated clock on the wall. Five minutes late. That wasn't a big deal, was it? Even for a man who always kept a tight schedule and valued punctuality. She frowned and then looked out the window again.

"See anything interesting out there?"

She turned as Patience walked into the living room. Ruby let the curtain fall. *"Nee."* She walked to the couch and plopped down. If any other person was late, she wouldn't be concerned. But this was Christian. Mr. Punctuality. *Also Mr. Can't Make Up His Mind.*

"Is something wrong?" Patience sat down in the chair across from her.

"Where are the *buwe*?" Ruby asked.

"Outside playing with Timothy. It won't be long before it will

be too cold and dark in the evenings for them to play outside."
She gave Ruby a sly look. "Nice change of subject, by the way."

Ruby sighed and put her elbow on the arm of the couch. She
cradled her chin in her hand. "I was waiting for someone. But
he's not coming."

"He?" Patience sat back in the chair and folded her hands in
her lap.

"Chris Ropp. He was going to pick me up and take me out
for ice cream tonight."

"At that new place on Clarendon?"

Was she the last person to know about the ice cream shop?
She nodded. "*Ya.*"

"I hear they have great hot fudge sundaes."

"Apparently, I won't find out tonight," she muttered.

Patience crossed her legs. "He's probably running a little
behind."

"Maybe." Ruby glanced at the clock again. It was almost ten
past now. He wasn't coming.

"I didn't realize there was something going on between
you two—"

"There isn't!" Goodness, she sounded like a screech owl.
"There isn't," she repeated, tempering her volume.

Patience nodded. "I see. Why don't we work on a puzzle
while you're waiting?"

Glad for the distraction, Ruby nodded. Patience went to the
cabinet on the other side of the room where she and Timothy kept
their games and puzzles, along with a few of the kids' smaller toys.
She pulled out a box and then closed the cabinet door. "This one
won't take long to do," she said as she placed it on the coffee table.

Ruby sat down on the floor and opened the box. The picture

on the front was of a lovely farm scene, with a bright-red barn in the distance and bales of hay dotting the landscape. She dumped the puzzle pieces on the table, and soon she and Patience were fitting them together.

They were partway through when the boys and Timothy came inside. "We're a little dirty," he said, looking sheepish.

Ruby looked up and Patience gasped. "A little?"

The boys were covered in mud, their tiny white teeth showing through the dark dirt on their faces as they grinned. "Did you guys roll in the mud with the pigs?" Ruby asked, getting up from the floor.

"They might be cleaner if they had." Patience rolled her eyes at Timothy, who was none too clean himself. *"Buwe,"* she said, taking Luke from his father and shooing Tobias toward the stairs.

"I'll help you with their baths," Timothy said, laughing.

"You'll need one *yerself.*"

Ruby looked at the puzzle and then at the window again. Maybe she should check for a phone message, just in case. He did have that cell phone the school board gave him. But when she slipped outside to the shanty and dialed up voice mail, she heard nothing. Christian definitely wasn't coming. She should have known better than to agree to go with him in the first place. Back in the house, she tried to concentrate on the puzzle again, but it was hard to focus. He had a lot of nerve standing her up like this. It wasn't a date, but they did have plans. He could have at least called.

She grimaced. He was getting a piece of her mind tomorrow at church, that was for sure.

The next morning Ruby wasn't as upset, but she was still

annoyed. She had also decided not to bother scolding Christian. Instead she would ignore him. She'd learned her lesson not to trust him anymore. Whatever friendship or relationship they had, it was over.

She helped Patience get the boys ready for church, and soon they were on their way. When they arrived at Abigail and Asa Bontrager's, Ruby kept her focus on the barn where they were holding the service. Of course, she said hi to people as they were passing by, but she didn't look for Christian.

Ruby sat down on the bench beside Patience, the boys between them. Tobias leaned his head against Ruby's arm. She patted his knee and waited for the service to begin.

By the time church was over, she was feeling better. She enjoyed the singing, and the sermon was a reminder of what was important—keeping her focus on God. She hadn't been doing that lately. In fact, her focus had been on herself, mostly. And Christian, of course. But not on her faith. *I'm sorry, Lord.*

They were staying for the meal afterward, and Ruby offered to help put out the food. "*Danki*, Ruby, but we've got plenty of help," Abigail said.

Ruby looked at the women in the packed kitchen and nodded. She'd probably spill something anyway. She went outside and walked over to the other side of the barn, on the opposite side of where the men talked and the children played. She leaned against the rough slats and sighed, crossing her arms over her chest, disappointment washing over her. Even though she was mad at him, she was disappointed she hadn't seen Christian in church. He might have been sitting out of her sight line. Or maybe he decided not to come today, although that would have been surprising. She couldn't imagine him skipping a service.

She needed to stop thinking about him so much. That was her biggest problem. He was taking up too much of her mental energy, which she needed to turn to God. She needed to start following his will, not her own. "That starts now," she whispered, looking up at the cloud-filled sky. "*Yer* will be done, no matter what."

After a few moments of silent prayer, she turned to go back to the house. Surely lunch had started by now. As she turned the corner of the barn, she struck something solid, and she felt the feeling of deja vu. *Christian.* She took a step back from him and frowned. They had to stop meeting like this. Also, she remembered she was supposed to be ignoring him. "Excuse me," she said, not looking at him as she started to move past him.

But he grabbed her by the shoulders, stopping her. "Thank God I found you!"

She looked up at him, this time paying more attention, and she was shocked at what she saw. His eyes were wild. He wasn't wearing a hat. He wasn't even wearing church clothes, and it looked like he'd slept in the clothing he was in. His face was unshaven too. She'd never seen him so unkempt before. Or so panicked. "What's wrong?" she asked, touching his forearm.

"It's Selah. She's gone."

Christian had never felt more panicked and out of control. Ever since he'd discovered Selah was gone, even his pulse had been out of control. But now, seeing Ruby, it slowed slightly. He hadn't known what to do, except to seek her out. "I don't know where she is," he said, his voice breaking.

Without a word she took his hand and they went behind the barn. She held on to him as she asked in a calm voice, "What happened?"

"I spent yesterday in Barton," he said, spilling everything out in *Dietsch*. "I had errands to run. When I came back in the afternoon, I was getting ready to come pick you up . . . I'm sorry about that, by the way."

"Don't worry about it."

"I went upstairs to tell Selah I was leaving. The door to her room was partway open, and since that was unusual, I went inside. Everything was gone. Her clothes, her books, a little rag doll she's had since she was a child and brought with her from New York. There was no note, nothing to let me know when she'd left or where she'd gone. I didn't panic at first. I figured she went back to New York. She'd been so unhappy here, even worse the past week. For a while I thought she was doing better."

He shook his head. For a few days after the pie debacle, Selah had kept her word about trying to do better. She cooked, cleaned, and made conversation. Then she lost her temper when he asked her why they were having green beans with meat loaf—they'd always had peas with that particular entrée—and she was back to giving him the silent treatment. That had been agreeable to him, since he was consumed with thinking about Ruby. What a mess he'd made of that. He'd been wanting to talk to her, to try to sort things out. He missed her—their lessons, their conversations, the way he could be himself around her. But he'd also hurt her, and he had to make amends. When Martha suggested they go have ice cream, he jumped at the chance, and he was pleased Ruby had agreed to go. He thought they might be on the right track.

Then Selah disappeared.

"What happened after that?" Ruby asked.

Her question brought his thoughts back into focus. "I called *Mamm*, and she said she hadn't heard from Selah in a couple of weeks. I didn't want to worry *mei* parents, so I made up some excuse for being concerned and told them she was probably just out with friends." He ran his hand through his hair. "I don't even remember what I told them exactly."

"And then what?"

"I went looking for her. I spent most of the night trying to find her without bothering anybody. I still wasn't one hundred percent sure something was wrong. But I felt that it was in *mei* gut."

"So you came here."

He nodded. "I didn't know what else to do. I still don't. I had just pulled up in *mei* buggy when I saw you by the barn." Without thinking, he squeezed her hand, the guilt he kept at bay rising within him. He'd left Selah to her own devices when he knew something was wrong with her. This was his fault. He should have done something—

"It will be okay, Christian." Ruby moved closer to him. "Remember, Selah's an adult."

"She's *mei* little *schwester*," he choked out.

"But she's also an adult. I'm sure she'll contact you soon."

"What if she doesn't?"

"Christian, she hasn't been gone that long. Maybe she went to visit another friend in a different district or town. That's why she took all her things with her."

"Then why wouldn't she tell me that?"

Ruby didn't respond. Finally, she said, "I'll sit with you until you hear from her. I'll let Timothy know I'm leaving."

He almost collapsed with relief. For once, he didn't want to be alone, his thoughts churning with blame and culpability.

"Wait in *yer* buggy," she said, her voice calm and soothing. "I'll be right back."

Christian climbed inside the buggy to wait for her. People were busy at the tables, set up outside since it wasn't too cold yet. Fortunately, it seemed no one had noticed him. He rubbed his hand over his face, feeling the stubble on his chin. He knew he looked like a mess. For once, he didn't care.

Ruby climbed into the buggy. "Let's *geh.*"

They had just left the Bontragers' when Ruby asked, "Do you want to drive around again and look for her?"

"I don't know where I'd look."

"Did you talk to Martha?"

He nodded. "I stopped by last night. When I asked her if Selah was there, she said no. She also said she hadn't seen her in a few weeks. Like I did with *mei* parents, I minimized *mei* explanation to her. I didn't want to upset Martha."

"That was kind of you," Ruby said.

He was barely paying attention to the road. Fortunately, his horse knew the way home.

"You don't have any idea where she would have gone?" she asked.

"*Nee.*" He gripped the reins. "She doesn't confide in me." *And I haven't been paying enough attention to her.*

They were quiet the rest of the way back to his house. Even though they weren't talking, he still took comfort from Ruby's presence. When they arrived and got out of the buggy, she said, "I'll make some lunch."

He nodded his thanks and put up the horse and buggy. When

he went inside, she had already put a sandwich and a handful of pretzels on a plate and set it on the table. "When was the last time you ate something?"

Christian sat down. "Lunch yesterday. I think." He wasn't hungry, but he logically knew he had to eat something. He took a bite of the sandwich. Turkey and cheese.

She set a glass of tea and an apple in front of him and sat down next to him.

"Aren't you going to eat?" he asked.

"Later."

He took the sandwich and tore it in half. Messy, but it would do. He handed her half. "Here. Eat this."

"It's *yers*—"

"Eat."

She took the sandwich and took a tiny bite. Christian could see the worry in her eyes, too, even though she was trying to hide it. Surprising, since she and Selah weren't exactly friends.

"Did you check Selah's room again?" Ruby asked after she finished the sandwich. "Maybe she left some kind of clue about where she went."

"I did. There was nothing there. She took everything with her."

Ruby frowned. "I don't think there's much we can do, other than wait. At least not right now. If she doesn't come back by tomorrow, you'll probably have to let Freemont know so he can get some of the men to help find her."

He nodded, also recognizing what she'd left unsaid—they may have to get the police involved. It was bad enough he'd brought Ruby into it. This was his business. His family. He should be able to handle this alone. But he couldn't.

Ruby took his hand. "Let's pray for her, Christian," she said softly.

He closed his eyes and prayed harder than he had for anything in his life.

CHAPTER 16

*R*uby looked at Christian as he slept on the couch, his breathing steady and deep. She let out a soft sigh, glad he was finally able to catch a nap. She'd been here with him for the past four hours, trying to keep his mind off Selah. They attempted to play cards, but neither of them could focus. Then they went for a short walk, but Christian didn't want to go far in case Selah came back. He'd tried to read, but he couldn't. And that's when Ruby knew something was wrong.

At first, she didn't understand why he was so upset. Yes, Selah had packed up everything and hadn't left a note. She'd been inconsiderate. But she wasn't a little kid. Christian was acting like she had disappeared off the face of the earth. Ruby was fairly sure he would get a phone call from his parents at any time, telling him Selah was there. Or from one of her friends.

Ruby got up and pulled the quilt off the back of the couch and covered him with it. He stirred slightly and then stilled.

She couldn't help but crouch next to him. A hank of his hair had fallen over his forehead, and she was tempted to brush it back. But she didn't dare wake him. He was exhausted from lack of sleep and worry. Her heart was moved by the way he cared about his sister. She hadn't realized his feelings could run so deep. At times he didn't seem to have feelings at all. But he did. And that caused a spark of attraction to light up within her.

Her cheeks grew hot and she rose. Oh, this wasn't good. And what kind of person was she, thinking about Christian that way at a time like this? Or at all?

She went into the kitchen and got a glass of water. Although she told herself not to think of him, she couldn't stop, especially the memory of their kiss. She still didn't know why he'd kissed her. It didn't make any sense. You only kissed people you liked. People you loved. And while Christian obviously cared deeply for his sister, he didn't care for Ruby except as a friend to seek out when trouble came. Sometimes she wasn't sure he even liked her very much.

"Why did you let me fall asleep?"

She whirled around, water sloshing out of the glass. She set it down on the counter before she did any damage and put her hands behind her back. "You were tired. You *are* tired." There were shadows beneath his bleary eyes.

"Doesn't mean I should have slept." He dragged himself to the table and sat down. Then he looked at her. "I'll take you home."

He didn't look like he should be alone. "I can stay here."

"No." He straightened his posture, looking a bit like the usual Christian. "I have taken up enough of your time," he added in English.

"You haven't, and there's *nee* need to be so formal. I thought we were—are—friends."

He paused. "We are."

She walked over to him and sat down. "This is what friends do. They're here for each other. They care about each other."

His gaze met hers, and she saw something in them that made her heart warm. "*Danki* for being *mei* friend, Ruby."

"You're welcome," she said, smiling. Maybe he did like her, at least a little more than she'd thought.

A knock sounded, and Christian jumped up from the chair. They both went to the living room and opened the front door. Martha's father stood there. "Chris," he said, and then gave Ruby a nod. "Martha sent me."

"She did?"

The man nodded. "She wanted me to tell you in person instead of calling. Selah is at our *haus*."

Christian tried not to pace while he waited in Martha's living room.

Ruby had insisted she'd walk home. He wanted to say so many things to her, but wanting to see Selah right away, without saying a word he got into his buggy and followed Martha's father.

Now he was waiting to see if his sister would come downstairs. Martha's mother was in the kitchen, kindly staying out of the way. Martha's father came down the stairs. "I let *mei dochder* know you're here," he said. Then he left the room.

Why was Selah doing this? Not only had she worried him

sick, but she had brought Martha's whole family into their private business. Much like he had brought in Ruby. But that was different, wasn't it?

At the sound of footsteps on the stairs, he looked up. Martha met his gaze as she came down. "Hi, Chris," she said, her tone kind.

"Is she coming?"

Martha shook her head. "She says *nee*, but I think she wants to see you."

"Is she okay?"

"I'm not sure. She's not saying much about what happened."

That sent another wave of panic through him, but he held his ground. He had to approach this carefully or he'd lose Selah for good.

"Why don't you *geh* upstairs?" Martha said. "The worst thing she can do is tell you to leave. My room is the second on the right."

He would leave, if Selah asked. He nodded and went upstairs. He paused at Martha's door. What should he say to his sister? He was angry, but worry was overriding that emotion. He closed his eyes and said a short prayer for wisdom before walking inside.

Selah was sitting on the bed, but her back was to him. Her shoulders were slumped, and he thought he heard a quiet sniffle. He also noticed she was wearing English clothes. He wondered about that, but he didn't dare ask for an explanation right now. "Selah?"

"I told Martha I didn't want to see you." She didn't turn around, and her voice was thick, as if she had just swallowed a spoonful of peanut butter.

"I know. But I'm here anyway." When she didn't respond he moved closer, hesitating when he reached the bed, but then he went around it and sat down next to her. He didn't say anything for a long while, sensing that his words right now would make the situation worse.

"I'm sorry," she finally said in a hoarse whisper.

"Apology accepted."

She turned toward him, her eyes red-rimmed, a wadded-up tissue in her hand. "That's it?"

He held out his hands. "What else should I say?"

"You could yell at me, for starters."

"Why would I do that? It wouldn't change what happened."

"It's what I deserve!" She jumped up from the bed and faced him. "Don't you ever feel anything, Christian? Were you even worried about me when I was gone?"

You have no idea. "Of course I was."

"Then why aren't you angry? Why aren't you dragging me back home?" Tears streamed down her cheeks. "Why are you being so calm? So *nice*?"

His heart seemed to constrict. It was hard to see her this way, crying, looking like she hadn't slept any more than he had. "You don't need me to yell at you," he said, keeping his voice even.

"*Ya*, I do! I need . . . I need . . ." She started to sob.

Christian was at a loss. How could he help her? Comfort her? He rose from the bed and went to her. Her face was in her hands as she cried. He lifted his arms, paused, and then put them around her shoulders. "It's okay," he whispered, patting her back. "Whatever it is, it's okay."

She leaned against him and sobbed against his shirt. He didn't move, determined to hold her as long as she needed him to. Finally, she lifted her head and looked at him. He reached over and pulled a tissue out of the box on a nightstand. "Here."

She grabbed it and blew her nose. "I got *yer* shirt wet."

He looked down at the damp spot just below his right shoulder. Then he shrugged. "This shirt isn't exactly clean, anyway."

Selah looked at him again. "You haven't shaved," she said. "And *yer* hair is a mess."

He tried to smooth it down, but then gave up.

"Are those the same clothes you had on yesterday morning?"

He nodded.

Her eyes softened. "You do care."

Again, his heart seemed to pinch. "Of course I do. I apologize if I've said or done anything to make you think otherwise." He paused. "Is that why you ran away?"

She sighed, and then she plopped on the bed.

He sat down next to her. "Why did you leave?"

"Because of a *mann*." She looked down at her jeans and sweatshirt. Her hair was loose and reached her waist. It was also tangled. "I've been seeing someone," she said, looking at him. "An English *mann*. I met him in Barton when we first moved here. He was nice, handsome, and I felt *gut* around him. Hopeful. I thought he was the answer to everything."

"What do you mean?"

"I'm so unhappy," she whispered. "I have been for a long time, long before I came here with you. And I shouldn't be. I have a *gut* life. I thought when I joined the church things would be right, that I would feel that happiness and peace other people seem to have so easily. But I didn't." She looked down at her lap. "I thought having a fresh start in a new place would help, but that didn't happen either. Then I met Oliver. He was fun. I sneaked away to meet with him at night even though I knew it was wrong." She blew out a breath. "Yesterday I thought if I went to him, if I left the church and told him I wanted us to be together, then I would be happy. I know it sounds stupid and wrong, but at the time I felt desperate."

"What did he say?"

Selah paused. "I don't know. I didn't see him. I stood outside his *haus*, but I couldn't make myself go to the door. I went to an all-night diner instead. Then I came here. Deep inside I knew I was making a mistake. That I had made so many mistakes." She looked at Christian, her eyes filled with tears. "What's wrong with me?" she whispered.

He put his arm around her shoulders and she leaned her head against him. He'd had no idea she was going through this much turmoil. He also didn't completely understand it. It seemed like she didn't understand it either. "We'll figure this out," he said.

"How?"

"By going back to New York and talking to *Mamm* and *Daed*."

She lifted her head. "*Nee*. I don't want to do that. They won't understand."

"Maybe not, but we can start there. Selah, I think you might be depressed."

She pulled away from him. "I'm not crazy."

"I'm not saying you are. Depression doesn't equal insanity. But it is a real thing." He moved his arm from her. "I'll *geh* with you."

"What about *yer* students?"

He smiled. "I happen to know an excellent substitute teacher. They'll be in *gut* hands."

Selah sniffed. "You'd leave *yer* job to help me?"

He nodded. "Of course. I'm willing to learn what I need to do to help you." He half-smiled. "You know I'm always eager to learn."

She threw her arms around him. *"Danki,* Christian. I love you."

He hugged her back. "I love you too."

Ruby sat in the hickory rocker on Timothy's front porch and looked out at the yard. It was chilly this evening, and the sun was setting behind the horizon. She glanced at the book in her lap, but she hadn't really been reading it. Her mind had been on Christian and Selah, praying that everything was okay.

A stronger wind kicked up, making her shiver and pull her dark-blue pea coat closer to her. She should have brought out a scarf. She closed the book and rose from the chair as a buggy pulled into the driveway. The driver brought the horse up short and then got out. When Ruby saw it was Christian, she dropped the book in the chair and went to meet him.

"Is Selah all right?" she asked when she reached him.

He nodded. "For now."

Ruby searched his face in the dim light of dusk. He looked exhausted. He also wasn't wearing a coat. "It's cold out here. Do you want to come inside?"

He shook his head. "I only came to ask a favor before I talk to a neighbor about boarding Einstein. First thing in the morning I have to *geh* to New York for a little while. Could you take over *mei* class for me, for at least a week?"

She didn't hesitate. "Of course."

"The substitute folder is on *mei* desk." He paused. "The only thing I can tell you is that Selah needs me."

"So you're both going back."

"*Ya.* Will you tell Timothy and the school board it's an emergency situation?"

"I will."

Relief crossed his face. "Also, about Selah running away—"

"I won't tell anyone."

"*Gut.* Martha's family agreed not to either." He looked down at her. "*Danki.* I knew I could trust you."

Something moved inside her. Not pride or happiness, or even satisfaction. But she was glad she could help Christian. She was glad she had earned his trust.

"If you'll give me your phone number, I'll be in touch and let you know when I'll be back."

Ruby had a pencil and her calendar in her apron pocket. She ripped out a page she'd never used. "Here's both our shanty number and Patience's new cell phone number. She just got it for emergencies."

"Thank you," he said when she gave him the paper. "You might have to come up with a few more lessons for the students in case I'm gone longer than a week."

She was suddenly doubtful. "A-all right . . ."

"Ruby."

She looked up at him, and through the weariness and stress on his face she saw a calmness. "*Ya?*"

"You're a *gut* teacher. I believe that. You need to believe it too."

That made her chest feel lighter with happiness. "*Danki.*"

"I have to get back home. I dropped Selah off before coming here." He started to back away. "When I come back, we have some things to discuss."

She nodded, not completely sure what he was talking about

but not wanting to pry. Selah was his priority now, and she admired him for that. "Have a safe trip."

He nodded, and then he climbed back in the buggy. She watched him leave before going inside.

As soon as she was in the house she found Timothy and explained the situation. He frowned. "He left just like that?"

She nodded. "Like I said, it's a family emergency." That was the truth.

Timothy looked at her. "I sense there's more to this."

Ruby bit her lip but didn't say anything.

Finally, he said, "All right. Tomorrow I'll let the rest of the board know about Christian leaving and you substituting again. Just promise me one thing."

"What's that?"

"*Nee* pets!"

She laughed. "Trust me. I learned *mei* lesson."

CHAPTER 17

*S*elah sat at her parents' kitchen table, her hands in her lap,
while her mother filled a glass with water from the sink.
She stared down at the oak table, wishing she hadn't listened to
Christian when he insisted they come here. When they arrived
from Birch Creek this morning, he'd said very little to *Mamm*
before leaving the two of them alone to talk. As usual, when it
came to her mother, she didn't know what to say.

Mamm set the glass in front of her, sat down, and then folded
her hands on the table. "I haven't heard from you for over two
weeks," she said, looking straight ahead.

"I'm sorry."

"I haven't heard from Christian either, except when he called
Saturday to ask if I'd seen you." *Mamm* touched the side of her
white *kapp*. "Out of sight, out of mind, I see."

If she wasn't so tired, Selah would have rolled her eyes. Her
mother could fan a flame of guilt in an instant. And if she'd
wanted to talk to them, why hadn't she called them?

"I still don't know why you felt the need to leave." *Mamm* finally looked at her. "Christian's decision, I understand. But *yer* home is here."

It doesn't feel like it. Birch Creek didn't feel like home either. Neither place was right. Nothing was right. Tears rolled down her cheeks. She sniffed and wiped them away.

"Selah?"

She looked up. Her mother's tone had changed, and a flicker of concern flashed in her eyes. Selah sniffed again and straightened. "You're right," she said, grasping for the composure her brother seemed to constantly have. "I shouldn't have left."

"Why are you crying?"

"I'm not." She blinked and glanced away.

"Did something happen to you in Birch Creek? Is that why you've returned?"

Selah almost laughed at how alike *Mamm* and Christian were. Formal, direct, detached. But she had seen a different side of her brother since their move. He was also compassionate and caring. Her mother was, too, in her own way. But Selah needed more. More of what, she didn't know. "I don't know what's wrong with me," she whispered.

"Wrong with you?" *Mamm* pushed up her silver-rimmed glasses. "There's *nix* wrong with you. You're fine the way you are."

"What way is that?" Selah turned to her.

Mamm blinked. "You're . . . you." She stood from the table. "Now, stop talking nonsense and unpack *yer* things. You can help me prepare lunch. *Yer* father is working from home today."

But Selah didn't move. She stared at the glass of water in front of her. She didn't want to unpack or help with lunch, or even take a sip of water. She wanted to shrink in her chair until she was . . . nothing.

"Selah, did you hear me?"

She didn't respond. *Mamm* wouldn't understand. No one could.

"Selah?" *Mamm* put her hand on Selah's shoulder.

Her eyes remained fixed on the glass of water.

Mamm grabbed a chair, moved it closer to Selah, and sat down. "Now you're worrying me."

Her anxious words broke through Selah's haze. It wasn't like her mother to express worry. She looked at her. "I'm sorry."

"It's okay." She patted Selah's hand awkwardly.

But her tone had a slight softness to it, reminding Selah of the few times over the years her mother had comforted her, mostly when she was a little girl. As she grew older, she'd experienced less comforting and more insistence on keeping her emotions to herself, the way Christian did. The way *Mamm* usually did. But *Mamm* wasn't doing that now, and that gave Selah a bit of courage. "Christian thinks I'm depressed," she said.

A flicker of surprise entered *Mamm's* eyes. "What do you think?"

Tears slipped down her cheeks again. "I don't know."

After a long silence, *Mamm* said, "Is that why you left? Because you're depressed?"

Selah shrugged. "Maybe. I'm not sure . . . about anything."

Her mother took a handkerchief out of the pocket of her apron and handed it to Selah. "Are you in . . . trouble?" she asked, averting her gaze.

Knowing what she meant, Selah shook her head and stared at the tabletop again. *"Nee."*

Mamm nodded, and there was no mistaking her relieved expression. "Would you be willing to talk to someone?"

Selah lifted her head. "What do you mean?"

"I should have seen the signs," *Mamm* said, her voice quiet, as if she were talking to herself and not Selah. "*Yer aenti* Keturah went through the same thing when she was *yer* age. I just didn't think . . ." *Mamm* shook her head. "I didn't think it would happen to you."

"What?"

"Depression. Keturah has struggled with it her entire life."

Selah was shocked. Her aunt was one of the sweetest, happiest people she knew. "Really?"

Mamm nodded. "Would you be willing to talk to her about how you're feeling? I don't know exactly how she's managed to cope with it, but I know she'll give you *gut* advice." *Mamm* paused. "She's also a *gut* listener. Unlike me."

Selah looked at her mother's hands. They were clasped again, but the knuckles were white. When was the last time her mother had comforted her? Reassured her? She couldn't remember. Then she realized it didn't matter. Her mother was here for her now, and that gave her hope. "*Ya*," she said, wiping her eyes with the handkerchief. "I'll talk to her."

"And I'll keep this conversation between you and me. *Nee* need for *yer vatter* or *bruder* to know anything about it."

Selah nodded. "*Danki.*"

Mamm relaxed her hands. "We should pay Keturah a visit now. You don't have to explain anything to her right away unless you want to, but I think being around more *familye* will be a nice activity. The men can fend for themselves for lunch."

This was the mother she was used to, a woman who took

control and planned the next step. That had irritated her in the past, but now she welcomed it. "*Ya*," Selah said. She even managed a small smile. "I think so too."

Christian adjusted his hat as he walked toward the barn. Ambled was a more precise word, and if he could avoid going to the barn at all, he would. But his mother had told him his father was sharpening his tools out there. Since Christian's goal was to make sure Selah and their mother talked, he had little choice but to say hello to *Daed*.

He stopped a few feet in front of the barn door, remembering the last conversation they had, which had turned into an altercation. How would their encounter turn out today? Christian didn't want to compound his sister's problems, so he took a deep breath, determined not to let his father get to him, no matter what he said.

Christian entered the barn, which was divided in half—two stalls for horses, one of which was empty, and the back half, which was his father's workshop. He'd seen Hank, *Daed*'s horse, nibbling on grass in the small pasture next to the barn when he and Selah arrived. He could hear the faint scrape of a blade sharpener as he ventured to the workshop.

He paused and watched his father sharpen a hickory knife on a small whetstone on top of an old table pushed against the barn wall. His father was archaic in his trade, using tools that had been handed down from his grandfather. A meat cleaver, a scraper, and several smaller knives were laid neatly on the table next to the stone. *Daed*'s shoulders were hunched as he bent over the stone. Christian waited until he was finished, not wanting to surprise him. His father could become engrossed in his work to the point of forgetting his surroundings.

When *Daed* picked up the blade for inspection, Christian cleared his throat. *Daed* turned, his brow lifting. "What are you doing here?" he said, placing the knife on the table and picking up the cleaver. He ran his thumb across the top of the metal edge, without cutting himself. Christian had tried to emulate that one time and ended up with several stitches. His father applied the blade to the whetstone. "Don't you have a job to do?"

"I have a capable substitute working in my stead." During the bus ride here, he'd thought about Ruby and the students in his classroom, but he didn't worry about them. He trusted Ruby, grateful she allowed him to keep his focus on addressing Selah's difficulties.

"Still using fancy English, I see." *Daed* ran the blade against the stone again.

Christian cringed. The sound had always given him the shivers. "Is this better?" he said, switching to *Dietsch*.

Daed shrugged. "Suit *yerself.*" *Scrape.*

Deciding to ignore his father's testy attitude, he said, "I see you're doing well."

Scrape.

"Do you, uh, need some help with anything?" Christian asked.

"Doing fine on *mei* own." *Scrape.*

Christian clenched his teeth. "I will be here for a few days, so if there's anything I can do—"

"I guess chasing little *kinner* around all day isn't what it's cracked up to be." *Daed* eyed him.

"I don't chase *kinner* all day," he said, feeling his hackles rise.

His father knew every button to push, and sometimes Christian suspected he enjoyed the results. He breathed in again. "As a member of the school board, you know firsthand how important a *gut* teacher is for the success of the school."

"So *yer* school's not successful."

"I didn't say that."

He turned back to the stone. "Then I'll ask you again. Why are you here?"

Scrape. Christian was tempted to grab the whetstone and throw it out the barn window. Instead, he shoved down his growing irritation. "Selah and I wanted to see how you and *Mamm* are doing." He'd let Selah decide what she wanted their father to know about the real reason.

Daed turned in his chair and laughed. "How we're doing? We're fine. In fact, better than fine." He narrowed his gaze. "Now we're free to do as we please."

Christian flinched, as if his *daed* had threatened to throw the cleaver at him. He also recognized the subtext of his words. "I'm sorry I couldn't be the *sohn* you wanted," he said, fighting to keep the wobble out of his voice.

Scrape.

"How long are you going to resent me for choosing *mei* own path?"

The blade hovered above the stone. *Daed* set it down. "I don't resent you," he said.

You could have fooled me. "Disappointed, then."

"I won't deny that." He picked up the hickory knife he'd previously sharpened. "Do you know how old this tool is?"

Christian did, but he remained silent, knowing what his father was going to say next.

"Four generations. Four generations of butchers, dating back to Europe. A trade that has kept food on the table and clothes on our bodies." He turned, still holding the knife. "A trade you rejected because it wasn't *gut* enough."

Stunned, Christian said, "Is that what you think?"

Daed shrugged again, his expression vacant. His father was the more expressive of his two parents, but right now he was so emotionless Christian wanted to shake him. "The Ropp men don't use fancy words or read fancy books," *Daed* continued.

"I'm an anomaly."

"Whatever that is." *Daed* set the knife down and picked up the cleaver again. "As you can see, we're fine. You and *yer schwester* can *geh* back to Dirt Creek—"

"Birch Creek—"

"And get on with *yer* lives. *Yer mamm* and I are getting on with ours."

He should just turn around and leave. His father was angry, despite his flat expression. And in a way, Christian understood. He'd had expectations for his son, and Christian had failed to meet them. *Daed* had worked side by side with his family until they retired—or in his grandfather's case, had passed away. Now his father was alone in his workshop. Yes, he worked with customers and other butchers, but his business was his own. And he had no one to pass it down to.

Christian had wrestled with this before telling his father about his decision to be a teacher. A burden had been lifted from him with the revelation, but perhaps a different one was now on his father's shoulders. "I'm sorry," Christian said, sounding sincere. He took a step forward. "I wish things could be different."

"You made *yer* decision."

"Just like you made *yers*."

Daed looked at him, a flicker of emotion crossing his face. "I didn't have a choice. I wasn't going to turn *mei* back on *mei vatter* and *grossvatter*. I wasn't going to throw away everything they taught me."

Christian's guilt escalated, but he remained resolute. "What about *Onkel* David? He left the business."

"He didn't have to stay."

"Because the business was *yers*." *And it was supposed to be mine.* He shook his head. He and his father could speak in circles about this and resolve nothing. "I see *nix* has changed," he muttered.

"*Nee*. It hasn't." *Daed* faced the whetstone again. He picked up the cleaver. *Scrape.*

Christian left the barn, tempted to call a taxi to take him to the bus station right away, but that wouldn't be fair to Selah. He would stay here as long as she needed him to. But as soon as he was confident she would be okay, he was going back to Birch Creek—where he belonged.

By the middle of the week, Ruby was tired, but fulfilled. The students had asked a few questions about when Christian was coming back, but after her second day of teaching, they'd had no more inquiries. She stuck to his plan and had even spent most of the time after school today working on the class schedule for next week in case Christian was delayed further. She really enjoyed teaching, even the difficult parts of it.

The discipline was especially challenging. She found a tack in her chair this morning, just before she sat on it. That would have been worse than the gum, and she was not amused. When no one confessed, everyone got five extra spelling words to study for their upcoming test on Friday. They would learn that she took their education seriously.

When she arrived home, Patience was in the kitchen making supper. "Where are the *buwe*?" Ruby asked, setting her books and papers on the counter near the mudroom door. She had a lot of work to grade tonight after supper, and she was looking forward to it.

"At the Beilers'," she said. "Joanna and Naomi offered to watch them today while I went to check on Irene. They're keeping them tonight."

"How is she doing?"

"*Gut*. I also found out Emily Beachy is expecting."

So Fanny, Samuel, and Caleb would have another sibling in the future. "You really are going to need some help."

"*Ya*, and God will provide it in his time. He always does."

"That's true." Ruby paused. She had been thinking about her own future lately. "I think he's provided something for me."

"Oh?"

"Patience . . . I want to be a teacher."

Her sister-in-law set down a carrot and her peeler and faced her. "I think that's an excellent decision."

"You do?"

"You obviously enjoy it. I'd say love it. And you're so *gut* with *kinner*. The *buwe* have missed you this week."

Ruby's heart warmed. "I missed them too. And you're right. I do love teaching."

Patience leaned against the counter. "What are *yer* plans, then?"

"First," she said, picking up her papers and books, "I'm going to focus on *mei* students until Chris comes back. They're *mei* priority right now."

With a smile, Patience said, "It's *gut* to see you content and confident."

Confident? Ruby thought about that as she went upstairs to put away her things. She'd never thought of herself as confident, but she did feel that way now. She was starting to believe what Christian said. She was a *gut* teacher, she had control of the class, and most of all, he trusted her. If that didn't give her assurance, nothing would. *Thank you, Lord.*

After supper and cleaning up, she spread the stacks of papers on the table and started to grade them. She heard Patience's cell phone ring from the mudroom. "I'll get it," she called to Timothy and Patience, who were in the living room. She went to the mudroom and picked up the phone. "Hello?"

"Hello, Ruby." Christian's deep, steady voice came through the receiver.

She smiled. "Hi. How are things?"

"They're okay. I should be back in Birch Creek by Saturday. Let's meet by the tree, and you can inform me about school this past week."

"Okay." She paused. He sounded brisk and businesslike. "How are you?"

"I'm well. Thank you for asking."

Her shoulders slumped. She shouldn't have expected anything different. Then again, what had she expected when she asked him how he was? For him to say he missed her? To ask how she was doing? That wasn't Christian. "Your students are also well," she said, imitating his formal speech.

"I'm sure they are. I have to hang up now. I'll see you Saturday. At four o'clock?"

"That will be fine. Good-bye." She set the phone on the charger. At least he was able to come back, which meant Selah must be doing better. She had prayed this week for them both, and it looked like God had provided something else—an answer to those prayers.

Christian hung up the phone and walked out of the shanty and back up to the house. He'd wanted to talk to Ruby longer, but he wasn't sure what to say. Most of the time it was easy to talk to her, but sometimes—like after he'd proposed and after he'd kissed her—it was awkward. It had been awkward for him again. *Because I miss her.*

Since being back in New York, he'd had a lot of time to think. But this time instead of thinking about teaching, his students, or improving his mind, he was focused on family . . . and Ruby. He didn't just want to talk to her about his classroom—although he definitely wanted a summary of the week. But he hadn't been worried about his students for a moment. He had meant it when he said he trusted her.

He'd also thought about his relationship with his father. They had avoided each other since their last conversation and didn't engage when they were in the same room, not even at mealtimes. His father wasn't willing to meet Christian halfway, and Christian couldn't force him to. Despite how much he wanted things to be different, he had to accept that *Daed* may never accept his decision, and their relationship might always be strained. He walked into the house. Selah and their mother were sitting at the kitchen table, talking. "I'll come back" he said, and then he started to leave the room.

"Christian?" Selah said.

He turned. "*Ya?*"

"May I talk to you?"

Mamm patted Selah's hand and rose from the table. "I'll *geh* wake *yer vatter*. I'm sure he's asleep in the chair in the living room by now."

Christian didn't say anything. He'd seen *Daed* snoring away in his old chair when he came into the house. It was the reason he'd decided to go into the kitchen.

Mamm paused. She looked at Christian and then at Selah. "It's *gut* to have you both home . . . even if it's just for a little while." She touched Christian's arm and left.

He sat down across from Selah. He'd noticed an improvement in her appearance since they'd arrived home. She was dressed when she came downstairs in the morning now, her hair up and wearing either her *kapp* or a kerchief. Her complexion seemed a little brighter, and her eyes were less dull. That's why he'd already decided he could return to Birch Creek at the end of the week. "What do you want to talk about?"

Selah ran her finger across the table. He also knew she'd not only spent time talking with *Mamm* but had visited their *aenti* Keturah, more than once. Perhaps being back around family had a positive effect on her.

Selah finally spoke. "I went to a doctor today. *Aenti* Keturah recommended it."

His brow lifted, but he remained silent. That was a surprise, considering their parents went to doctors only in emergency situations. He was also surprised that their aunt had such an influence over Selah's decision. As far as he knew, she wasn't enamored of doctors either.

"What did the doctor say?"

"She thinks I am depressed and suggested I have therapy. She also said I can take some medications, but she wants me to try talking to someone first. She knows a counselor she highly recommends." Selah swallowed. "I'm not sure I want to talk to a stranger, especially someone who isn't Amish."

He understood her trepidation. They were private people, even among the Amish. It would be difficult to talk to an outsider about anything particular to their culture.

"But I'm going to try. *Aenti* also suggested I talk to Samuel."

That surprised him too. Samuel King, their bishop, was a kind man who was always available whenever he was needed. "I imagine he will supply you with plenty of helpful Bible verses," he said.

Selah nodded. "He does like to quote Scripture. I used to dismiss a lot of that, but now I really need those words."

"This all sounds *gut*." It sounded better than good, but he didn't want to put any pressure on Selah. She would heal on her timetable, and God's.

"I'm really sorry," she said, her expression sincere. "I've been a terrible *schwester* to you, and I'm glad you feel okay about returning to Birch Creek on Saturday. I'm going to be fine."

"You don't need to apologize," he said. "I understand."

"That still doesn't make it right." She sighed. "I need to apologize to Martha and her *familye*. And to Ruby. I really wasn't fair to her."

"She understands too."

Selah looked at him, her brow lifting in a mirror image of what he knew to be his usual gesture. "Did you tell her what happened?"

"*Nee.* I would never break that confidence."

"You're a *gut mann*, Christian. And a great *bruder*." Her expression turned sly. "But you need some help in the romance department."

Not this again. "I've given up on that."

"Why? You already asked Ruby to marry you."

"A mistake on *mei* part."

"Ouch. Don't let her hear you say that."

"I'm sure she wholeheartedly agrees."

Selah looked at him. "Did she tell you that?"

He shook his head. "Not in so many words."

"In any words?"

"Well . . . *nee*."

She reached over and bonked his head.

His hand went to his forehead. She'd barely touched him, and it didn't hurt, but he was surprised. "What was that for?"

"Because you're so dense for a brilliant *mann*. Can't you see that you and Ruby are perfect for each other?"

Something stirred inside him at her words, but he tamped it down. His feelings—whatever they were—didn't matter. "This is quite unexpected, considering your opinion of Ruby."

"I've reconsidered. She's exactly what you need."

He gazed at the clock above the wall. In the center sat a plump rooster, a rather whimsical decoration for his staid parents.

"I guess you don't want to talk about Ruby anymore."

Christian turned to his sister. "You are correct."

"All right, new subject. How are you and *Daed*? Seems like

you two can barely stand to be in the same room together since we've been back."

This time he looked at her squarely. "I don't want to talk about him, either."

Selah nodded. "All right. I will respect that." She rose from the table. "But when it comes to Ruby, you need to figure out *yer* future with her. And that's all I'm going to say about that."

"But—"

Selah left the kitchen, leaving Christian with his jumbled thoughts. He looked at the platter of apple cake squares in the middle of the table. They were covered in plastic wrap, but that didn't stop him from lifting it up and taking one. As he bit into the moist cake, he thought about what Selah said. Frankly, he had no idea how she would have come to that determination, considering she hadn't seen him and Ruby together that much.

He finished off the treat and cleaned up the crumbs. It didn't matter what Selah thought. Ruby had refused his proposal. But there was still the matter of the kiss. She had wanted to talk to him about it, and he needed to explain himself. He wanted her to be free to pursue Seth, or any other man she thought was suitable husband material. Just because he had given up on his plan to marry didn't mean she had.

But something twisted inside of him as he thought about Ruby being with anyone else.

Ruby waited as she stood beneath the tree's branches. It was mid-November, and almost all the leaves had fallen. The sky was cloudy, and it was cold. She snuggled into her scarf and put her gloved hands in the pockets of her coat. Maybe they should have agreed to meet somewhere warmer. She crouched next to the canvas tote bag that said *#1 Teacher* on the front next to a bright-red apple. She saw it yesterday when she went to a department store in Barton after school. It was whimsical, but also appropriate for Christian. She doubted he'd think so, but she bought the bag anyway.

She heard the rustle of leaves and looked up. He was walking toward her, his hat low on his head, a scarf also around his neck. She stood and threaded her fingers together as the brown leaves whirled around her ankles.

He stopped a few feet in front of her. "Hi," he said.

"Hi." Before any awkwardness could settle between them, she picked up the tote bag. "Here," she said, handing it to him.

"What's this?" He eyed the front of it. "Number one teacher?"

She nodded and smiled. "The students took their spelling tests yesterday. I graded them and put them in a folder, along with *yer* lesson plans and some of Malachi's extra work."

"Thank you."

"Don't be surprised to see extra words on the test." She explained about the tack in the chair.

"They tried that on you too? I had one in my seat the second day. It seems like a rite of passage for teachers."

She smiled again. She liked hearing him refer to her as a teacher. She also realized that she still liked him, despite everything. She had missed him while he was gone, and not just because she could have asked him for advice during some of the more trying times in the classroom this past week. But her feelings for him didn't make any difference. She had already chosen her path. "How is Selah?"

"Better. She's going to be okay."

"I'm glad to hear it. I was praying for you both."

He looked at her. *"Danki."*

She thought she heard his voice slightly crack as he slipped into *Dietsch*, but that could be from the wind. She shivered in her coat.

"Are you cold?" he asked.

"Ya. It's cold in November, you know."

"We've been working on our Christmas program," he said.

"I'm sure it will be a *gut* one." She rocked back on her heels. "Ruby—"

"I'm going to become a teacher," she blurted. "I've been thinking and praying about it, and it's something I really want to pursue. Thanks to you giving me another chance, I think I've found *mei* calling."

He didn't say anything for a long moment. Then he said, "That's . . . great."

"Don't worry, I'm not trying to get *yer* job," she said, wanting to reassure him. "Now that you're back, I'm going home to Lancaster to get some training. I'm also going to prove to the people in *mei* community that I can be a *gut* teacher, so if an opening comes up they'll hire me. If there is no opening, then I'll apply to other districts."

"Sounds like you have everything figured out."

"I do." She grinned and blew out a breath. "I feel at peace."

"What about . . . Seth?"

She waved her hand. "That was a foolish idea, looking for a husband like that." She met his gaze, and for some reason butterflies started fluttering in her stomach. "You can't force a marriage to happen. A relationship takes time to develop, and a marriage needs love."

"Except when love is irrelevant."

Ruby stared at him. She shouldn't be surprised at his response, but she was. "How can it be irrelevant? We're talking about marriage. Two people spending the rest of their lives together. Having children, creating a *familye*, being there through the *gut* times and bad . . ." She shook her head, the butterflies in her stomach disappearing. "How can you say love doesn't matter?"

"History has shown—"

"I don't care about history. I'm talking about me." *About us.* But there wasn't an *us* where she and Christian were concerned. Despite everything, she wanted there to be. "I'm leaving on Monday," she said, lifting her chin, pretending her heart wasn't fracturing inside. Her mouth turned to cotton as she added, "Since there's *nee* church service tomorrow, I'll say *mei* good-bye now." She waited for him to respond, hoping he would ask her to stay, offer to take her for ice cream, and this time they would go. Tell her that he wanted her here in Birch Creek. That he wanted her to be with him.

He looked at her, his gaze impassive. Then he said, "I'm gratified that you have everything settled in your mind, and that you have developed a plan to achieve your goals. Have a safe trip to Lancaster."

She lowered her head, forcing her trembling chin to stay still. He was speaking English again. "*Danki.*" Then she looked at him. He had rejected her, but that didn't completely change how she felt about him. She was probably a fool to still care for him. *I'm always a fool, anyway.* "I hope you find *yer* happy ending, Christian," she said, sincere. "Whether it's with Martha or someone else." She turned and walked toward Timothy's before she broke down completely.

Coward. That's what he was, a coward. He watched Ruby leave as he held on to the silly tote bag she'd given him. He never would purchase something so frivolous himself. But he held on to it tightly as she walked away, fighting with himself about whether to go after her.

But what could he say? He didn't love her. He liked her. He cared about her well-being. But he wasn't in love with her. And from what he could tell, she felt love was important. She had stated her parameters for marriage, not to mention her career goal—which he thought was a good one. There was nothing he could do, or say, to convince her to stay.

He trudged home, trying to convince himself this was all for the best. While his mind accepted it, his heart ached. He walked inside his house and put the bag on the kitchen table. Somehow, he would have to let her go. He should be grateful he didn't love her, or it would be twice as hard. The sting in his heart would hurt twice as much. Yes, it was a good thing he didn't love Ruby Glick. Because if he did, he'd be in agony.

For three months Ruby had been in Lancaster learning everything she could about being a teacher. She also got a job working as a housekeeper at a local bed and breakfast. She'd managed to mess up only a few times. She'd splashed a small bit of bleach on an antique quilt in one of the rooms, but fortunately it wasn't noticeable. She still confessed to the owner, a woman in her sixties who was brusque but fair. "Accidents happen," she said. "As long as the quilt isn't ruined."

There were a few other mishaps, but for the most part she did her job well. On Saturdays she spent the day in the local library reading all she could on education methods and application, even getting books ordered through inter-library loan. She also discovered a local teacher's group, where several Amish teachers from nearby districts met to exchange ideas and methodology. She asked to attend the meetings, where she made some new friends as well as gained new information.

During the first Saturday evening in February, Ruby was sitting at the kitchen table reading up on discipline procedures in the classroom. Her mother walked in. "Would you like a cup of tea?" she asked Ruby.

Ruby nodded, but she didn't look up from her book. *"Danki."*

Mamm put the kettle on the stove, and then she pulled her navy-blue sweater closer to her body. "The wind is brutal out there."

"It is? I hadn't noticed."

Her mother sat down and put her hand on Ruby's book. "How about we chat for a few minutes until the water boils?"

Ruby closed the book. "All right. What would you like to talk about?"

"You. You've changed, *dochder."*

She smiled. "For the better, I hope."

"In some ways, *ya."*

Ruby frowned. "And in others?"

"You've been keeping to *yerself* since you got back from Birch Creek. You used to like to *geh* to singings and frolics, but you haven't been to a single one."

"I have plenty to keep me busy," she said. "*Mei* job, and studying."

"And that makes you happy?"

"It does." And she was telling the truth, for the most part. She was happy, and she had a sense of satisfaction and peace she hadn't had before. But something was still off. Things with her and Christian had been left unfinished. Or was that wishful thinking on her part? She hadn't heard from him since she left Birch Creek, and if he had wanted to talk to her he could have asked Timothy for her address and phone number. To be fair, she also hadn't contacted him, although she'd been tempted. But what would be the point? Their good-bye had been permanent, and she needed to accept that, even if a part of her didn't want to.

"I'm perfectly content with what I'm doing, *Mamm*. I've started looking for teaching jobs since Julia doesn't have any plans to leave the school here anytime soon."

"She will when she gets married."

"But she says that's a way off, and I don't want to wait. I want to start teaching, *Mamm*. I believe I'm ready."

Mamm smiled, her eyes crinkling at the corners like it always did when she was pleased. "I believe you are too. You've shown a lot of maturity since you've been back home. Any school would be blessed to have you as their teacher."

She leaned back in her chair, returning the smile. *Mamm* didn't compliment easily. Neither did her father. Knowing that they had noticed the change in her and approved meant so much. "*Danki*," she said, her throat growing tight.

The whistle sounded. "The water's ready." *Mamm* got up, and a few moments later she put a cup of chamomile tea in front of Ruby. "Don't stay up too late," she said.

"I won't. *Gute nacht.*"

Ruby worked for a little while longer, until she heard a knock on the door that connected the kitchen and back porch. She glanced at the clock. Who would be here at this hour? When she opened the door, a blast of cold wind hit her. "Selah?" she said, peering at the bundled-up woman in front of her.

"May I come in? It's freezing out here."

"*Ya*, of course." Ruby gestured for her to come inside and then closed the door behind her. "What are you doing here?"

Selah held a small tote bag. "I came to see you."

"How did you know where I lived? And do you know what time it is?"

She nodded. "I asked Patience for *yer* address," she said. "And I know it's late, but the bus was running behind. I was lucky to get a taxi here."

Ruby was confused by all this, but she didn't forget her manners. "Do you want something to drink? *Kaffee?* Tea?"

"Tea would be wonderful."

Ruby put the kettle on as Selah took off her coat, bonnet, scarf, and gloves. She put the bonnet on the table and Ruby picked up her other clothing. "*Geh* ahead and sit down. I'll hang these up."

After putting Selah's outerwear away and making her a cup of tea, she joined Selah at the table. "I'm so surprised you're here," Ruby said.

"I'm a little surprised myself. But I needed to talk to you." She glanced down at her hands as they cradled the small mug. "I owe you an apology. Several, actually."

"You don't owe me anything."

Selah gave her a half-smile. "I knew you would say that, because you're so nice. I haven't been nice to you, however."

"Water under the bridge." Ruby waved her hand.

"Not for me." She looked at Ruby. "I'm sorry for how I treated you. You didn't deserve *mei* rudeness. I've been going through some things, some personal business, and I shouldn't have taken that out on you."

"You came all the way here to tell me that?"

Selah nodded. "*Ya*. I thought I'd be here early enough to find a hotel or a bed and breakfast. I'm sorry to invite myself—"

"You can stay here," Ruby said, smiling. "As long as you want."

"I have to *geh* back tomorrow, but *danki*." She smiled.

Ruby nodded, still trying to wrap her mind around the fact that Selah had come all the way from New York to apologize to her. She also noticed that Selah was different. The expression in her eyes seemed softer, and her words didn't carry the harsh tone they used to. She had changed, and Ruby could tell it was for the better.

Selah looked at the books on the table. "I hope I didn't interrupt anything important." She read the title of one of them. "*Discipline for the Elementary Classroom.*" She turned to Ruby. "Teaching books?"

"*Ya.*" She told Selah about her plan to become a teacher.

"That's perfect." Selah clasped her hands together.

"Why?"

"Because Birch Creek needs a teacher."

Ruby frowned. "What happened to Christian?"

"*Nix*. But four families moved to the district over the winter, and the school is bursting at the seams again. I called him last week, and he had just told the school board they needed to hire a second teacher for next year. They were already planning to add on to the building over the summer, Christian said. I thought they should hire someone now, but Christian thinks the students have had enough upheaval this school year. He said he could handle it until April when the school year ends, but they need another teacher by fall."

Ruby got up from the table and picked up her mug, her hand a bit unsteady at the mention of Christian. "I'm sure they'll find someone by then."

"Why don't you apply?"

She set her empty mug on the counter but didn't answer Selah.

"Is it because you'd have to work with Christian?"

Ruby turned around. "*Nee*," she said, swinging her hand back and almost knocking the mug onto the floor. *That was close.* "Of course not. Christian and I are . . ."

"What?" Selah said, cocking her head "What are you and Christian, exactly?"

"*Nix*," she said softly. "We're *nix*."

Selah shook her head. "I don't believe that."

Ruby turned around and put the mug in the sink, unsettled by Selah's conviction. But Selah hadn't witnessed Ruby's last conversation with Christian. The way he'd politely and unemotionally told her good-bye. If she had, she would feel the same way about the situation Ruby did—resigned. She picked up the teakettle. "Would you like some more tea?"

"*Nee.* I would like to stay on subject." She paused. "Unless it's too uncomfortable for you."

Ruby set down the teakettle and forced a smile. "Why would it be uncomfortable? There's *nix* to discuss, anyway."

"Then you wouldn't mind working with Christian next year."

"I didn't say that."

Selah sighed and got up from the table. "What am I going to do with you two?"

"What?" Ruby asked, confused.

"Far be it from me to put *mei* nose in *mei bruder*'s business—or *yers*—but it seems you both need an intervention, for *yer* own sakes."

She could only imagine what that meant, but she still didn't want to discuss Christian. Ruby went to the table and picked up Selah's mug. "We usually eat breakfast around six," she said. "I think we're having pancakes tomorrow."

Selah chuckled. "You even change the subject the same way." She moved in front of Ruby. "See, this is why you and Christian belong together. He's too stuffy and you're—"

"Clumsy? Flighty? Incompetent?" Maybe Selah hadn't changed at all and this was a weird ruse to hurl insults her way.

"*Nee*, Ruby," she said, her tone kind. Then she smiled. You're sweet. Optimistic. A breath of fresh air, which *mei bruder* desperately needs."

Her stomach fluttered again. *Stop it*. She couldn't let her thoughts and feelings get in the way of reality. "I'm sure he's forgotten about me by now."

"Hardly. Although he won't admit it. Like you, he says there's *nee* point discussing it."

Well, that didn't make her feel optimistic at all. But hadn't she'd known that all along? Why had she let a few words from Selah give her a glimmer of hope? *Because I still care about him.* "He's right," she said, this time unable to keep the disappointment out of her voice.

"Christian is right about a lot of things, but this isn't one of them." She touched Ruby's arm. "You should apply for the teaching job. The students love you, and I know they miss you. Christian did mention that. And I know he misses you too."

Ruby sat down at the table. Hearing that the students missed her did fill her with happiness, but that was quickly tempered by the idea of working with Christian in the close quarters of a classroom. She couldn't do it. Not with how she felt. This was too important an opportunity for her not to be completely honest with herself. She still had feelings for Christian, and she couldn't give her best to her students if she was preoccupied with her fruitless emotions. That wasn't fair to them, to her, or to Christian. He needed a teaching partner who would help him, not be in the way.

She looked up at Selah. "I can't," she said firmly. "That isn't the job for me. I'm sure Christian would agree."

"But—"

"It's getting late." She stood. "I'll get some extra quilts for the bed in Timothy's old room. Do you need anything else?"

Selah's gaze was downcast as she shook her head. "That should be fine."

Ruby went to her. "I appreciate what you're trying to do, Selah. You care about *yer bruder.*" A lump formed in her throat, her feelings overcoming her common sense. "I do too," she whispered, unable to ignore the truth. She hurried out of the kitchen before she said anything else she might regret.

Selah frowned as Ruby disappeared from the room, just as if her dress were on fire. Then she sighed. Why were these two so stubborn? Then again, they were also both a bit odd in their own ways. Why wouldn't they be odd about their relationship?

She picked up her tote bag, grateful that she hadn't pushed Ruby too much or she'd be sleeping out in the cold. Not that Ruby would have done that. She didn't have a cruel or petty bone in her body. Selah couldn't say the same about herself. But with the help of *Aenti* Keturah and her counselor, who had counseled a few other Amish clients, and with lots of prayer and spending time with God, Selah was changing. The sadness and confusion still laced her mind, but it wasn't as all-consuming as it had been. Now she had hope, for the first time in a long time.

She also had hope for Ruby and Christian, if she could help them get over themselves. And she wasn't wrong when she said Ruby would be wanted back in the Birch Creek school. But both she and Christian were so focused on denying their feelings that they were missing out on several wonderful opportunities. And now that she was learning one of the keys to battling depression was to help others, she was determined to do something about these two. *I'm not sure what, though.*

"*Yer* room is ready," Ruby said as she reentered the kitchen. "Do you want to take some water or tea upstairs with you?"

"*Nee*, but *danki.*"

Ruby picked up her books and turned off the kitchen lamp. She clicked on a small flashlight and Selah followed her to the room. She turned on a small lamp on the nightstand. "I'm right next door if you need anything."

Selah fought the lump in her throat. Ruby was such a good person, and her brother deserved someone like her. He deserved *her.* "*Danki*, Ruby."

"*Gute nacht.*" Ruby smiled before she left the room.

Selah set her tote bag on the end of the bed. She'd brought only the essentials—a nightgown, fresh underclothes, and a toothbrush. She did have to get back to New York tomorrow. But as soon as she arrived home, she'd make new plans to go to Birch Creek. "Just let me know what I need to do to bring them together, Lord," she whispered, closing her eyes. "Right now, I'm out of ideas."

CHAPTER 18

*C*hristian leaned against the doorjamb of the schoolhouse entrance as the last of his students poured out for the day. Finally, it was Friday. He felt a little guilty looking forward to the weekend so much, but it had been a long, hard week. It was March, and the children were already getting spring fever. Not to mention they were crammed into a school building that was only a year old but already too small. The residents of Birch Creek would have to build another addition over the summer. Maybe even a separate building, which would be a good idea for when they hired another teacher. Since the teacher would likely be female, it would be easier and more appropriate if they worked in separate buildings.

He waved to Malachi, Judah, Jesse, and Nelson before the boys ran down the road. He hadn't given any homework over the weekend, hoping the children would work and play out most of their energy before Monday. He turned and faced the school building. Inside, his classroom was a mess. It was hard to keep thirty-five students under control and occupied and still keep things tidy, particularly on a Friday.

Christian went inside, picked up the broom, and started sweeping the scraps of paper and dirt and dust on the floor into a pile. He filled and emptied the dustpan and then put it and the broom away and sat down at his desk. He picked up his #1 Teacher tote bag and put a stack of papers and his lesson plans inside. Normally he would work on them there, but he needed some fresh air, and today was unseasonably warm and sunny. He supposed he had a bit of spring fever too.

He went home and walked through the back door. To his surprise Selah was sitting at the table. He smiled and went to her. "I didn't know you were coming to visit."

"I wanted to surprise you." She grinned back and got up and hugged him.

He looked at her. He hadn't seen her since Christmas, although they had talked on the phone a few times. She looked brighter, her smile genuine and not forced. He couldn't stop his smile from growing, knowing that she was doing well. "I don't have much to make for supper," he said. "Unless you like peanut butter and jelly."

"Living like a true bachelor, then. It's okay. I haven't had peanut butter and jelly since I left Birch Creek. I'll *geh* to Schrock Grocery in the morning and fill *yer* pantry." She started for the living room. "Why don't we sit on the front porch? It's too beautiful out to stay inside."

Christian agreed, and a few moments later they were sitting on the two chairs on the porch. "How long are you planning to stay?" he asked.

"A couple of days." Her gaze landed on the birdfeeder he'd

put out last week. Two robins and a cardinal were jockeying for the food. "Although it's so nice here, I'm tempted to visit a little longer."

"Oh." He stared at the cardinal, who had been pushed aside by the robins. "I thought you might be moving back."

She paused. "I'm not ready yet. But maybe someday." She turned to him. "Tell me about you. Have they found a second teacher yet?"

He shook his head. "There seems to be a shortage of teachers right now."

"That's unfortunate." She let out a heavy sigh.

"What was that for?"

"I know the perfect teacher." She sighed again. "Too bad she turned down the job."

His sister was starting to sound as if she were a tragic Shakespearean heroine. "Who?"

Selah looked at him with an artful expression. "The one and only Ruby Glick."

He raised his brow, hoping he appeared unaffected at the mention of the woman he hadn't been able to stop thinking about since she'd left for Lancaster. "They offered her the teaching position?"

She shook her head. "*Nee.* I mentioned it to her when I visited her a month ago, though."

"You went to see her?" He had to stop himself from asking about her, even though he was highly curious. More than curious. Desperately wanting to know about her was more accurate.

"*Ya.*" Selah looked down at the porch floor. "I needed to apologize for how I acted toward her."

"I presume she accepted your apology?"

"Of course she did. She's too nice not to. I also told her about how the school was filling up again and that the board would need to hire another teacher."

He had told Selah about that when he called her in January, never suspecting she would pass that information along to Ruby. In fact, it hadn't dawned on him that the two of them would ever speak to each other again. "Um, what did she say?"

"She didn't want the job."

"I see." He rubbed his palms over his pants legs, surprised that they were a little damp. His heartbeat felt a tad bit accelerated too. "I'm not surprised." *But I am disappointed.*

"For the record, it wasn't because the position is in Birch Creek, or because of the students, or even because she has doubts about her teaching ability."

"She shouldn't doubt that," he mumbled.

"She's apprehensive about working with you."

Christian took that in. He wasn't surprised. They hadn't parted on the best of terms. "I guess that's that, then."

"I guess so." She drummed her fingers on the arm of the chair. "Too bad someone can't convince her otherwise. She'd be perfect for the job, you know."

"I know."

"And it's a shame she has to turn down an excellent teaching job because . . ." She gave him a pointed look. "Because of her potential coworker."

Now he was rubbing the back of his neck. "She won't listen to me." He got up from the chair and started to pace. "And even if she would, I would probably make things worse by talking to her. I seem to have a gift for that."

"Color me shocked, Christian."

Christian stopped walking long enough to see his sister smirk. "What do you mean?"

"You've never shied away from a challenge before."

"Are you forgetting Martha?"

She waved her hand. "If you really cared about Martha, you would have made that work." Her gaze met his, not wavering. "You can't tell me you don't care about Ruby."

He opened his mouth, but then he closed it and went back to pacing. "My feelings are immaterial."

"*Yer* feelings are important. So are hers." Selah stood and arched her back. "It's been a long trip. I think I'll lie down for a while. After supper I'm going to Martha's." She touched his arm. "I promise I'll be back."

He nodded. "I know you will."

Selah went inside, and Christian thought about what she said. Setting his personal feelings for Ruby aside, he fully believed she would be the best person for the teaching job. There was no doubt about that. It distressed him to think that she was giving up a prime opportunity because she didn't want to work with him. Admittedly that stung a little bit, but he couldn't resent her for it.

He also couldn't let her turn down the perfect job because of him.

Christian sat back down and stared at the now-empty bird-feeder. Next week was a short school week, as the students had Friday off. He could make a quick weekend trip to see Ruby and talk her into taking the job. They would discuss logistics. He wasn't making this decision because of Selah, even though he knew his sister wouldn't let up until he agreed to talk to Ruby. He was doing this for Ruby, and for the benefit of the schoolchildren. And he would ignore the annoying pounding of his heart that seemed to happen when he was around her.

Ruby sipped on a glass of iced tea as the sun started to set. She'd come out on the back patio a little after supper to pray and enjoy the early spring evening, which was slightly chilly but better than being cooped up inside. It wasn't the same as sitting under the huge oak tree back in Birch Creek, but she felt a sense of peace here now, and she was grateful for it.

The back door opened, and she glanced over her shoulder. Her father came out with his own glass of tea and sat down next to her. "Nice sunset," he said, stretching out his legs.

"It is."

"I figured I'd see you at the kitchen table studying *yer* books again."

Ruby shrugged. "I needed to take a break."

He nodded. "It's *gut* to have a rest every once in a while. You've been working hard on *yer* studies."

She was surprised he'd noticed. "I enjoy learning." Which was something she hadn't realized about herself. She'd been an average student in school, but she'd found it boring sometimes, which had led to her getting into trouble more than she should have. But having her own course of study in a topic she was interested in—that was satisfying. *And I have Christian to thank for it.*

Christian. She thought about him often. A little too often for her own good. She figured it was because of the teaching connection. But that didn't explain why he came to mind when she wasn't working on her education studies. Or why she wondered if he was okay. Was he eating enough? Did he and Selah work things out, or were they back to arguing again? Did he still sit under the beautiful oak tree and pray?

"Ruby?"

She looked at her father. *"Ya?"*

"Everything all right? You got quiet all of a sudden."

She chuckled. "Which is so unlike me."

"Oh, you've had *yer* quiet moments."

"Usually after I got into trouble."

Her father turned pensive. "You're not the only *kinn* to ever get into a few scrapes," he said.

"Timothy certainly didn't."

"*Nee,* but he takes after *yer mudder.*" He gave her a cryptic smile. "You, I'm afraid, take after me."

Surprised, she said, "You would get into trouble when you were younger?"

"Definitely. Pretty much up until I married *yer mamm.*" He paused. "But there's a difference between you and me. You've always got *gut* intentions. I rarely did. I was a mischievous *bu.* Gave *mei* parents fits sometimes."

Why hadn't her father told her this before? "I'm sorry for all the problems I caused you."

He waved his hand. "Let all that stay in the past, Ruby. We forgave you. Consider it forgotten." His smile widened. "I suspect now that you've found *yer* calling, things will *geh* a bit smoother for you."

"I hope." She still hadn't found a job, and it was nearly April. Even if she wasn't hired anywhere, she'd already decided to offer tutoring services to any students in the community who needed them. She had a plan B, which was a miracle, since she'd never bothered with having a plan A before.

The back door opened, and her mother stepped out. "Ruby, you have a visitor."

She turned. "I do?" She wasn't expecting anyone.

Christian suddenly appeared behind *Mamm*. Stunned, Ruby just stared at him.

"I think this is *mei* cue to *geh*." *Daed* stood up, yawned, and went to the door. "You're Christian Ropp, *ya*?"

Christian lifted an eyebrow. "*Ya*."

"Figured as much."

Her parents went inside, and then Christian came outside. He stood near the house, and Ruby didn't move. She was too surprised to say anything. She also couldn't keep her eyes off him.

"Hello." He cleared his throat. "I'm sorry I came by without prior notice."

Still formal as always. Which she would have found endearing if she hadn't reminded herself that she wasn't supposed to find him endearing anymore. She stood and lifted her chin, ignoring the pitter-patter rhythm in her heart. "Surprising people must run in *yer familye*. Selah came here unannounced several weeks ago."

"I know." He took a step forward. He wasn't wearing a hat, and she noticed his hair was a little on the long side. She could also see a bit of five o'clock shadow on his face. Which was strange, since Christian was always meticulous about his appearance—and everything else. The only other time she'd seen him askew was when he was upset about his sister.

"Did something happen to Selah?" she said, alarmed.

He shook his head, frowning. "*Nee*. She's fine."

"Oh. *Gut.*" She blew out a breath. "I thought maybe that was the reason you're here looking a little . . . uh, disheveled."

"Impressive use of vocabulary." He ran his hand over his unshaven chin. "And accurate. Although you could have simply said messy."

"I've been studying." Despite trying to keep her emotional distance from him, she couldn't help but smile. "I have a vocabulary book on *mei* desk. Along with a dictionary."

"*The* Webster's Dictionary?"

She chuckled. "Why, Christian, did you just make a joke?"

He smiled. "I suppose I did." Then his smile faded. "Jocularity aside, I'm here to talk to you about something of a serious nature."

She took a step back, her good humor disappearing. "The teaching job."

He nodded. "Selah told me you refused to apply. I was surprised to hear that."

"Why?"

"Because you want to be a teacher. It's an available job. The logical decision would be—"

"I'm not interested in logic!" Suddenly she remembered why she was irritated with him in the first place. "Christian, we can't always make logical choices."

"Why not?"

"Because the heart isn't always logical."

He pressed his lips together. "And *yer* heart is saying to stay away from Birch Creek."

She nodded. "There's *nee* reason for me to *geh* back."

"On the contrary. *Yer bruder* and his *familye* are there. I believe you and Martha also became friends of some sort. Even Selah misses you, although she's living back in New York now."

"What about you?"

His Adam's apple bobbed up and down. "What about me?"

"Do you . . . miss me?" She wished she hadn't asked the question. But now that it was out there, she needed to know his answer.

"I suppose there are moments, brief moments, of course—"

"Forget it." Her eyes burned. She should have known better than to ask him about his feelings. She knew he had them, just not for her. He was here only to persuade her to apply for the job because it was the reasonable thing to do. And rationally, he was right. It was the only teaching job available. But like a nitwit she had allowed herself to hope he had come here for a reason that had nothing to do with her teaching and everything to do with each other. *Stupid, stupid.* She plopped down in her chair and crossed her arms.

"That's quite petulant of you." Christian moved to stand over her.

"I still have *mei* petulant moments." She uncrossed her arms, feeling childish. She refused to fall into bad habits. "I appreciate *yer* trying to help me gain employment," she said, keeping her tone even. "But I'm still not going to apply."

"Is the reason . . . Is it because of me?"

She looked up at him. He was rubbing the back of his neck so hard she thought he might rub off his skin. His gaze stayed pinned to the ground. Never had she seen him so uncertain. Not when they played horseshoes, not when his raspberry pie hit her in the face, not even when he kissed her. Now he was tapping his foot, and his hand moved from his neck to his suspender. He started to fidget with it. Wait, Christian didn't fidget. Which gave her an opening.

Ruby shot up from the chair and faced him. "Why did you kiss me?"

He took a step back, his brow shooting up as he looked away. "Why are you bringing that up now?"

"Because you never answered me when I asked that question months ago." She moved closer to him, determined to get an answer from him this time. "Why, Christian Ropp, did you kiss me?"

Christian thought his heart was going to hammer right out of his chest. He'd been a bundle of nerves since leaving Birch Creek earlier today, enough so that he not only forgot to shave, he also left his hat on the kitchen table. Right up to the moment he knocked on Ruby's front door, he'd nearly changed his mind. But when he saw her sitting there with her father . . . When she turned around and looked at him . . . his emotions went haywire.

And they were still firing in all different directions, even when he fell back on what he'd always been able to trust—logic. But what he was feeling wasn't logical. It was disconcerting. A bit frightening. And for some unfathomable reason, very right.

Until she asked him about the kiss. And she did deserve an answer. He opened his mouth. No sound came out.

"I'm not letting you leave until I get an answer." She crossed her arms again. This time instead of looking petulant, she looked cute. *Cute.* He'd never used that word in his life. Yet it was the perfect word to describe Ruby. He tried to speak again, and once again, he couldn't say a word. *What is wrong with me?*

Ruby threw up her hands. "This is getting us nowhere." She

stood on her tiptoes and kissed him on the mouth. Lightly, quickly. But long enough to make his knees buckle.

"Why did you do that?" he asked, amazed he managed to formulate the question, especially since he still felt the tingle of her lips on his.

"To refresh *yer* memory." She smirked, looking quite satisfied with herself. "Now, why did *you* kiss me?"

"Because . . . because . . ."

Her lovely eyes turned dull. "Never mind." She turned her back to him. "Christian, *geh* home."

She was right. He wasn't going to convince her of anything. It was hopeless because she wouldn't listen to reason. She insisted on playing games, asking personal questions, bringing up the irrelevant. Why had he bothered to come here in the first place? He would call a taxi right now and wait at the station as long as necessary for the next bus. Ruby Glick's employment wasn't his responsibility. It wasn't as if he cared about her.

He stilled. His heart thumped even harder, as if he'd run the entire distance from his house to Ruby's. *I care about her.* And admitting that felt freeing. The exact opposite of how he felt holding his feelings for her in. He swallowed and lifted his hand. It hung in the air for a moment, hovering over her shoulder, before he lightly touched her sweater.

She turned, her eyes wide with surprise. "Christian?"

"I . . ." He gulped. Everything washing over him was new, and he could barely make sense of it. But one thing was clear—he couldn't leave her without telling her how he felt. "I kissed you because . . . because I wanted to."

Her expression turned soft. "You did?"

"*Ya.*" And he wanted to kiss her now. But he didn't dare. He moved his hand to his side, both arms straight next to his body. "I'm sorry if I crossed the line when I did."

"You didn't cross a line," she murmured, taking a step closer to him. "But, Christian, people don't kiss unless they like each other."

He nodded. "I know."

"I mean as more than friends."

"Ruby, I'm not an infant. I do understand how human mating rituals work."

"You make it sound so romantic." She sighed. "I just want to make sure you know what you're saying. What you're feeling."

Christian paused. Then he took her hand in his. Her skin was soft, warm. Her hand fit in his hand perfectly. "I know what I'm feeling," he said, meeting her eyes. "I don't understand it completely. I'm not sure how to express it yet. All I know is, I care for you. A lot. And I don't want to be the reason you don't take the job in Birch Creek."

"Apply, you mean."

"That's just a formality." He rubbed his thumb over the top of her hand, barely aware he was doing it but unable to stop. "Once you tell the board you want the position, they'll hire you immediately."

"*Danki* for saying that, Christian."

"I don't say it lightly." He let go of her hand. "If you can't work with me, then I'll find a teaching job somewhere else."

"*Nee.*" She grabbed his hand. "You love *yer* job and *yer* students. You can't leave."

"I will, if it means you'll take the job."

Ruby couldn't believe what Christian was saying. He couldn't give up his job for her. That didn't make any sense. "You're being illogical, you know."

"Perhaps." His eyes softened. "But as someone wise just told me, you can't always make decisions based on logic."

She released his hand and tentatively put hers over his heart. "You have to follow this."

He swallowed. "*Ya*. You do."

She moved her hand away, her heart suddenly swelling with emotion for this man. No, not any emotion. Love. And while Christian hadn't told her he loved her, the sacrifice he was willing to make said everything. "Keep *yer* job, Christian."

"But—"

"And I'll apply for the teaching position."

His body almost went limp. "Seriously?"

She nodded. "Seriously."

Relief flashed over his face. He really was handsome, even more so now that he was letting her see how he felt. "I'm glad you changed *yer* mind," he said. "It was the—"

"Logical thing to do?"

He shook his head. "The right thing to do."

They both could agree on that. "I just have one more question," she said.

"Which is?"

"Can we revisit that kiss again? I think both of us need a redo."

"I'm agreeable to that."

"You'll have to move a little closer," she said with a grin.

He closed the space between them. Then he surprised her by cupping her cheek with his palm. "Is this better?"

She nodded. "Much. Also, nice technique. Have you been practicing?"

"I don't have to. Something about you makes everything feel natural." He bent down and kissed her. Her heart turned to mush. He was a romantic after all.

Eight months later

"I can't *geh* downstairs like this—*hiccup!*" Ruby started pacing back and forth. This was a disaster, and she thought she'd put those behind her by now. Just like Christian said she would, she got the teaching position after only a five-minute interview. Over the summer the community had added on to the school building again, putting a divider between the two large class-rooms. Ruby had the early elementary students in one room, and Christian had the older students in the other. For the past two months they had run each classroom like separate schools. Which was good for them both since they weren't married—and she found Christian a significant distraction.

Then he proposed to her—for the right reasons this time—and she eagerly said yes. Now it was mid-November . . . and her wedding day.

Hiccup. "I can't believe this." She turned to Martha and to Selah, who had returned several times over the past year for vis-its. The three of them had become good friends, and they were both her attendants. Of course, neither of them had a massive case of hiccups. "I'm not even nervous," Ruby added.

"Are you sure?"

"*Ya.*" And she wasn't, except for a few butterflies in her

stomach. All right, a whole swarm, but that didn't make sense. She loved Christian. He loved her, and after a bit of stuttering he was able to tell her he loved her. Now he said it all the time. For such a stuffy person he was quite the romantic. Who would have thought that? She smiled as she remembered their kiss last night. Sweet, but lingering, and full of promise. *Hiccup.*

"Do you want a glass of water?" Martha asked. "Sugar water always works for me."

"You can pinch *yer* nose." Selah demonstrated. "I also read somewhere that if you stand on *yer* head they'll *geh* away."

Ruby paused, considering it. No, what a ludicrous idea. She plopped onto the bed. *Hiccup.* "Everyone's waiting."

Martha put her hand on her shoulder. "Don't worry about it, Ruby. Everyone gets the hiccups."

"Not"—*hiccup*—"like"—*hiccup*—"this." *Hiccup.*

Selah clapped in front of her face.

Ruby jumped. "What did you do that for?"

"I'm trying to scare you." She looked at her expectantly. "Did it work?"

Ruby stilled. She stood up and walked around the room. "I think it did." She clasped her hands. "They're gone." She hugged Selah and then Martha. *"Danki!"*

"Now come downstairs and get married," Selah said.

The two women left, and Ruby went to the mirror above the dresser in Timothy and Patience's spare bedroom. She had lived here since May. After today, she'd live with Christian in his small house. They had already talked about expanding it for when they had children, should the Lord bless them in such a way. While it was the logical step after marriage, it was also the right one. They had also decided to postpone their honeymoon until next spring, once school dismissed for the summer.

She smiled at her reflection. She couldn't keep him and everyone else waiting. She left the room, went to the top of the stairs, and started to descend into the living room, where guests were crowding in for the ceremony. Ruby reached the middle of the staircase and then—

Hiccup!

Her hand flew to her mouth. Oh, *nee.*

A few chuckles went through the crowd. Her gaze flew to her brother, whose expression was a mix of amusement and pity. She was used to that from him. Martha and Selah's faces were pinched, and she could tell they were trying not to laugh.

Then she saw Christian. He wasn't laughing. He was gazing at her with love.

Her hiccups forgotten, she hurried to him. She was his bride, and she wasn't going to keep him waiting any longer.

EPILOGUE

$\mathcal{S}$ eth Yoder opened the door to the shed he'd constructed more than a year ago. He'd found the wood scattered in an open area in the woods about half a mile away and had thought of building it there, but something didn't sit right with him about the place. He couldn't put his finger on why, only that he knew he had to locate his shed elsewhere, yet far away enough from home that it wouldn't be found. And it hadn't, until Christian Ropp showed up.

He shook his head and grinned as he walked into the shed, the battery-powered sensor lights he'd installed flickering on. Christian and Ruby's wedding, which he'd attended, had been last week. That was one odd couple, he had to admit. Christian had his hands full with Ruby, and vice versa.

Seth looked around his woodshop, the familiar feeling of guilt coming over him as it always did when he was here. He mostly came here on Sundays, and today was no exception. He wasn't a carpenter, and the shed wasn't the sturdiest building, but it suited his needs. He looked at the array of woodcarving tools on the pegboard in front of him and then at the stack of fresh wood on the worktable beneath the pegboard. Sawdust piles surrounded him, and he knew he needed to get rid of them soon. He would haul them to a bigger pile he'd created farther into the woods. No one ever came this way, and even Christian, as smart as he was, hadn't figured out what Seth did here. Seth wanted to keep it that way.

He picked up a chisel and held it in his hand. It felt a part of him, the way all the tools he used to make his carvings did. Carvings he'd kept secret and worked on only on Sundays when he could get away from the house. So far, his excuse of taking a Sunday walk had been fine with his family. But it wasn't fine with God. He wasn't supposed to work on Sundays. He wasn't supposed to deceive his family or anyone else. He owed God, his community, and especially his father an apology and a confession—things he couldn't bring himself to do.

He sighed and started work on a pasture scene he'd been carving for the past two months. When finished, he would add the decorative plaque to the rest of the projects that had never been out of his workshop, much less seen by anyone. He didn't know what to do with his creations, only that he had to create. If he didn't, he would wither inside.

He wanted more than anything to carve for a living, but he knew that wasn't practical. He had to think about the future, and his future would be secure. He and his family had lived through hard times, through near starvation. He wouldn't do it again, and he would never put anyone else at risk of it either. Even though he wasn't in a relationship and he wasn't interested in one right now, eventually he wanted to get married. God would have to take care of that part, since the pickings were slim in Birch Creek.

Seth paused and lifted his straight gouge. Why should God do anything for him when he was purposely breaking the Sabbath? Did he deserve any blessings when he was being so selfish?

His fingers gripped the handle of the gouge. He couldn't put it down. Couldn't walk away from the one thing he loved above everything else.

He continued to carve.

ACKNOWLEDGMENTS

*a*s I was writing this book, I threw out a question to my Facebook friends, asking them for examples of student mischief. I received so many great replies, but the one that struck me was when a student brought a chicken to school. Thus, Bring Your Pet to School Day was born. Thank you to all my friends who shared their school misadventures. It's my favorite social media interaction to date.

Thank you also to Becky Monds and Jean Bloom, the best editorial team ever. Also, a huge thanks to my brainstorming buddies, Eddie Columbia and Kelly Long, for listening to my free association phone calls.

And of course, thanks to you, dear reader. Christian and Ruby's story is close to my heart, and I hope it becomes close to yours.

DISCUSSION QUESTIONS

1. When Ruby arrived in Birch Creek, she struggled with self-esteem. At the end of the book, she had gained confidence. What do you think brought about this change in her?

2. Did you ever have Show and Tell day when you were in school? What kinds of things did you bring to show your teacher and classmates?

3. Both Ruby and Christian had the same plan—to find a spouse. If you were to give each of them advice about their plans, what would you tell them?

4. Who is your favorite character in *The Teacher's Bride*? Why?

5. Ruby had found her purpose in teaching. What do you think your purpose is, and how did God lead you to find it?

6. Christian has a difficult time emotionally connecting to people. What do you think he'll learn from Ruby when it comes to social interaction?

7. Selah struggles with depression. If you have a family

member or friend with depression, how have you helped them?

8. Ruby and Christian are completely opposite personalities, yet God brought them together. What are some other examples of God using opposite or unusual circumstances to bring about something good?

Don't miss a charming tale of falling in love
while pursuing the dreams of your heart in the
next Amish Brides of Birch Creek novel!

The
FARMER'S
Bride

ZONDERVAN®   AVAILABLE JUNE 2019

Read more from Kathleen Fuller in her Amish Letters series!

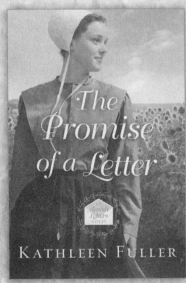

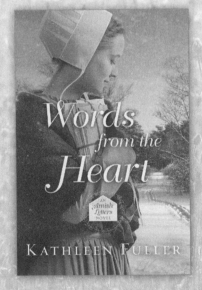

AVAILABLE IN PRINT AND E-BOOK.

ABOUT THE AUTHOR

 With over a million copies sold, Kathleen Fuller is the author of several bestselling novels, including the Hearts of Middlefield novels, the Middlefield Family novels, the Amish of Birch Creek series, and the Amish Letters series as well as a middle-grade Amish series, the Mysteries of Middlefield.

Visit her online at KathleenFuller.com
Twitter: @TheKatJam
Facebook: WriterKathleenFuller